W9-AJN-166

too
shattered
for
mending

also by peter brown hoffmeister

This Is the Part Where You Laugh

too

shattered

for

mending

Peter Brown Hoffmeister

ALFRED A. KNOPF
NEW YORK

THIS IS A BORZOI BOOK PUBLISHED BY ALFRED A. KNOPF

Text copyright © 2017 by Peter Brown Hoffmeister
Photo of landscape copyright © 2017 by Pete Ryan/Getty Images
Photo of boy copyright © 2017 by Farhad Ghaderi/Arcangel

Visit us on the Web! randomhouseteens.com

Educators and librarians, for a variety of teaching tools, visit us at RHTeachersLibrarians.com

Library of Congress Cataloging-in-Publication Data is available upon request.

ISBN 978-0-553-53805-2 (trade) — ISBN 978-0-553-53807-6 (lib. bdg.) — ISBN 978-0-553-53816-8 (ebook)

The text of this book is set in 11.25-point Revival 565 BT.

Printed in the United States of America
September 2017
10 9 8 7 6 5 4 3 2 1

First Edition

Random House Children's Books supports the First Amendment and celebrates the right to read.

To my mother,

Pamela C. Hoffmeister,

for her love of books and art,

and for all the stories she read aloud to me

. . . but the great redtail

Had nothing left but unable misery

From the bone too shattered for mending, the wing

   that trailed under his talons when he moved.

We had fed him six weeks, I gave him freedom,

He wandered over the foreland hill and returned

   in the evening, asking for death . . .

—Robinson Jeffers, "Hurt Hawks"

late october

in the wilderness

I know the smell of pine loam moldering in the fall.

Watch a coyote hunt a house cat in the Chinese cemetery.

Native rainbow trout shake their heads at a ⅛ Rooster Tail spinner at midday, swallow it come evening.

I know that Rowan loves JT, even after he beat her.

the wanderer

Rowan smells like water. I told her that once. I said, "You smell like an eddy." I was thinking of the North Fork of the Clearwater. The backcountry runs, rocks and pools, clean enough to see the trout cut to shadow.

Rowan was drinking a Monster in front of the Mini-Mart. She said, "A what?"

She'd sliced the knees out of her jeans, scissored them way back to the side, and I kept looking at all that exposed skin.

I said, "Like an eddy on the river, when you wade in. You know?"

"When I wade in?"

"To fish," I said.

She tilted her head, and the hair she'd pulled up bobbed to the left. "So I smell like a fish?"

"No," I said, "not like a fish. You smell like an eddy."

She smiled, already shaking her head, laughing at me.

I said, "Messing with me, huh?"

It was last school year. I was a freshman then, a year younger than her. I'd gotten more work in the cemetery and

I imagined that I'd take her out, do something nice for her. Rowan was with JT but I tried to ignore that.

Rowan finished her Monster and threw the empty down on the cement. "I'll see you around?" she said, and made a fish motion with her hand.

the running kind

Sheriff's deputy pulls off the asphalt of the Idaho 11. Drops his Clearwater County cruiser into the flats next to the trampoline. Willa stops jumping and watches. Exposes her teeth, sticking her tongue through her front gap.

The deputy gets out. Walks over to me where I'm searching for chicken eggs in the overgrowth. He says, "Are you the kid they call Little?"

I stand up straight. Say, "Yep." Let him see my full height: six foot five and still growing.

"All right." He nods. Looks up at me. Taps his badge. "I'm Deputy White. Sheriff's Department."

I know who he is. Know where he lives, up Walker Road toward the National Guard school. Know his mustache and his cruiser.

Deputy says, "Have you seen your grandfather lately?"

I shake my head.

"Not at all?" he asks.

"Not at all."

Deputy White stares off to the northeast, the cemetery

rows, the plots and headstones like teeth bucking up out of the ground. He says, "For how long?"

I have the chicken eggs in my left hand. Pick the stuck grass between them with my right, look in the same direction as the deputy, across the graveyard. Say, "Weeks maybe? I don't know."

Deputy White hooks his thumbs in his utility belt. "You think he's gone down the Grade?" He means to Orofino, along the Clearwater River. A meth run.

I shake my head again.

The deputy says, "You don't know or you won't say?"

"Can't," I say, " 'cause I haven't seen him." I shift the eggs in my hand like a pitcher choosing a baseball.

The deputy has his hands on his hips. He's looking past the cemetery now, staring into the hills, the lodgepole pines beyond the Baptist church, the first trees after a slash fire, all the same shade of high green, low gray.

He says, "So that's how it's gonna be, then?"

I don't say anything. There's nothing to say to that.

Deputy White points at the big house. Derlene's out on that porch now. Uncle Lucky too. "Okay," the deputy says. "If y'all do see him, you tell him I'm looking for him and we need to talk. He's slipped up, and I'm following. You got that?"

"Okay," I say.

Derlene and Uncle Lucky don't say anything at all. Their faces are sacks of Quikrete. Cigarettes smoking between their fingers.

"Now y'all don't forget it. I want him talking to me real

7

soon, you hear?" The deputy nods at us like he's being friendly but he unsnaps his holster with his thumb while he smiles, and when he walks to his driver's-side door, he circles around the back of his cruiser so he can keep us in front of him. This is the angle the law takes here. Keep your back to the wall. A man could catch a potshot easy.

three days after

Big, I thought I saw you walk up from the shallows to the ballfield, Highway 11 around the turn to Main Street, your head down the way you always walked as if there was something important on the ground in front of you that needed focus. But you didn't have your bucket with you, and I knew it was only my head bothering me. There was no one in the grass along the road. I blinked, and there was no one next to the ballfield either. The night became the morning, all in one moment, and the dew on the early-fall grass was like metal shavings sprinkled by God.

Light east-west wind, the clouds running laterals in the opposite direction. I looked over at the house, stick frame propped on cinder blocks after being moved from Weippe. A four-foot ground gap. If I crouched down, I could look under the house and see the cemetery at an angle. The cemetery out back. A garden of the dead. All those planted and none to spring up. I'd come outside to pee in my favorite spot, out by the stop sign, but seeing you made me forget.

It was three days after, and I could still feel my hands shaking. I looked down and my fingers wouldn't straighten.

shantytown

I drive south through town over the rise, past the Timber Inn, the Outback, and Sammy's, head south to the 250 split, the Judge Town road. It's not far out but I pass the main houses and the one good place with the fish pond, up the road toward the old Cardiff Mill, past Brown's Creek.

There's a few places I could ask, but some I wouldn't want to, and I roll up on gravel to a place I've been to with Big twice before. It's a yellow house with a five-foot TV satellite dish in the middle of the driveway on 8" x 4" wood blocks, and I stop the truck in front of the dish.

A man walks out, duck-footed, feet pointed in two different directions and his head craning all ways to see if I've got anyone with me in the cab or laying flat in the back.

My window's already rolled down. I don't get out. I say, "Have you seen Big McCardell?"

"Who's asking?"

"Little McCardell."

The man's finished looking in the cab and the bed of the truck, and he knows I'm alone now. He rubs his eyes with the palms of his hand. "Not for a bit," he says. He keeps rubbing at his eyes.

"You know what he was last doing here? What he was running?" This is what I really came to ask.

The man stops rubbing his eyes. Looks at me close. "Hey now. Those ain't the kinda questions people ask around here." He shifts one hand behind his back and holds on to something I can't see. Says, "You know who's in that cabin behind me?"

I shake my head.

"Right," he says, "you don't. And you don't wanna know. 'Cause people that know, well, they sometimes disappear."

"But I gotta ask. I gotta know about my own granddad's business."

"Kid, I don't think you understand what all I'm sayin'."

I look at the house. See movement at a window. A blind pulled down quick.

The man says, "I seen real young before, and I get that. That's how we all growed up. Just don't mix young with stupid. Right?" He still has one hand behind his back.

I pop the truck in reverse. "I'll go ask around elsewhere." I start to back up, and the gravel under the tires crunches.

The man calls out, "It don't matter for me 'cause I ain't affected, but I wouldn't ask too many elsewheres if I were you. You understand?"

The next three places I stop are abandoned, no cars and no answers at the door, and Judge Town isn't a place where you

11

check a door and walk in if it's unlocked. You never know what you might find inside a house, and you wouldn't want to get caught by whoever's staked a claim. So I drive back home to my trailer to eat, to get some sleep, to head to school in the morning.

born to lose

Dyslexia in school is like trying to ride a four-wheeler with the back axle broken. If I can get it to drive at all, it's just a matter of time until a bump takes the wheels off.

Grade school, I remember seeing other kids excited and raising their hands, asking what we were doing next, and I was just hoping to God there wouldn't be anything next because I didn't have a chance of finishing what was in front of me.

But the worst was always math. Math is a trick they play on you when you're a kid. You'll never win. Grade school, I'd be in class wondering why the teacher made up *problems* for us.

High school's supposed to be different, but it isn't. Without Mr. Polchowski—my Room 2 teacher during study hall—I wouldn't have passed a single math class in all of high school. To be honest, I wouldn't have passed science either. Science has math in it, among other things. Last week, in science class, I asked a kid what a word was in our textbook, and he said, "That's Latin, man."

Latin, I thought. *I don't think there's even a country where they still speak Latin, so what's it doing in my textbook?*

Today in study hall, Mr. Polchowski says, "Listen to me. You've got to make time for your homework *at home*, you know?"

I don't tell him how hard I tried to do my math homework last night because it doesn't look like I tried at all. I sat down and wrote out all 13 problems but only answered one of them, number 6. The others didn't make any sense to me.

"Okay," I say.

"Okay?" Mr. Polchowski adjusts his ponytail. "You always say 'Okay,' but then you don't do it. Look," he says, "I understand that math isn't your favorite subject. But that's why you have to do your homework. It only gets harder if you *don't* do it. If you put something off, it makes a thing worse."

"Okay," I say again. I know I should've come after school yesterday to get more help, but I always want to go right home, just get away, and so most of the time I do.

Mr. Polchowski taps the desktop. "Let's get your homework out and see how much we can get done during this study hall period. All right?"

"All right."

I have a see-through red plastic sheet that I cover my page with, and it helps the problems come into focus underneath, so I use that. Together, Mr. Polchowski and I work on math for the next 45 minutes. We don't get to all the problems, but we get most of them done, and I feel a little bit better about things when the bell goes off.

the chicken

When I get home, I find a yellow chicken carcass under the front of the trailer, one of the Buff Orpington egg-layers. This hen's missing her undercarriage, like a small-block Chevy without a bottom end. I look around. Search for clues. Think, maybe raccoon? Maybe a weasel? I pace off five steps and walk the circle, each part of the clock as if I'm doing a search and rescue for a lost hunter.

I find bobcat prints in the mud patch near the gate, all four feet gathered together where he set to leap at the base of the corner post. I put my index finger in the mud print, imagine his jumping with a full belly, making a pistol out of my other hand and pulling the trigger.

I go back to the chicken carcass, grab it feet-first, and sling it into the yard can. I look around and count ten chickens now, plus one rooster. Hope no more egg-layers get took.

mrs. trepp

Willa and I are sitting on the trampoline, doing homework. I look at that fading bruise on her face. It doesn't seem to bother her. She's doing her subtractions page and getting through it pretty quick. I'm trying to do an algebra problem, but the equation makes no sense to me, the numbers and Xs shifting all over the place. I pull out my red cover sheet but it doesn't help much.

"Little," Willa says, "look."

"Hold on a second. I'm trying to do this math problem."

"No, trust me, look. It's Mrs. Trepp."

I look up, and Mrs. Trepp is coming along the 11 from the west in the right-side driving lane. She's in her wheelchair. She has her lawn mower out in front of her, in gear, and she's gripping its handle and gas bar. She's still an eighth of a mile down the road, but we can already hear the mower's engine rumbling.

Willa says, "How fast do you think that thing runs?"

"I don't know. Maybe three miles an hour?"

Willa giggles. "And it just pulls her along, huh?"

"It's a self-propelled mower, so she doesn't have to push it."

Willa says, "I heard she's run that to Weippe before."

"I don't know about that. It'd take at least a couple hours."

Willa raises her eyebrows and stares at me, meaning she believes what she heard.

Mrs. Trepp rumbles by, passing the front of our house. She never looks at anyone. She wears those big sunglasses that old people wear over their glasses, sort of like safety glasses a person might wear on a construction site, but tinted dark, not clear or yellow. I used to wave at Mrs. Trepp when I was younger, but she never waved back or turned her sunglasses toward me, so I stopped.

As she passes, I look at her arms, the muscles and tendons flexing. I say, "See that? Her arms are strong."

Willa makes little clicking sounds between her teeth. Says, "I know it's wrong to say, but she *better* have strong arms . . . because she doesn't have any legs."

Mrs. Trepp drags up the hill past the Mini-Mart, the Timber Inn, the Blue Moose, and the Vug. Then she disappears over the hill.

Willa says, "Where do you think she's going?"

"Sammy's Grocery, probably."

"Oh," Willa says. "I guess everyone needs groceries, huh?"

Willa and I go back to doing our math homework. My algebra problem still isn't working out. I want to rip the textbook in half and throw it into the road. Maybe burn it after it's been run over a few times.

Willa says, "Wanna hear a joke?"

I'm not really in the mood for a joke, but I say, "Okay," because Willa loves to tell jokes so much.

"All right," Willa says. "What do you call a cow who works for a landscaping company?"

"I don't know," I say. "What?"

"A lawn moo-er." Willa starts giggling, and she falls back on the trampoline. Then she does a lawn mower sound in her throat and makes a real serious face. Stares forward with her arms out straight. "Who am I, Little?"

"Mrs. Trepp?"

"Exactly," Willa says, and starts to giggle again.

I've never met a girl as serious or as silly as my cousin Willa. She can go from a frown to a smile and back to a frown again quicker than anyone on earth.

girl from the north country

The first time I saw Rowan was last year. She was a sopho-more at Timberline and I was a freshman. I was in her math class at the start of the year because the school people had gotten something mixed up, and somehow they'd placed me in Advanced Algebra instead of Remedial Algebra Skills. I didn't understand any of the concepts the teacher talked about, and they transferred me down two levels after that, but that was three weeks later. Until I was moved down, I sat next to Rowan.

Timberline High School sits between our two towns, Pierce and Weippe, and since Rowan was from Weippe and I was from Pierce, I'd never seen her before. She was thin in a sort of underfed way, and her clothes were loose, cheap hand-me-downs from someone three or four sizes bigger than her, but she had a real pretty face, and the way she moved was sort of like a long-limbed cat. It's hard to describe, but people noticed her. She wore thick black mascara and black eyeliner too, and it made me think of Queen Cleopatra in the book Mrs. Q read to us in fourth grade when we were learning about the Egyptians. Rowan painted eyeliner in sharp little lines to the outsides of her eyes, and all that black eyeliner made the green in her eyes brighter than it already was. I thought she looked perfect like that, and I had a hard time taking my eyes off her.

Math was never good for me, but in the advanced class everyone was speaking a language I didn't know a single word of. I was just over six foot four last year, in a room full of freshmen and sophomores, and I felt like a grizzly shifting his weight through a crowded lunchroom, knocking cafeteria trays and spilling milk. My chair made a loud screeching sound every time I moved in my seat, and the whole class would look at me whenever I did anything.

JT was the best football player in the school that fall, a preseason All-State selection at strong safety, and that only made me more of a curiosity. The little brother of a hero. I was on varsity too that year, partly because of JT and partly because of my abnormal size. I didn't mind hitting people, and JT made me do some tough workouts in the summer to get ready for the season, but the playbook wasn't something I understood. The plays looked like a bunch of letters and lines scribbled all over the place, crossing each other everywhere, and in a bunch of different colors, and I couldn't memorize any of the offensive or defensive packages. I told the coach that the playbook made no sense to me, but he said, "You just need to buckle down and learn up then, son. Spend more time with it," so I took it home and studied it, even put my red plastic sheet over the pages, but nothing helped. There wasn't anything in the world that would make the playbook read like a story to me.

One night at practice, my positions coach said, "Jesus

dammit, Little, if you go the wrong way one more time, then the whole fuckin' team's gonna run wind sprints after practice." I went the wrong way again two plays later because I was trying to do what was in the playbook and not really trusting what I felt might be right, and everyone glared pretty hard at me as we started our line runs after the last drill.

But JT said real loud, "I don't give a shit about this extra running. These sprints are only making us faster as a team, right, so I'm fine with this," and he winked at me after he said it. So then the team was okay with the sprints, and no one gave me too hard of a time after practice. But football stayed rough after that, and the coaches kept yelling at me.

Rowan sat next to me those whole three weeks I was in the advanced math class. I thought she was beautiful with those cat's eyes, and I didn't care too much that I couldn't understand the math that was being taught in the class as long as I could keep sitting next to Rowan. She was good at math, always getting the right answer on the board when she was called up by the teacher, but the way she slumped her shoulders and rolled her eyes as she walked back to her seat, the whole class could tell that she hated it, or hated the teacher, and that only made people like her more. I hoped she'd be called up every day so I could watch her walk, watch her shift her hips in her big, loose clothes. She'd write her equations in a loopy handwriting, then walk back down my aisle like she was coming to get me.

I know it sounds dumb but I liked to imagine that she'd

walk back to our seats and take my hand. Lean down and whisper, "Let's get out of here, right now, you and me, okay?"

And I'd say, "Yeah, okay," and we'd walk out of class, and the teacher would yell for us to come back, but we'd just laugh and run outside, keep running across the road, up Grasshopper Creek. Then my ideas would kind of get the better of me and I'd imagine Rowan asking me if I wanted to skinny-dip and I'd say okay. She'd take off her clothes in front of me and she'd be thin and tan, like she spent all her time naked in the sun, and she'd take off her bra last, and she'd cover her chest with her hands before she'd laugh and run into the water, throwing her bra over her shoulder, and I'd struggle with my clothes and want to catch up to her, hoping to get a glimpse of her nakedness underwater.

But then we'd be back in math class and the teacher would be calling my name for the third or fourth time and some of my classmates would have started to giggle and I'd say, "Oh, sorry. Wait, what?" and I'd look at Rowan and she'd be smiling too.

tall man

Driving early to school toward Weippe. I'm looking for the turnoff to the house Big took me to once when I was seven or eight. He had a cut hand that night, an ACE bandage sopped with blood on the palm side, and I could hear the wet each time he unstuck it from the steering wheel. I was thinking about his hand, wondering how he cut it—not asking questions because he wasn't in a talking mood—and I didn't notice where we turned. Suddenly we were off the 11, and we made two more turns before we got to a yellow house with three men sitting on the porch drinking clear liquor out of jars.

The turn's what I'm looking for now, something familiar, something to remind me, and maybe that yellow house might tell me what Big was into lately. I'm driving the truck slow, looking left and right on the highway, and that's when I see the worker, a man in his late 30s or early 40s, unloading corrugated roofing from the back of an '85 F-250.

There's something about the man—his height maybe, the way he looks a little like JT—that makes me let off the gas all the way. The truck coasts, and I slide by him, see his black hair, his tan skin, see him yell something to the man up by the house.

I like to drive with my windows down until it snows each year, so when I pull over I can sort of hear the two men saying stuff, but I'm not too close and I can't quite tell what they're yelling back and forth. The taller one—the one that looks like JT—I think he's speaking another language, maybe, and I watch him until he stops pulling roofing from the back of the Ford and just stares at me in my truck. Even that look is something I've seen on JT's face, and I wonder if the man looks at all like me too, but that's a hard thing to tell. I never can see myself the way other people do.

The man's still glaring at me, standing there at the back of his rig, so I put my truck back into drive and leave, drive the rest of the way to school.

sailor on a concrete sea

In English class, I can listen to everyone talking about the book we're reading, and I can sort of understand what's happening even if I haven't read all of it. The English teacher doesn't like kids like me—he went to some fancy college in California and I overheard him once say to another teacher that "trailer trash are the hardest to teach"—but I understand his class well enough, and I can pass it just because stories make sense.

Same with history. Stories there too. But sometimes I still get lost when it comes to dates and memorizing, and when that happens, I lay my red cover sheet on top of the textbook page like Mr. Polchowski tells me to do in every class, but it only helps sometimes. I want to ask the history teacher more questions like Mr. Polchowski says I should, but I don't want to annoy her, and the rest of the kids in the class seem to be understanding what's going on, so it seems like I should be okay if I just listen better.

But the last class of the day is Art I—Drawing—and that's a great class. First off, I like to draw. I'm not good at drawing but I like doing it, and Mrs. F doesn't care how talented a person is. Her grading system is all about hard work, and I don't mind working hard on a drawing even if it doesn't look good in the end. I just like being able to earn an A in a class by working hard. It's the only class I have an A in—ever—so I always try my best, and Mrs. F is always coming around and saying something like "Good work so far. Now try to shade one side of that face more than the other as if that was natural light coming across a room. Does that make sense to you?" And it does.

So I work on shading, and my drawings sometimes turn out okay and sometimes they don't. Every student draws one face each day, and I'm getting better at faces as the term goes on. Also, Mrs. F lets us listen to music after she's done teaching a drawing concept or showing us famous examples from one of her big art books, and this tiny little sophomore girl named Zaylie—who sits next to me—always gives me one of her earbuds and then cranks up her rap music, and we listen to rap while we draw, and that's my favorite part of every school day.

When I get home, I'm in a good mood from art class, and I ride Willa's ATV down to the public library, across the street from Studio 205. I walk in and out of the book stacks, but I don't pull anything off the shelves. I can't find what I'm looking for. I scan the book titles, but all those books next to each other make me feel like I'm trying to count individual pine needles in a clearing in the forest. The titles start to run together, and I lose track of what I want.

The librarian walks over and says, "Can I help you find something?"

"Uh," I say, "no thank you, ma'am," and I walk out into the overcast day, get back on the four-wheeler, and ride home because I don't know if I'm ready to tell anyone yet what I want.

little gray donkey

Saturday, a '78 Chevy pickup turns in, pulling a horse trailer. The driver parks it in the flats. He's a short, balding man I've never seen before, which is odd. There's maybe 350 people in Pierce and I've seen them all. Every single one. So this man must be from Weippe or Judge Town.

The man wipes his hands on his jeans. Looks nervous over his shoulder like someone might be coming up behind him at any moment to hit him in the back of the head. He yells in the direction of the house. "Hey now, Big?"

I'm behind the trailer, fixing a fence line that a deer nudged from the post. I pound a staple. Look up.

The man says again, "Big?" He turns in a circle. "You here?"

I walk over to him. "What do you need?"

"I just need to talk to Big is all. I got some things that, uh . . ." He stops talking. Looks over my shoulder at the house.

I wait.

The man wipes his hands on his jeans again.

I say, "Yeah?"

"Well, is Big here?"

"Nope."

The man looks at the house as though I might be lying. "He really ain't here?"

"Nope," I say again.

"Well, when's he coming back?"

I shake my head. "No idea."

A log truck hits its Jake brakes in front of the Idaho 11 sign. We hear the pump-hiss. Watch the truck rumble across the Orofino Bridge.

"Are you Little?" the man says. "You look a lot like him."

I don't wanna hear that comparison, but I say, "That's what people call me."

"Can I give the stuff to you, then? You think that'd be good enough?"

"Good enough for what?"

The man wipes his hands on his jeans again. "For my debt, for what I owe."

"You've got money for Big?"

"Money"—he nods—"and something else. Here, I'll show you." He takes an envelope out of his back pocket. Hands it to me. "There's $800, straight up, but that ain't all."

I count the bills. All in 20s.

The man says, "You didn't really have to count that. I'd never make the mistake of shorting Big, if you know what I mean."

"Well, maybe you'd miscounted?"

The man laughs. "Oh, no. When it comes to Big, you count three times to make sure it's all there." The man wipes his hands on his jeans again.

I can't figure out what he's wiping off. I say, "What's the other thing you were talking about?"

The man walks back to the horse trailer and opens the doors.

I lean to look inside. It's one of those trailers with latch windows that slide, but none of the slides open. The only light coming in on the end of the trailer is from the slits up high. I can't see well. I say, "What is that?"

"It's a donkey," the man says. "Well bred. Trained to pack. Perfect for a solo hunt, country you can't get a machine into."

"A donkey?"

"It's worth at least $1,500. Best animal on the trail, bar none. You give it to Big, okay?"

I shake my head. "I don't know."

"Oh, no," the man says, "I'm sure he'd want it. You add that to the 8 and it makes 23. Since I owed only $2,000, that makes us more than squared. Ain't that right?"

"Paying more than you owe?"

The man holds his hands up in the air. "Just wanna settle. That's all. You let Big know how much I wanted him to be happy with how things turned out."

"By giving him a donkey?"

The man looks at me like I'm turning down a free six-pack. He says, "No, not just a donkey. It's a real top-quality donkey. Let me lead him and you'll see." The man steps in and takes hold of the rope. The donkey pulls back and kicks the rear wall of the trailer, a sound like a sledgehammer against a tin roof, and both of us jump. The man says, "Watch yourself. He'll kick a hole right through you if he's bothered."

I step way back.

The man pulls him out, and I see the donkey's long ears and short legs. Dark lips curled back. I say, "I don't want him."

"Well, it ain't up to you. It's for Big to decide, you hear? Say Sullivan brought him."

I keep shaking my head. "But you're giving him to me right now. So I'm saying no."

The man's still holding that lead rope, and the donkey doesn't seem bothered anymore. He's not showing his teeth, and he's dropped his head a little. The man says, "It's only for you to give it to Big, right? Don't you understand what I'm saying, kid?"

I don't like it when people ask me if I understand, and I don't like it when people act like I'm just a kid. That's all I get in school, and I don't need any more of it. But this whole deal is for Big, so there's nothing to do about it. I say, "All right, then. I guess."

The man hands the lead rope to me. "You tell Big he only needs two acres at most for a donkey. Maybe less, even. So he can fence a spot in right up there, for example." He points past the graveyard to the Baptist church's flats.

"Yeah, whatever." I wave him off. I don't want this man to tell me what to do.

"So we're square?" he says, and wipes his hands on his jeans one more time.

"I guess so."

"Well, all righty then. Remember, tell Big it was Sullivan." The man taps his chest when he says his own name. Then he walks to the front of his truck, gets in on the driver's side, and starts it up. Now that he's given me the donkey, he's moving like it's bar time on a Friday afternoon. "And tell Big hey for me, okay?"

I watch the man drive up onto the road, the empty horse trailer rattling as he pulls it over the lip of the asphalt. Then he turns left up Main Street and disappears over the rise, into the center of town.

I didn't know what they were. You were drinking Wild Turkey and Coke, half and half, shaking the can in your hand, and I could hear the most-way-gone sound, the tink tink tink of the bottom ounce bouncing around in that red-painted aluminum.

You came into the trailer stumbling, put your arms out to balance but touched nothing, and it looked like you were trying to walk across a slippery log over a creek. I took your elbow but you pulled it away and said, "Don't fuckin' . . . ," and sat down heavy in one of the kitchenette chairs.

It was one of those nights last year—freshman year—when I was trying to do homework but it wasn't going well, none of the algebra answers coming easy, and I folded my textbook closed and pulled it into my lap. That's when you set them on the table, both of them, whatever they were.

I thought they were dried peach halves or apricots maybe. Sitting there, they matched, but I didn't recognize that at first. You turned them until they were symmetrical, mirroring, and it wasn't until you said, "He just *really* wouldn't listen. You know?" and you smiled, and then I knew.

I stood up from the table like I didn't want them to touch me, and I held my math textbook to my chest as if it was something I cared about.

You drank the rest of your mix. Set the can empty—sideways, not upright—on the table and it rolled to the middle until it stopped against one of those ears.

always on my mind

I find a long length of nylon rope behind the house in the shed and tie the donkey to a post. He doesn't pull or fight me. He looks bored. I can't figure out his eyes. They're like the math section on that sophomore PLAN test they made me do in school a couple of weeks ago.

I leave the donkey tied to the post by the shed. Go back to the trailer. Hide the $800 behind the particleboard slat where JT won't find it when he gets out. I had $557 saved up already for the land, so now there's more than $1,350. It's not the $5,000 I need to make my plan happen, but it's partway there.

I push the loose nail back into place, run my fingertips over the seam to see that the board's flush, then get my tool belt and fence staples and walk out. I've got a spool of barb-wire under the shed roof. I find a half-length two-by-four and pick that up. Snap the belt and jack the spool. Then I walk out past the west edge of the cemetery, through the gap at the Baptist church property line. The church land is shaped like a messed-up rectangle, and I walk the south line of fence first to look for gaps.

Along that fence line, there's a stand of eight noble firs planted by someone with an odd sense of humor or a weird idea of forestry. There used to be ten noble firs, but the last two years Big had me diminish the herd at Christmastime.

After the noble patch, there's a fence gap, wire on the ground on the south side, plus another gap on the east. I mend there. Run a double line all the way around the turn. Then I walk the reeds above the seasonal spring, the long grass, and jump water twice before I work along the north.

In the tree gaps where there's dry space, some of the poison oak has pushed up to four feet, the leaves crinkling to red this time of year, fall, the oil dripping like tears off eyelashes. I brush past the growths, nervous, knowing I can scrub my hands and arms with creek sand after, but I still don't like getting near it or touching it.

The only clean double line of fence is on the west, so I don't have to fix that at all. But at the other gaps, I spool high and low, pound staples at the posts. It takes an hour to fix the run to an acre plus.

I go back and get the donkey, lead him up, stop at the gate, and show him his new home. I say, "What do you think?" and pat him on the neck. But he starts when I touch him, kicks at the air behind him, and I take a few steps away. Wait and let him calm down again.

After a minute or so, I take the lead rope, more careful this time, and guide him into the pen. As long as I'm pulling on the rope and not touching his coat, the donkey doesn't kick. I walk him over to the noble fir growth and say, "Home, sweet home?" Flip and loop the lead rope at his neck to shorten it.

Then I go down to the trailer and get a bowl of water. Carry it back up to the pen. The donkey's still standing by the noble firs. I say, "You can drink out of this bowl or you can drink out of that seasonal spring over there. And if you're hungry, eat some of this long grass for now." I don't know why I'm talking to him. The donkey doesn't say anything back.

I walk down to the creek, sliding on the steep bank. I kneel and scrub the wet sand over my arms and hands to cut the poison oak oil. I get the sand between my fingers and rasp the grit back and forth. Lace my fingers together like I'm folding my hands to pray.

When I dip my hands into the creek and look, I think I see the pink water of blood.

riverboat rowan

Sunday evening, I make two grilled-cheese sandwiches on the stove. Cut slices off the cheddar block, lay the bread slices in heated butter and flip them when they brown. Slide them onto a plate, then grab a carrot and pour a cup of water. Sit down at the kitchenette table to eat.

There's a knock at the door. I say, "Hey, Willa," but when I open the door, it's Rowan.

She's leaning against the side of the trailer. "Hey," she says. She has a big black coat on. Way too big for her.

"Oh," I say, and nothing else.

Rowan raises her eyebrows. "Can I come in?"

"Yeah," I say, "sure." I step back to let her through the door.

She slides past me into the space, smelling like coat mold and liquor. I close the door behind her.

"You all right?"

She nods. "Can I sit?" She's leaning against the wall.

I point to the seat across from me, and we both sit down. I look at her. Her trademark eyeliner is smeared like small bruises.

I hold out my plate. "Want a sandwich?"

"Thank you." She takes a grilled cheese, bites, and chews. Talks with her mouth full. " 'S'really good."

I want to ask again if she's okay, ask her where she's been sleeping. I heard from someone at school that she hasn't been home for a while, and I want to ask her about that too, ask her if she and her daddy aren't getting along. But Rowan makes me too nervous to say what I want to say. And when I look at her, at her smeared eyeliner, her green eyes, her cheeks and lips, my stomach twists. Tightens. We eat our sandwiches, and it's hard for me to chew and swallow. With her there, I don't want to eat anything. I don't even feel hungry.

I snap my carrot in half. Offer the bigger half to her, and she takes it.

She says, "I always liked you," and smiles. But her eyes are glassy.

I take a drink of water. Push the cup to her side of the table, and Rowan drinks the rest.

I say, "JT's almost out."

Rowan takes a deep breath. Exhales and nods. "I heard that."

"So will you two, you know . . . still be together?" I don't know why I ask that. It's not even something I want to talk about.

Rowan nods, then shakes her head. Says, "Maybe?"

I get up and refill the water cup. Take a long drink at the sink. "Have you gone to see him?"

"No," she says. "I didn't know what to do about that. Do you think I should?"

"I don't know."

"Because it wasn't . . ."

I remember her two black eyes. The cut across the bridge of her nose. How I couldn't picture him hitting her, open-handed or not. I'd seen him hit a lot of people, but never a girl.

I say, "Maybe it'll be better now."

"Maybe," she says again. She wipes her face on her sleeve, and her eyeliner smears some more. She stands up. "I just wanted to say hello to you. Hadn't seen you in a while."

I say, "You could come to school tomorrow." I stand up and follow her to the door. "With me. I could give you a ride in the morning."

"No," she says, "I don't think so." She walks like a river-boat, tilting back and forth with each crosscurrent. I wonder how much she drank.

"I could pick you up wherever you need. Wherever you've been . . ."

"No," she says. "Thanks, though." She opens the door. Then she turns around, and she's close to me. She reaches up and takes my face in her hands. Pulls me down. Kisses me on the lips, and her tongue touches my bottom lip, quick, like when a dragonfly bumps you coming up a creek along the water. I pull back, and there's Rowan's breath of liquor and grilled cheese. Our faces still close.

Right away I wish I could keep kissing her, but I don't know how to make that happen. I don't know what to do, and I just stand there.

Rowan steps away. Smiles at me, her eyes wet, and she

wipes her face with her sleeve again, this time jagging a line of eyeliner down her cheek.

She jumps down off the step, out onto the grass, stumbling a little. She laughs and says, "Thanks for the food."

"Yeah," I say, "no problem."

Rowan walks across the yard in the evening light. Holds up her hand. Calls out, "See ya," but doesn't turn around again.

I hold up my hand too, but she's turned away and walking fast. She walks across Canal Street, past the historical signs to the four-wheeler bridge, and crosses the Orofino there. She keeps walking along the Idaho 11 in the dark. I don't understand where she's going, but I don't say anything, don't yell to her. I just watch her go.

ghost riders in the sky

Three months after I got transferred out of advanced math, I still hadn't gotten up the nerve to talk to Rowan, but then I saw her and JT together at a school basketball game. Somehow I'd missed it before. I didn't even know they knew each other, but they were well past knowing each other by then. Rowan was leaning against JT, had one of her long arms looped around his waist, her thumb hooked on his belt underneath his letterman's jacket.

I walked past them on my way to get popcorn at the concessions stand and I pretended like I didn't even see them there. But JT said, "Hey, Little," and nodded his chin at me and I nodded back.

Rowan and JT were always together after that. In the hall. In Big's truck. Or Rowan waiting after football practice and them walking off somewhere together.

The first time she came to our trailer I pretended she'd come there for me, but pretending something like that is like eating a clump of dandelions when you haven't eaten anything at all for three days.

it is what it is

In the morning, before school, I find another chicken carcass. Gutted same as the last ones. No bobcat prints this time, but I know it's him because of the hollowing at the underside. The hen count is down to nine now, and I wonder if I'm gonna have to sit up for the cat. I'd rather not shoot him, but there are things in this life that aren't asking what I want.

I dump the carcass and start collecting morning eggs. Three from the grass, and I stop at the sound of Derlene puking off the porch. I watch from where I am.

She retches, bent over. Turns her head and says, "You gettin' a good show?"

I shake my head.

She puts an index finger over a nostril and blows a nose chunk. Says, "I know you've been eatin' off my stamps."

"So?"

"So you better come at life a little more grateful." Derlene clears her other nostril. Shuts her eyes to a headache.

I say, "I'll think about that."

Derlene raises an index finger. Points at me. Then

43

switches to the middle finger and holds that up as she ducks inside the house.

I go back to egg hunting.

Uncle Lucky comes out a minute later, a morning miracle. He walks down the steps, careful and slow, as if his head is a china teapot, already starting to crack. He's wearing a short-sleeved button-up, his hair combed for the first time in a week.

I say, "Where are you headed?"

"To apply for jobs. Make copies in Orofino."

I pick the stuck grass off the eggs in my hand. "What kind of jobs?"

"Nothing in particular," he says. His hands are shaking, and I know he'll catch a shot in town as soon as the interviews are done. "But I gotta keep applying for jobs if I wanna stay on unemployment." He smiles at the old joke, one brown tooth showing at the front of his mouth.

"Well," I say, "I hope you get one of them." It's been five months since his last temp.

Lucky spits in the grass. "I can't say that I'm too qualified." He winks and pulls out his car keys, walks over to his Buick Skylark.

I look at the house and see that Derlene's come back out on the porch. She's sitting on the top step, smoking a Marlboro Red, seeming uninterested.

I walk back to my trailer to cook up some scrambled eggs.

the gambler

After school, I get a flake of alfalfa from the neighbor Henshaw's shed, go up to the donkey pen, and Willa follows me. It rained earlier, and the donkey looks miserable. He's in the middle of that little stand of noble firs, coat wet and mane wet, reminding me of the black bear. I'm thinking about the heavy smell of the bear's fur as we skinned him.

Willa says, "It doesn't look like the donkey enjoys this rain."

"Huh?" I say. I was still way back in my mind with the bear on top of the snow in February, his blood and fat staining a circle bigger than I could've ever imagined.

"But I like it," Willa says. "I like the rain a lot. I like playing in it and I like the smell of it. And I like the mud it makes." She reaches down and sticks her index finger into a rained-out gopher hole, swirls that finger around like she's mixing a straw in a milk shake.

I point at the donkey. "Well, you're right about him. He doesn't like it one bit."

Willa stands up. Wipes her finger on her jeans, leaving a brown smudge. "Can I ride him?"

"The donkey?"

"Yeah."

"This donkey isn't a pet," I say. "I'm not sure if he's safe."

Willa puts her hands on her hips. "Well, what did the man say?"

"The man who left him?"

"Yeah."

"He said the donkey's trail-broke, but . . ."

"So he's broke," Willa says. "And broke is broke, right?"

I don't know much about horses, and I know even less about donkeys. Trail-broke could mean a lot of things. Also, I wonder if donkeys take a saddle, or if people ride them bareback.

Willa starts to push through the small trees. Says, "I'm riding him."

The donkey's backing away and snorting at us.

"Willa, he really looks pissed."

"He'll be fine," Willa says. "I have a way with things."

Willa may only be ten, but she sometimes reminds me of that middle-aged woman who works behind the counter at the Mini-Mart, raspy-voiced, always walking out in front of the store and glaring at the sun.

Willa backs the donkey up against the last few trees near the fence.

I say, "Haven't you ever heard about cornering animals?"

She turns and smiles at me. "That cornered animals are easier to catch?"

"No," I say, "that they might bite your face off or rip your arm out of its socket. Stuff like that."

"This is a donkey, Little, and how's a donkey gonna rip my arm out of its socket?"

I realize that I still have the flake of alfalfa under my arm. All this time I forgot about it. I turn and drop the flake underneath a pine tree, and even though it doesn't really make a sound when it hits the ground, it's like some sort of bell is rung in the donkey's head. He starts and does a little trot past Willa and comes running up to me and the food. He puts his head down and starts eating.

Willa says, "Do you think he'd care if I grabbed a handful of his mane?"

"Right now? Yes."

"No, not now," she says. "When I'm riding him." She walks around the back of the pine tree, puts her foot on an old branch knot, and bear-hugs the trunk to pull herself up. She shimmies and stands, reaching high for the first branch. When she gets it with one hand, she lunges and catches it with her other hand too. Then she swings her legs up above her head, over the branch, pulling herself up into a seated position.

"Willa, what are you—"

"That's the first half of the plan," she says. She climbs and steps around the tree until she's on the near side, directly above the donkey.

I say, "This isn't a good idea."

But she ignores me. She slides down. Puts her arms around the lowest branch and swings her legs out into the air, windmilling them above the donkey's back, then drops. The donkey's neck arches like someone's stuck a bull thistle up his butt, then his head rears back.

I yell, "Jump off, Willa! Quick!"

But she wraps her little hands in his mane and clutches

the donkey with her knees and elbows. The donkey takes off running, snorting and zigzagging all over the place.

"Jump off! Just jump off quick!"

But Willa doesn't jump. She holds on tight, rides that donkey to the far side of the pen, through the water and along the fence to the northwest corner, then back again along the fence going the other way. The donkey stops to kick, puts all his weight on his front hooves and kicks back with his hind legs again. Willa grips tight and stays locked on his back, then the donkey runs again. I can see the huge smile on Willa's face, even from a hundred feet away.

Willa's just lifted her head up when the donkey stops, and it stops hard, and Willa flies forward like a football popped out of a running back's hands. Willa looks so small in the air, and when she hits the ground, face-first into a gopher mound, divoting, her legs and arms roll over the top of her head in an awkward-looking somersault.

She rolls and skids, and before I can get to her, she's shaking and sobbing, curled into a little ball. The donkey is behind her, head down, snorting, seeming like he might charge her or stomp on her. "Willa!" I yell. "Are you all right?" I run up to her. Push the donkey's face back. Push it hard. Say, "Get! Get away now!" And I kneel down, put my hand on Willa's shoulder. "It's gonna be okay, Willa. You're gonna be all right."

She's got her face in her hands.

Then she rolls over onto her back, and I see that she's laughing, laughing so hard that her whole body is shaking. She laughs for a long time, then says, "Did you see that, Little? Did you see me ride him all over the place?" The left side of Willa's face is covered in mud. It's like some kind of shading exercise on a drawing in my art class, thick brown all over. Willa's laughing, and I see she's even got mud on a couple of her front teeth.

"Are you okay, though? Not hurt at all?"

"Oh, heck no. I landed in soft mud." Willa's still laughing. "Hey, Little," she says, "wanna hear a dirty joke?"

"A dirty joke?"

"Yeah," she said, "a white horse fell in the mud."

I shake my head. "That's not very funny."

"Wanna hear a dirtier joke, then?" Willa wipes the back of her wrist across her face and smears the mud to her ear. "The white horse fell in again," she says, and rests her head back down on the ground, her whole body shaking with laughter once more.

come along and ride this train

At school on Tuesday, I'm worrying about math even after math class is over. No matter what I do, it doesn't make sense. Numbers and lines and letters scribbled everywhere.

I look for Rowan in the halls but I don't find her. So I dip into Room 2 to talk to Mr. Polchowski. But he has a substitute, some old lady with a weird red growth on her neck, something that looks like a chewed-up glob of Skittles stuck to her skin. I slip back out before anyone notices I'm there.

I eat lunch outside. Egg salad sandwich. Thermos of milk. Watch two kids duck down into the alders by the creek to smoke weed before fourth period.

I get up and walk back inside the school, on to my next class.

In art, fifth period, we're working on texturizing hair, hard lines, soft lines, and shading. Mrs. F demonstrates smudging with her middle finger. I try to draw Willa the way her face was covered in mud. It doesn't look like her, but it sort of looks like someone, sort of like a real person, so that's good enough for me. That's improvement.

Zaylie comes in late. She sits down and whispers, "My boyfriend's an asshole."

"Yeah," I say, "I know who he is."

Zaylie glares at me. "You shouldn't say that. He's not really an asshole."

"What?"

"He's just a *little* bit of an asshole . . . today. But whatever. It doesn't matter." Zaylie looks at her iPod screen and starts scrolling through songs. "What should our soundtrack be today?"

I look at the screen, but I don't know the people she's looking at. I say, "How 'bout that guy?"

"Too old-school for today," Zaylie says. "We need something newer. Something better."

"Something fast?"

"No." She keeps scrolling down her lists. "Maybe something slow. Maybe something that makes us feel like we're gonna get out of this town someday."

"Okay." I go back to shading the hair on my picture of Willa. Then I look at Zaylie.

She bobs her head back and forth. "Maybe Drake? Maybe 'Tuesday'?"

"Tuesday?"

"Right. It's ILoveMakonnen featuring Drake? It's so terrible that it's good. And we're on a Tuesday right now. Working hard on the weekends."

"Wait, did you say *on* a Tuesday?"

"Exactly." Zaylie hands me one earbud. "Club is going up. That's our future."

I have no idea what she's talking about. I put the earbud in.

Zaylie says, "Now we're ready to draw, right?" She picks up her pencil.

"Okay," I say. Then we listen to "Tuesday" three times in a row. By the third time through, Zaylie and I are mouthing the words, leaning into each other, singing quietly so Mrs. F doesn't get annoyed at us.

When I came outside, I didn't know anything about what you were doing. You were leaning over the trunk of your Trans Am. The other guy was someone from Judge Town, long-haired, and I didn't know his name even though I'd seen him before. I started to walk up, but then I stopped because you didn't say, "Come on over here, Little," the way you normally did.

You held a rolled-up dollar bill in your hand like a cigarette. There was something on the trunk. I couldn't see what.

"Is he cool?" the long-haired man said.

"Don't worry," you said. "He's real tall but he's not even eleven yet." You put the rolled-up dollar bill to your nostril and leaned over the back of the car.

The man stared at me like I was a mosquito that needed squashing.

I would've gone back inside, but JT was with a girl in the trailer and I hated listening to their sloppy eighth-grade kissing and the way the girls always said, "I don't know if I wanna do that yet," and JT always said, "If you just relax, you know you're gonna like it."

The other option was to walk through the cemetery, which I was afraid of back then. Fifth grade, and I kept thinking about all those bodies in the ground. Sometimes, at night, I'd start thinking about the rows of graves behind the trailer, what each body looked like underground, how rotten they were, whether or not they still had hair, or what their eyes might look like.

In the other cemetery across town, the Chinese cemetery, I knew people had dug up their relatives from a hundred years ago and sent them back to the country where they were born, and I didn't like to think about that either.

walk the line

I wake up on Saturday and feel an itch between my index and middle fingers. I spread those fingers, and a sore cracks open, a line of pink, yellow in the middle. I must've not scrubbed all the poison oak oil off the last day I worked. I look at the sore and consider bleaching it. Sometimes I use a Q-tip and hold the bleach on until I'm sure it'll scab up.

JT's getting released in a week, and I have to go visit him. I promised Saturdays, so later I'll drive down the Grade along the Clearwater to Orofino. Visit him at County. But first, I drive Big's truck around to the back of the cemetery, all those dead people I don't even think about anymore. Mr. Reynolds, the manager, told me to work on three family plots today, to clear bull and Canada thistle, make a slash pile, burn back roots, and clear poison oak nubs.

I start cutting and clearing, dragging and building piles. It's hot work with gloves and a coat on to avoid the oak, and I'm sweating heavy as I use the burner to scorch. The rash on my hand is worse inside my glove. I can feel the pink spreading between my fingers, the sores branching out. I want to rip my gloves off and itch my fingers, but I know that'll only make things even worse. I stop and shake my hands. Breathe deep. Think about the next thing I need to do for work.

I like to do work and not think too much, just use my body. Focus on whatever the job is I've gotta do. Sometimes when things start coming into my head, and I start to wonder about my mom or something, or my dad, and I start to picture all the different places he could be, I like to go over the simple steps of the job and just think about those steps and nothing else.

I see that a family plot has cracks in its wrought-iron enclosure, so I focus on that. I mix the toothpaste compound, talk through the steps out loud so I can't think of anything else. I say, "Mix gray and red, then smear the paste into the cracks. After that, you push it down into the open holes in the candle holders. Then you take a rag and wipe it smooth."

I enjoy the chemical smell of the paste, like inhaling gas fumes at the Mini-Mart pumps.

The work takes four and a half hours, and I write my start and end time in the little notebook Mr. Reynolds leaves for me in the box nailed to the bottom tree. When I go back to my truck on the road next to the cemetery, the deputy's cruiser is parked behind it.

I wipe my face with my work gloves, forgetting about poison oak. I look around. See the cruiser but not the deputy. I say, "White? You around here?"

"Yep," he says. He's crouched down, behind the rear bumper of Big's truck. He fingers the metal. "Would you look right here and tell me what you see?"

"Right where?"

"Here," he says, and beckons me with his finger.

I walk back there and stand above him. Tilt my head.

He's tapping his finger against the metal. "Would you say that this is a spot of blood or what?"

I lean in. Look over his shoulder. "I don't know." And I don't. It could be paint or rust or blood, any of them.

"Right here. Look close." He points to a dull-colored spot. Brownish red. He says, "Wouldn't you say that looks blood-like?"

I say, "I don't know," again.

"You don't know?" Deputy pulls out a little flip pad. Writes shorthand. "Well, crouch down closer, then. Take a good, hard look at it."

I don't want to, but I crouch close, right next to the deputy.

"Right here." He points at the dot.

I say, "Is that red enough to be blood?"

"Yep, for sure"—the deputy almost touches it with his fingertip—"that's what blood looks like when it's dried."

"Oh."

The deputy rubs his face as if he's real tired and it's late at night. He stands up and looks off across the cemetery toward my trailer and the big house.

I watch his face. Think about the story I heard, that he got a divorce not too long ago, six months maybe, that his wife left him for a foot doctor from Lewiston.

When the deputy turns back around, I pretend I wasn't watching him. I look off the other way. We're next to the part of the cemetery where the people were buried in the

1800s, some of the oldest graves, grave markers that are just flat stone rectangles on the ground. If you didn't look too hard, you'd see only grass and weeds. You wouldn't know there were bodies underneath.

"You know what," Deputy White says, "I'm wondering what Big is up to."

I nod with him. "Me too. I've been asking around."

"And," he says, "I'm wondering why you have his truck."

"Because he left it at the house," I say. "He drove off in the Trans Am a few weeks ago, so I just keep using his truck until he comes back."

"Headed in which direction?"

"Which way did he go? Toward Weippe, I guess, or Judge Town. Something down the road that way." I point south. "That's all I saw."

"And nobody knows more than that?"

"Like I said, I've been asking."

Deputy White puts his hands on his utility belt. Says, "Hmm." Then he doesn't say anything else. So we both stand there. I don't know what I'm supposed to say, and I keep thinking of things that wouldn't come out right.

Finally, Deputy White says, "You finished with work for today?"

"Yep."

"And where're you headed after this?"

"Orofino."

"To . . ."

"To see my brother."

"JT"—Deputy nods—"he's still in county lockup, right?"

"For another week. Then he should get his release."

Deputy reaches into his shirt pocket and gets out a package of sunflower seeds. Puts a handful in his mouth, then holds the bag out to me.

I take a few and put them in my mouth.

Deputy cracks the seeds and spits the husks. Says, "Well, good luck to him, then. Tell him to stay out of jail after this."

"All right."

" 'Cause he could still get offers, you know."

I say, "Maybe, maybe not."

"Too much talent anyway." The deputy moves some seeds with his tongue. Sets a pouch in his cheek. "Too much talent to just rot in a jail cell for the rest of his life. He'd've been first- or second-team All-State if there was any team around him for sure. But he had to do everything, go all over the place and wear himself thin. I seen that a few times now with different kids."

I chew my seeds and spit the husks into the weeds. I don't say anything because I don't like talking about JT's football days.

Deputy says, "Tell him to keep lifting and training, okay?"

"Okay," I say, and fish in my jeans pocket. Take out the truck keys. Then walk to the driver's door.

Deputy White says, "Don't forget to tell him he's still got a chance, you hear that? Sometimes people gotta hear it."

I nod and get in. "Yeah," I say, "I'll tell him that."

He walks up and puts his hand on the open truck door right before I pull it closed. Stands there and leans in. Tilts his head down and spits seed husks onto the ground.

I'm sitting in the driver seat with the keys in my hand, not sure if I should start the truck or not.

Deputy White spits again. "You might need to hear that too," he says. "Sometimes kids get dipped in a world that isn't gonna be kind to them. You understand?"

I nod.

"But you still got a chance. Maybe make a different thing happen." He puts his finger in his mouth and fishes out a few seeds that got stuck up in his gums. Wipes the husks on his pant leg. He shakes his head. "Don't do a repeat of someone else's life."

"I won't."

"Well, I seen a lot of kids think that they won't, or say that they won't, but if a griddle's spittin' out pancakes, sometimes the pancakes just keep on comin'."

Deputy White steps back and shuts my truck door for me. Pats twice on the hood and walks away.

didn't it rain

I take the Greer Grade to the drop-down along the Clear-water River and the 12. Storm clouds build in the southwest, roiling cumulonimbus, white anvil high and dark blue underneath. Near purple.

The jail's on Michigan Street, above the courthouse, across from a coffee trailer, and I smell roasted coffee and baked goods as I get out of the truck. I look down to the Camas Prairie Railroad tracks, the changing yard, switch sets. Look up and see the thunderstorm closing in, a single, enormous column, as if it's come to destroy the earth.

But the rain doesn't hit me before I go into the courthouse. I walk upstairs through the metal detector to the check-in window and sign in. Show my ID. Then I sit down on a bench against the wall. There's nothing to look at but the people around me and the signs on the wall. This is what Mr. Polchowski is always calling a good reading opportunity, but I didn't bring a book.

A man comes to the visitor check-in window. He has light brown skin and he's strong like he's spent his whole grown life in a weight room. He has symbols tattooed all over the back of his shaved head, words in Spanish, and I think about my dad. Wonder where he is. Wonder what he looks like.

A deputy with a huge gut walks up to the young man and says, "Nope." Shakes his finger. Puts his hands on his hips.

The younger man looks at him. I picture the two of them late at night, in an alley behind a bar, and there's no way that this heavy-stomached deputy wins that battle.

The deputy says, "I know all 'bout those signs right there." He points at the back of the man's head.

"What are you talking about?" The younger man has a Mexican accent, and hearing the accent makes the deputy smile in a mean way.

He says, "Those are gang symbols, fella. You and I both know it."

A second deputy sees the two of them talking and walks over from the other end of the hall. Puts his hand on the pistol grip of his Taser.

"Nope," the first deputy says again. "You ain't visitin' today. Maybe next time you'll get smart and wear a hat to cover those up." He mimics the motion of pulling on a stocking cap. Talks a little louder than he did before he heard the accent.

The younger man says, "But I'm not doing anything wrong."

"Don't matter," the deputy says. "You just gotta scoot anyway. You understand *vámonos?*"

The younger man puts his index finger in the deputy's face, the muscles tightening through his forearm and up into his shoulder. "Are you telling me how to wear my clothes? I am not a criminal."

The deputy brings that mean smile out again. He says, "With those tattoos all over you? I seriously doubt you're not a criminal."

The other deputy unholsters his Taser and holds it in his hand, and all three of them look at it for a moment.

The younger man shakes his head, but he puts his finger down and walks to the door. Then he turns and backs out of the door, holding up his middle finger.

"I'll remember that," the deputy calls out. "I'll remember that I seen your stupid Mexican face the next time you're arrested."

It's still a little while until visiting hours start. I watch the deputies talk to each other, tell jokes, put their thumbs in their utility belts, and walk over to mess with the woman who works behind the counter.

Finally, a third deputy steps out from behind the big metal door with a clipboard and says, "Gavin McCardell?" and then looks up.

I raise my hand.

"Are you here to visit Jonathan Thomas McCardell?"

"Yes, sir."

"Well, come on now. It's this way."

Down the hall, JT's at the third phone booth. I sit down across from him, but we have to wait a few seconds for the phones to click on. He smiles at me and I smile back. He's built up pretty big now, gained a lot of weight back in the last two months, rounded out his shoulders again, brought the veins out on his arms.

The red light flashes on the wall, and we both pluck our phones off the hooks.

JT says, "Hey," and winks at me.

"Hey back," I say.

"How've you been?"

"Not bad, JT. You look strong."

He nods. "A lot of push-ups. I'm up to 600 every other day now. Rotate that with pulls and core."

I shake my head. JT was always good at motivating himself to work out. I was never as good at that. I mostly just work out when I work.

He says, "There's really not much else to do in here."

"Do they treat you good?"

"Pretty much." He rubs his face, clean-shaven now, none of his usual stubble. He says, "How's our wonderful extended family?"

"Good," I say. "Or good enough. Willa's good, at least." I don't know if I should tell him about Big yet. I still haven't decided.

JT says, "Just the usual with everyone else?"

I picture telling him about Big and also not telling him about Big. Two paths in my brain splitting like a two-trunked white pine.

JT smiles. Shakes his head. "Our family, huh?"

"Right." The phone feels oily in my hand. I rub my fingers on it. Then I think about the Mexican man in the lobby and the worker I saw running corrugated roofing the other day. I say, "Do you ever wonder about Dad?"

JT makes a face like I just spit in his bowl of soup. He says, "Why would I wonder about him?"

"Well, do you remember anything?"

"From when I was three?" JT smiles, but it's the smile I've seen right before he sucker-punches somebody at a party.

I say, "I guess I forgot you were only three."

JT shakes his head. "I don't remember much of anything."

"So he and Mom just . . ." I shift in my plastic seat. ". . . And then after Mom . . . he just took off?"

JT taps the glass like he's tapping my chest. He says, "You already know this story."

"Well, I guess sometimes I wonder if I'm missing something."

"Little, there's no conspiracy here. Just fucked-up people. Things happen and people die, right? Or they don't die. Either way." JT takes his phone and wipes it on his shirt. "This phone's fuckin' nasty. Can you feel all the oil?" He smiles and stands up. Hangs his phone back on the wall. So I stand and hang up my phone too. Then a deputy steps forward and takes JT under the arm like he's an old man who needs help getting up and down the stairs. JT looks back and smiles at me. Raises his eyebrows.

I wave and watch him go.

When I walk out of the courthouse onto the black asphalt, it's bright sunny and hot for October, but the ground is wet.

There must've been a rainstorm while I was inside, or hail that's already melted. I look for a rainbow to the northeast but the steep hills block my view.

The water on the ground is evaporating. Water-smoke hanging low. All that wet, but the plants in the landscaped borders are still yellow, everything dry and cracking open as if the world has shifted one step closer to the sun.

two weeks after

Willa's bruise is turning from a purple blue to a yellow now. Two weeks out. Streaked like a paint smear under her one eye. A dripping triangle. I touch the mush, and she squints. Says, "It doesn't even hurt now. Not anymore."

That night, when we were sitting at the kitchenette table, I told her to tell people she fell off the porch. We practiced telling the story back and forth, again and again, before she went to school the next day. Her hands shook, but she practiced.

After three rounds, Willa looked straight at me and said, "I was in a hurry to get to school. I grabbed my lunch off the table and ran out the front door. I was just about to run down the steps when my toe caught on the edge of a porch board, and I launched out over the steps, hit hard, face-first in the yard. Right here." She touched next to her bad eye. "On the grass, five feet down."

I said, "That'll work. Just tell it like that."

She practiced again. Her voice cracked the first few times, but then it smoothed out.

The teacher called the house after school, said she wanted to talk to a parent, but I erased the message. Uncle Lucky or Derlene wouldn't have called back anyway. They were down at the Flame Bar all night, buying double drinks at last call.

father and son

I ride Willa's ATV back down to the library. Walk in. Look across the different-colored book spines, one to the next, walk slow past red, black, green, red, black, orange, blue, blue, red, green, and so on. I shake my head. Stop and go back to read the titles. Don't know what section I'm in right now, everything sounding like a bad movie:

Quiver for Me Alone

If You Will Only Wait for Me

Seven Days with a Dark, Handsome Man

I walk to a new section. HISTORY.

I move on to the next section. GEOLOGY.

The librarian walks up. Says, "Can I help you find something?"

"Um . . . ," I say, "well, the thing is . . . I guess I wanna sorta see what Spanish is like. Does that make any sense?"

"Sure." The librarian smiles at me. "That makes sense. Let me help you."

She leads me over to a different section. The shelf reads WORLD LANGUAGES.

There are a lot of dictionaries there, and some thick

books that say FRENCH, GERMAN, ITALIAN, JAPANESE, and SPAN-ISH. She pulls two Spanish books off the shelf. Puts them in my hands. They're as thick as math books but don't have any numbers on them. I don't open them.

"Are those maybe the sorts of things you're looking for?" She taps the cover of the top book.

I nod slowly.

She says, "Are those not what you're looking for?"

"Well," I say, "I'm really not that . . ."

She smiles and waits.

I don't know if I should explain myself to her or not. It seems like a bad thing to tell a librarian I'm not a good reader. "See, the thing is, ma'am, I like stories a lot. And I like books that tell a story, like in English class or something . . ."

"Okay . . ." She nods, waiting for me to explain more.

"But the thing is, I'm really not that good of a student if it's not a story or an art class. Does that make any sense?"

She says, "Yes," but she tilts her head sideways like she doesn't fully understand me.

I say, "I guess I mean that these books look sorta like math books or science books or something. And I'm not real good at math or science, either one, you know?"

"Oh." She smiles. "Okay, yes, I understand. And I have an idea. First"—she taps the top Spanish book's cover—"these aren't like math books. See this first one? It's a joke, but it says *The Complete Idiot's Guide to Learning Spanish*. Now, I know that you're not an idiot of any kind—and that's the publisher's little joke—but what they want you to feel is comfortable. Not too overwhelmed."

I look at the cover and see what she's saying.

"See," she says, "it starts out quite simply, so you can feel accomplished right from the beginning."

"Oh, all right." I hand the other book back to her. Keep the idiot's guide.

"But the other thing I thought of is this. . . ." She motions to me to follow her. "I could give you a cassette series to work through at the same time so you could hear the language. Do you have a cassette player somewhere? I know tapes are kind of an old-timey thing these days, but our library's not too up-to-date."

"In my grandpa's truck I've got a tape player."

"Well then, perfect. You can check out the tapes and the book, and make sure you listen to the tapes a little at the start. I want you to get used to the sounds of the words, and start to hear how they form simple sentences. All right?"

"All right."

"Now let me see if you have a card with us or if we need to open a new account." She walks behind the counter and starts clicking keys on her computer.

Outside the library, I put the tapes and the Spanish book on the hunting rack on the front of my four-wheeler and drive back home. At the trailer, I sit down at the kitchenette table and crack the cover of *The Complete Idiot's Guide*, read Chapter 1: "The Top Ten Reasons You Should Study Spanish."

hurt

The next morning, I can feel the poison oak rash starting up next to my left eye. The beginnings of itch. The skin rising pink.

I'm making scrambled eggs when someone knocks on the trailer door.

I yell, "Come in!" and Rowan does.

Her hair is matted, but her eyes are bright. She looks more sober this time. She says, "Hey."

"Hey," I say, and point to a chair.

She sits. Puts her elbows on the table.

"Did you stay in town last night?"

"Yeah."

I flip the scrambled eggs. "Where'd you sleep?"

"Do you really want to know?" she says. "Well, let's just say that I'm keeping my sense of humor." She wipes her nose on her sleeve and looks at the smear of snot.

I slice cheese and lay it across the top of the eggs. "Your sense of humor?"

"Well," she says, "I learned how to break into places on You-Tube, watched nine different videos, and practiced on my own."

"Okay, so you're breaking into vacant houses now?"

With the mill closed, they're all over town.

"Sometimes," Rowan says, "but not usually. Not vacant houses."

"Then where?" I turn the burner off. Move the eggs one more time so they don't brown on the bottom.

"Museums. Historical locations." She sniffs and wipes her nose again.

"Really?" I split the eggs in half. Get a second plate from the drying rack. Put half of the eggs on the first plate, grab a fork, and hand that plate to Rowan.

She says, "I slept in the logging museum last night, on Main, and before that, the courthouse. I move around."

"The courthouse . . . You mean the original courthouse?"

"Yep." She eats a big bite of eggs. Chews and talks with her mouth full. "Built in 1861."

I scrape the rest of the eggs out of the pan onto my plate. Sit down across from Rowan. "But why museums?"

"Why?" She shrugs. "I don't know. It's funny to me?"

We both eat for a minute.

I look at Rowan's matted hair. Say, "Are you sure you're okay?"

"I'm doing fine," she says. "Not too bad, really. Not too bad at all."

"But what about sleeping? You have to break into places just to sleep?"

"I'm the Huck Finn of Pierce," she says. "Museums are my corncribs."

I take a bite of eggs. Say, "I haven't read that book."

"You should." Rowan squints, and her face gets real serious. "Twain's amazing."

"To be honest, Rowan, I don't read too much." This seems to be something I'm admitting a lot these days.

Rowan puts her hands flat on the tabletop. Spreads her fingers and looks at them. "That's too bad. If you read *Huck Finn*, you'd understand some things."

"Like?"

Rowan tips her head to the side the way she always does. This time a matted clump of hair slides off the top of her head and dangles next to her ear. She says, "For example, you'd understand that if you had my daddy, you wouldn't sleep at home either. Huckleberry knew to stay away from his Pap Finn, right?" She smiles when she says that, but we both get quiet.

I think about what her home must be like as I eat the rest of my eggs. How there's so many different types of trouble. My trouble's one thing. Hers another. And there's other lives out there in this town, or not even just this town, but the world, lives that are a different kind of hard.

I finish my last bite of eggs and scrape my plate.

Rowan finishes her eggs too. "Thanks for the food, Little."

"No problem."

Rowan leans forward and taps my plate with her fork. "I just sort of drop in on you, don't I?"

"Yeah, but I like it."

"Are you sure?"

Rowan's eyes are so bright green I want to swim in them. "Yeah," I say, "I'm sure. You can come by anytime."

I take my plate to the sink and notice the clock on the stove. "Oh, shit. I've gotta go to school."

"School?"

"Wait, and you do too, Rowan. Let's go."

"Me? To school?"

"Yeah. Come on."

She laughs. "I don't even know what I'd do if I went. It's been two weeks, maybe three, since I went in for one, single, awkward day, and everyone either stared at me or yelled at me about my attendance before that. To be honest, I don't even know my teachers' names this term."

"Well, then let's go. Today can be the day when you learn their names."

"Fine." Rowan stands up and steps over to the sink. Scrubs her plate quick with the sponge, rinses it, and puts it on the drying rack. Then she leans over and combs water into her hair with her fingers. Detangles the matted clump that was hanging from the top of her head. "Little," she says, "do you have a toothbrush I can borrow?"

"Sure." I go into the bathroom and get JT's. It doesn't look good, but I know Rowan won't care.

We brush together at the kitchenette sink. Spit down the drain and lean over the sink to drink out of the tap one after the other. "Thanks," Rowan says, and taps the toothbrush against the side of the sink. Sets it on the counter to dry. She reaches into her sweatshirt pocket and pulls out a baggie. Dips for a handful of pills and puts a few in my hand. "If you have a bad day at school, crush one or two of these and snort them."

"What are they?"

"Adderall. I got 'em from Judy at the Flame."

"You mean the younger bartender? Do you hang out with her?"

"A little. We party a bit. Or I stay at her place sometimes. And if I come in the back door of the Flame when it's open, she'll let me read in a booth. Most of the time, she'll even slip me drinks."

"Why?"

"We have a deal. She gives me what I want, and in return I tell her what happens in all the books her community college teachers assign."

"Oh." I look at the Adderall pills in my hand. Almost give them back because I know I won't take them. But Rowan never gives me anything. "Okay," I say, and put them in the pocket of my Carhartt. "Thanks."

I have the first Spanish tape in the tape deck in the truck, but I turn it off as soon as I start the engine. I don't want to explain to Rowan why I'm learning the names for colors in Spanish.

We drive with no music on, just the hum of the V8 under the hood, the low rumble on the flats and the higher growl of the engine when I drop the pedal to push uphill.

After the Judge Town turn, past the Chinese Hanging site, and through the curves that follow, Rowan puts her hand on my thigh. I look over when she does it, but she isn't looking at me. She's just staring out the windshield, looking straight ahead, and she doesn't say anything even when a redtail hawk drops from a tree in front of us and plunges into a field to hunt.

My very first memory is of you making us Quaker oatmeal on the stove. You pulled a chair up next to the counter and had me stand and watch, learning how to cook next to you. You cut pats of butter and stirred them into the bubbling mix, then spoonfuls of brown sugar tinting it dark. When you pulled the pot off the burner, you poured cream until the oatmeal was two small islands in a white lake.

You waited for the pot to cool and set out bowls and spoons for me and JT. You said, "This is Super Meal, boys," then poured us each a big bowl. I moved my chair over to the table and sat down in front of my food.

You said, "Eat this to get big and strong."

We both said, "Thank you," as we slurped our first bites.

"Eat this," you said, "and you'll be able to work all day in the woods."

But we didn't work in the woods. JT and I were seven and four that year.

We leaned into our bowls and ate. Ducked our heads. We always ate a lot, were always hungry, both tall like you, though even then you knew I would be taller than JT when we grew up. Sometimes people asked if we were twins, and JT would spit on the sidewalk when they asked that. Roll his eyes and shake his head.

That year, people asked if I was in the first or second grade, wondered why I seemed so slow. But I hadn't even started kindergarten. Wasn't yet five years old.

Next to the pot of Super Meal, you stood, leaning against the stove, wearing one of your red flannel shirts, finished drinking a Hamm's pounder. You leaned down to look out the window when a red-winged blackbird ducked by, then stood back up after it was gone.

We all lived in the big house then, even Derlene and Lucky. But they were young married and early drunks. Spent a lot of their time upstairs in their room. And there was no Willa yet. Not even on the way.

You were still leaning against the stove, not looking out the window anymore, but watching us eat our Super Meal. You tilted your beer can all the way up then, shook the last drops into your mouth, went to the fridge to open another.

That's what I remember.

I don't know if Rowan made it through the school day. I'm not sure if she went to any of her classes. I looked for her after my last period, but I never saw her.

When I get home, the poison oak rash is rimming my left eye like a pink moon. I go into the bathroom and rub Cortizone 10 on it and step outside for sunlight. Hope for dry. Then I go back into the trailer and make some food. Eat it.

I haven't seen Willa, and that's weird on a school day. She might wander and explore, but all paths lead back to the trampoline in the yard at some point. Not this evening, though. I haven't seen her jump once.

She took her ATV somewhere, and I drive around in the truck trying to find her. Drive up Walker Road by the National Guard school, then back down Canal, past the Baptist church, up the hill past the Timber and the Saw Shop, drop down to Clearwater at the Blue Moose, then the Orofino Creek run on Fromelt. But I don't see her any of those places.

I idle the truck and think. Three vacant houses to my left, real estate signs picketed in the front yards. I read the signs, and they say none over $30,000. One of the houses has an irrigation ditch half dug next to shrubs, the open ditch clicking something in my brain, and I think of where Willa might be.

I drive along Second Street, past the tire shop, and up to Stover. At the turn there, across from the New Life Fellowship Church, I see Willa standing on the hillside in the old Chinese cemetery. Her ATV's parked below. I pull over and park on the shoulder. Leave the truck and walk up the hillside.

Willa's sitting in an empty grave now.

I say, "It's kind of creepy how you hang out up here sometimes."

"There's no bodies left, Little. They all got dug up and sent back."

"Are you sure?"

"Lucky said so." Willa never calls him Dad or Daddy. Always Lucky.

"You know that him saying so doesn't make it true. I think there's bodies here for sure."

Willa shrugs. Pats the ground in the bottom of the hole she's sitting in. "Not in this one. I think it was a kid's grave. It's a little shorter than the others. That's why I sit in it."

I look across the slant. In between the trees, there are holes every few feet. Rows and rows where the dead used to lay. I say, "Willa, this is a creepy place."

Willa smiles with her gap-teeth. Nods her head fast. "I've been here a lot lately. Tell me again why there were so many Chinese?"

"Gold mining. Everyone struck it big around 1860, mined

all the easy-to-get gold out of the creeks. Then the Chinese came in after and mined the creeks again. Did the hardest labor."

Willa pats the pine needles in the bottom of her grave. "Did any of them make much money?"

"Some."

Willa lays back, settles herself in the grave, straight-bodied. The grave fits her perfect. She says, "How much does a real fat dead man weigh?"

"What?"

"I said"—she turns and looks at me—"how much does a real fat dead man weigh?"

"I don't know, Willa. How fat was he?"

"No, Little, it's a joke. A real fat dead man weighs a . . . skele-*ton*. Get it?"

I wince and look down the hill onto the dirt and gravel of Stover Street. The church across the street painted bright white. One steeple.

Willa says, "Didn't some of the Chinese people get murdered?"

Even though I know all about it, I say, "I don't know," and toe an old piece of granite, one of the broken grave markers from the 1800s.

Willa tilts her head toward me, still laying down, her head and feet just touching the ends of the grave. She says, "There's that Chinese Hanging spot on the road to Weippe, and then there's that miner's story, right?"

"Which miner's story?"

"You know all about it. Don't pretend you don't. It's the one about the Chinese miner who'd done pretty good and gotten a bundle of gold together. The story goes that one night, a group of men came to his cabin up near Shanghai Road. They busted in and said, 'Give us your gold, mister.' But he didn't. He wouldn't tell them where he'd hid it, and they didn't find it either." Willa shrugs. "But they killed him anyway."

I say, "How do you know about this stuff?"

Willa makes a little clicking noise with her mouth. Stares straight up out of the grave. "Kids at school."

I shake my head. "Don't those kinds of stories bother you?"

"Not really," she says. "It was a long time ago."

"But now? After . . . I mean, don't stories like that make you think of . . ." I lace my fingers together and put my hands behind my head. Look around on the hillside. The next two graves nearest where I'm standing also have old pieces of granite in front of them. And in front of those two, there's six empty graves across the lower slope.

I don't look at Willa.

She says, "Are you asking if it reminds me?"

"Never mind," I say, "I don't want to talk about it." I look at her then.

Willa sits up. "Are we ever gonna talk about it?"

"No."

Willa stands up then. With her legs down in the bottom of the grave, she's half as tall as normal, even younger looking. "So are we just gonna pretend forever? Is that what we're gonna do?"

I stare at her. Wonder how she can be so young and so old at the same time. I say, "We're not pretending. This is real life. We're in a real graveyard, and you're standing in a real grave."

I tap the piece of granite with my toe again, then I kick it and it rolls down the hill and catches in the bramble on the steep. "Real things happen, Willa. You know?"

When I say that, Willa starts to cry. She crosses her arms and glares at me. "I know what real life is. You don't have to tell me about it. You don't have to talk to me like I'm a baby, all right? I'm ten years old. I'm almost eleven now."

I look down at my feet. Where the granite was laying before, the pine needles are left dry and flat. I say, "I'm sorry. I'm sorry I said it like that."

Willa steps out of the grave.

I watch her walk around the next tree and angle between two bigger graves. "Look . . ."

"No. Don't talk to me anymore. I'm riding home."

She cuts left toward the corner of the graveyard, the only place where it's not too steep to get up or down the hill. She slips a couple of times on the pine needles while sidestepping downhill, weaving in and out of empty graves as she goes.

I want to yell to her to stop. I want to say we can ride back at the same time. I want her to turn around and wait for me. But I know that once Willa's made up her mind, there's no changing it.

accidentally on purpose

The day JT got his driver's license, on his 16th birthday, he drove us to the overlook and we walked up to the guard-rail gap above the steep. There's a wide shoulder there on that straightaway, so it'd take a car veering way, way off the road to make it to the guardrail gap. But I guess that's how it was.

He and I stood at the edge and looked down. Three hundred feet of steep hillside above the trees. The bottom of the ravine laying way below us. I guess the car came apart pretty good as it went through those trees. That's what I heard. And looking down, it made sense. Nothing could stay in one piece after a fall like that.

I said, "Do you wish they'd at least left the car down there?"

JT shook his head.

"No? You don't sort of wish we could hike down there and look at the wreckage?"

"We could hike down there, but there'd be nothing good to see. Even if that old car was there."

We stood next to each other. Stared down into the dark

green of the pine trees. It was foggy that day, and the shadows were like thick spiderwebs in the forest. I said, "Let's go down there anyway."

JT spit out into the gap, watched his spit travel 30 feet down. "That's not a good idea. It's real steep, Little."

"I know," I said, but started to hike anyway. I only took three or four steps before I slipped on the wet grass, fell to my side, and slid. It was a long slide, 40 or 50 feet until I hit a dirt mound that stuck out and stopped me. The slide happened so fast that I didn't even yell.

JT called down, "You all right?"

I scrambled to a seated position on top of the mound. "Yeah," I said. "I'm fine." I sat there and looked down to the bottom of the draw, the tops of the trees still below me.

JT said, "Little, you should climb back up."

Sitting there, I could see how steep it was below me, somehow even steeper than above. The momentum of a car going 50 miles an hour would take it out into open space. The car would bounce once, then go back out into nothing. I'd seen prairie falcons drop off the Grade and glide above a stand of green trees. I wanted to think of it like that. I imagined her car gliding, dropping smoothly through the air above all that color. But I knew better. I knew that a 1,500-pound car didn't look anything like a V-winged raptor dropping into space.

I knew how it really went.

The car bounced and turned over. The first tree it hit knocked a door off. All the glass exploded. The windshield. The side windows. My mom wasn't wearing a seat belt, and she didn't stay in the car for very long.

it's a sin to tell a lie

I set a baited fishing line and plant the pole in the rocks, then fish with a second rod and spinner, casting across the deepest part of the hole. I cast maybe 25 times and get nothing. I try to be patient and not itch the poison oak that's spread around my eye to make half of a pink set of goggles.

The PowerBait hooks the first trout, not big, but maybe nine inches. I turn its head back to pop the skull at the spinal column with my thumb, dump it in the bucket, then rebait the treble. Cast that line out and turn back to my Rooster Tail spinner.

It takes two hours to catch three smallish fish, not a good fishing evening, but it'll be something other than eggs to eat tonight.

As it's getting dark, a spotlight swings across the water and finds me. Stays pointed on me. I look over my shoulder into the bright and see the outline of the sheriff's cruiser. I reel in my line, and my Rooster Tail clicks at the eyelet. I don't recast, just wait for the deputy to come down the cutbank. He scrabbles over the rocks, steps down next to me. Says, "How you been?"

"All right," I say.

Deputy White points at the creek. "Any luck tonight?"

"Three small ones."

The deputy looks in my bucket. Tilts it so he can see the fish in the bottom. Stands up straight. Says, "Have you heard any news?"

"No," I say. Release the line and hear the clink of the Rooster Tail against the rocks at my feet. "I haven't." I reel up to within a foot of the last eyelet.

The deputy says, "I've asked around Orofino . . . other parts . . . and nobody's heard a thing. Not anywhere. Same in Lewiston and Clarkston too."

I cast my line across the top of the hole, watch the Rooster Tail plunk and sink with its drift. I can't follow it underwater in the near dark, especially with the spotlight shining past, but I can feel the lure coming across three or four feet deep as I reel, see the angle of the line, feel the resistance when it cuts the current.

Deputy White steps over next to my second pole, the baited line held by river rocks. I watch him nudge one of the rocks with his boot, the pole listing to the side. He says, "Don't you think that's odd?"

"That other pole?"

"No," Deputy White says, "not that other pole. I mean, don't you think it's odd that no one's heard anything about Big?"

"Yeah, I haven't heard anything." I turn and cast again. "But he's been known to do this."

"Hmm," Deputy White says, "are you sure?"

"Sure? Yeah, I'm real sure. He's been gone for weeks before."

I keep fishing but reel too fast, don't jigger the line enough, don't let the Rooster Tail sink along the bottom. I'm just casting and reeling as an action, a rhythm. The eddy lines in front of us are white at their edges from the shine of the spotlight.

When I was younger, JT told me, "Never say too much to grown-ups. Better to say nothing and let them worry about whatever it is they worry about." I think about that right now. Keep fishing. Hoping for the deputy to leave.

But he stays. Says, "When was the last time you saw him?"

I want to say we've already talked about this, but I don't say it since the deputy is the law. I flick my line across the top of the hole. Plunk the Rooster Tail just before the deep on the far side. Say, "I don't know."

Deputy White shifts his feet. "Son, do you know what obstruction of justice is?"

I reel, then cast again.

"Son, if you don't say what you saw, or you don't tell me what you know, you can go to jail just for that, just for making my job more difficult. See, I generally want you to do well, but I'm also okay with you going down if you decide I'm the enemy here. So have you been lying to me?"

I feel like the time JT held my head underwater when we were swimming and I wasn't sure if he'd let me back up again. I say, "The thing is, I've been asking around. It's just that nobody knows anything, or they won't tell me."

"You keep asking then," the deputy says. "You *have* to find something out. Do you understand me? There's no other option for you here."

"All right," I say. "I'll keep trying."

"Good. Then here's what's gonna happen. You're gonna keep talking to people up here. You're gonna keep asking around and trying to figure things out for me. You're gonna talk to family members, to friends, to people who work at the Flame, at Sammy's, at the Saw Shop. You're gonna talk to anyone who might know anything about Big, anyone who might've heard anything about what he was up to. Then I'm gonna come back and talk to you in a few days, and by then, you're gonna have something to tell me. You got that?"

I nod again.

"Once more, is that a yes?"

"Yes," I say.

"Well, okay then." Deputy White turns around. "Guess that's it for tonight." He scrambles up the bank, tumbling the rocks behind me.

I stand, facing the dark of the creek, watching the water swirl and circle under the shine of the spotlight. Then the deputy's light goes off and I stand in the full dark, unaccustomed to the black, taking a minute to figure out what is around me, what is water and what is solid ground.

the reaper

I walk to the Saw Shop the next morning. Go to the foreman, who's always been Big's drinking buddy. Say, "Do you
know me?"

He's sharpening a chain-saw blade with a six-inch round
file. He stops. Holds the file in the air. Says, "You're Big's
grandson, right?" He wipes his hand on his apron, a smear of
3-in-One oil.

"Yep," I say.

He points at the exit sign. "Maybe we should talk outside, then?"

We walk out into the mud lot, stop next to a huge puddle surrounding a white and orange Bobcat with a skid-steer
loader on the front. The foreman says, "You looking for your
grandpa?"

"Yeah."

"And you haven't heard anything?"

"No."

He hooks his thumbs in his apron and sniffs the air like
he's smelling for bear. "A bunch of guys were talking the
other night, saying no one's seen or heard."

"From Big?"

"Yep. Pretty weird," he says. "I mean, Big did his own thing, but not quite like this. He'd at least come in for a Friday card table."

"Even this last year?"

"Most Fridays," he says.

"And how long's it been since you've seen him?"

"More than a month." The foreman rubs his fingers together, the oily graphite shining a metallic gray.

I put my boot to the edge of the puddle, nudge the water, and the ripples carry under the Bobcat. "Do you know what he's into right now?"

"Into?" he says. "Are you thinking about working his business?"

"Maybe," I say. "Maybe he owes money. Or maybe he's *owed* money."

The foreman says, "Leave that shit alone. You just let that go."

I nod. Tap my toe against the puddle again. Watch the circles travel.

Neither of us says anything.

The foreman starts rubbing his index finger on his apron again, works to clean it. He rubs the finger pad, then the side, but the gray won't come off. "You know," he says, "there's another possibility?"

"What's that?"

"Well, what I'm thinking . . . or what I'm worried about . . . is that Big's not coming back. See, Big was into all kinds of stuff the last couple of years. He made some friends, but maybe a lot more enemies. He did things when people didn't pay up. All kinds of things. You know how it goes in this town, Judge Town, Weippe . . . all the way down. All the towns within an hour of here? They *are* what they are. No way to make them pretty." He spits in his hands and rubs them together.

There's a Tuff Shed behind the Bobcat. Roof-dented. I kick a pebble and it pings off the side of the shed. "So you don't think he's coming back?"

"No I don't. I'm sorry."

"No chance?"

"To be honest?" The foreman pulls his apron straight, smooths over the big front pocket, wipes his hands once more, and looks up. "What he was into? All those not-so-good people he was making deals with? No. No chance at all."

brand-new dance

In the middle of the night, the door to the trailer opens. I say, "Hey, Willa." But I don't hear her small footsteps. These steps are heavier. Boots. I open my eyes and swing my legs over the side of the bed. Try to see in the dark.

"Hey." It's Rowan's voice. She walks past me. Goes to JT's bed. I hear her moving the blankets back there.

I get back in bed. Close my eyes again. But Rowan comes back. She kicks off her boots next to my bunk. Peels her jeans. Takes off her sweatshirt. Gets into my bed, pulls the covers up over us. Then she scooches back against me. She only has panties on and a T-shirt, the backs of her long legs bare against the fronts of my thighs. She reaches for me, takes my hand, puts it around her, against her rib cage, underneath her left breast. I can feel the thump-thump double rhythm of her heart.

I want to kiss her neck. Want to feel her chest. Want to pull her closer. But she's breathing deep already, relaxing in my arms, and I try to make myself relax too, try to breathe as deep as she is and go back to sleep.

Rowan is asleep. Just like that. In my bed. Her long, thin body in front of me, pressed back against me.

I stare into the dark, the smell of her hair, her skin, her alcohol sweat. Her back against my chest, her legs against my legs. I stare off and try not to think about her, but it's impossible not to think about her with her here. Her body is all there is in this world in this moment, and I lie awake and hold her, hold Rowan sleeping in my bed.

It's at least an hour before I can relax enough to close my eyes again. Then I go to sleep. But it's a light sleep. Even in my dreams, I know Rowan's there. Feel her under my arm until she slides away.

And when I wake up in the morning, she's already gone.

the house is falling down

When I get home from school, Willa's sitting on the trailer steps. She says, "We're out of meat."

"In the big house?"

"Yep."

"Are you sure?"

"Yeah," she says, "I even checked the deep freeze." Her hair is stuck to her forehead by a dried glob of grape jelly.

"All right," I say, "is anybody in the house worried about that?"

Willa leans down. Spits between her gap-teeth. "They drank magic mushrooms this morning."

"Did what?"

"In their coffee. They said the day was full of crazy and maybe still is. And another chicken got killed, and a red one's out missing. So the count's seven."

"Wait, Lucky and Derlene told you that?"

Willa says, "I saw the chicken myself."

"No, about the mushrooms and the coffee."

"They said the world was so bright today they had to

wear sunglasses." She looks sideways at me. "Kept laughing like on a stupid television show. Every other thing they said."

I look up at the porch to see if Derlene or Uncle Lucky's sitting there. I wanna kill them both.

Willa does an imitation of Derlene when she's been drinking. Stumbles around the trampoline. Holds a pretend drink in her hand, spilling a little. Makes a face that Derlene makes.

I shake my head. Say, "So you walked home again today?"

"Had to."

"Why's that?"

Willa sits up straight. "'Cause Bobbie Simms was throwing stuff down on kids at the bus stop. He was sitting above us on the wall."

"That older kid Bobbie Simms?"

"Exactly," she says. "A year older and seems like two years bigger. He was throwing food, chewed up and not. So I didn't want to wait and get his chewed-up sandwich in my hair."

I point to her forehead. "Did you eat grape jelly today? 'Cause if not, he already got some on you."

Willa touches her forehead and feels the sticky. "Shit," she says, saying it just the way Derlene does, drawing it out.

"Don't cuss, Willa. Here, come on in. I'll help you wash up." I open the trailer door and usher her in. Sling my school-bag down and turn the sink on to warm. Willa leans, and I help her wash it out. There's a little jelly in her hair where it must've hit her head first, then slid down to her forehead.

I'm washing out the dried sticky when she says, "But what about meat?"

"Meat?"

"You know, we're out."

"Oh, right. But you've got other food?"

"Some," she says, "but meat's been out a week now. It's not like I complained right away."

"And this month's food stamps?"

"No, no," she says. "Derlene traded them a long time ago."

"Wait, she did that again?" I go get a towel. Come back and start drying Willa's hair. "She can't do that every month."

"She can and she did," Willa says. Wraps her hair up on top of her head like a beehive. "So what do you have in here?" She opens the fridge. "Any meat?"

"Nope. I've been eating the same three things—oatmeal, eggs, and grilled-cheese sandwiches—for the last month. Plus that huge bag of carrots we got a couple weeks ago from Henshaw."

Willa makes a face. She hates carrots. "But no meat?" She leans in and touches everything in the fridge as if leaning in and moving things around will change what they are. She rattles the ketchup and mustard bottles on the door.

"If I had any meat, I'd give it to you."

Willa makes a face, pouting her bottom lip. "But you don't, so it doesn't matter."

"I sure haven't come into any meat lately. And anyway, I still have all that bread and cheese from the last stamps we took from Derlene's purse. I put all that bread in the freezer, so we're good for a while."

Willa hears the word *freezer* and opens it up. Sticks her head in. Moves the frozen bread loaves and the ice trays.

I say, "First things first, next month, you tell me when

the stamps come, and I'll take half of them. We'll buy hot dogs and stew meat and hamburger, and all that. All right? Keep some of it in my trailer, and some with you."

Willa nods. "All right," she says, "but it's not food stamps time yet. Still two weeks away. What do we do about meat right now?"

I think about the money I've saved up in the wall space, but I shake my head at my own idea. I've made a promise to myself that I'll save that $5,000 for the land. The money only goes in, not out.

I say, "Maybe I could shoot us some meat?"

Willa turns quick. "Could you please, Little? Seriously?"

"The only thing is, we're between two seasons, and I didn't get a deer license this year."

"Does that really matter?"

"Yeah, it does."

"No, I mean does it *really* matter?" she says. "Think how many deer there are. Think how much forest. And we're down to seven chickens now. We might be outta eggs soon."

Willa has a way of wearing me down. I don't like to tell her no, and I usually don't. I say, "Maybe I could run up and see."

Willa stands tall and bounces on her toes. "Pinkie promise?" She holds out her little finger.

I keep my hand at my side. "I promise to go up and look, but that's all. I'm not promising I'll bring anything back."

"Deal," she says, still holding out her pinkie.

I wrap my huge pinkie around her small pinkie.

Willa clenches her fist and shakes our hands in unison. "Thanks. I know you'll shoot something. I just know it for sure. You're a good shot. You can do it. You'll get something for sure."

"I didn't say I'd shoot."

"Right," she says, "but I know you will. So you wanna hear a hunting joke?"

"Okay."

"Two duck hunters go out hunting one day but they don't get any ducks all morning, not a single, itty bitty duck. So the first hunter says, 'Why aren't we getting any ducks?' And the second hunter thinks about it. 'I don't know,' he says, 'maybe we're not throwing the dog high enough.'"

Willa laughs so hard that she leans on the sink and starts snorting a little bit.

And her laughing makes me laugh too.

i'm gonna try to be that way

I listen to my Spanish tape while I drive the East Fork toward Shanghai Road, along Canal Gulch, past the elk dump where the chopped hooves stick angled out of the ground like broken table legs. I follow the road east into Potlatch Corp. country, the creek split, three miles and pull to the ditch. I take the .30-30 from the rack, a Henry's edition, chamber five cartridges from the glove compartment, then sling the rifle and start hiking.

There's always a run of mule deer up here in this country of lodgepole pines, but it's steep, no movement without breaking a sweat. I got my first deer in a small meadow up this way when I was twelve and had to carry its quarters all day just to get to the ATV. I thought JT was hunting *with* me, but when he dropped down the ridge across from me, he kept dropping, and drove on out, and I found him at home later that night watching *Sunday Night Football* on the old black-and-white television Uncle Lucky let us have in our room.

◇ ◇ ◇

It's a foggy morning. I brush saplings, and my jeans get wet to my knees. It makes me think of following hunts when I was little, so cold I'd keep my hands in my armpits, walk like a boy in a straitjacket, but hike hard, following men from town, or older boys, anyone who'd have me along.

I'd always hope for a midday fire on the coldest days, but never ask for it. I didn't want to seem weak or needy.

I hike a few hundred feet, round a knoll, cut up another gully to the east, and don't see the road below me anymore. Up a half-mile from the Forest Service marker, the gully trail forks into braided runs, and I follow one to a water-filled bowl where there are animal tracks everywhere: deer, elk, and Shiras moose. I lean down. Large prints on one end of the puddle, a black bear drinking, two paws in, and his scat 20 feet back on a little hump.

I suck my finger and hold it up to feel the wind. It's running from the northwest. Walk to the southeast like I was taught, move uphill 50 yards, to a tangle of old downed lumber. I step over a log and slide down. Rest my gun on top, only my head up above, and feel the breeze gusting my face like it should.

I wonder at these moments how we come to like what we do, how some things sit easy with us like old men on a porch in summer. I can fish a river all year, in sunlight or in snow, even winter, sleeted down and waded in. I'll keep casting as my feet hang numb as concrete from the ends of my legs. Or hunting a ridge until I find game trails crossing, then waiting all day for that game to come. I know other people feel the way I do about certain things, but not many.

JT never liked deer hunting. He didn't like sitting in the cold or the wet, didn't like waiting behind his propped gun. He didn't want to stare above open sights or squint into a scope. He didn't want to stay in a deer stand. He wanted to keep moving, shoot at targets, shoot at clay pigeons, hunt birds and go home. He liked to snipe grouse with a .22 on Forest Service roads three steps from the truck, or knock the heads off chukars with a break-barrel .410, build a fire on the gravel road, and fry breasts in Krusteaz.

But I always liked the calm and the still. The slow of it. The smell of loam. Sun warming the thicket. Bird sounds: flickers tapping a tick tick, a raven's squawk, a redtail's dip between trees.

My eyes are heavy. There are pine needles near me, and I pull a few and put them in my mouth, fold them with my tongue and bite down halfway to suck the bitter the way I was taught. Vitamin C, and the bitter to stay awake.

A doe comes in below. I've got the wind with me, and she doesn't smell anything. She drinks, looks up once, then drinks again. I watch her through my open sights, the safety on. She walks away, downhill.

Another doe comes in, young and small and nervous. She turns her head at every birdcall. I know a doe that small can't be alone, so I wait for the others to appear, hoping for a buck. I look past her, right and left, see nothing.

Then two more step out of the gully. Each another doe. I

shake my head. Sight the larger of the two. Click my safety off. Whisper to myself, "What's the difference, right?" Groove the trigger with my finger, but I don't pull. I think and wait, hoping for that buck.

The deer move together, walking, crest the small hill, drop down into the next gully, and finally they're out of sight. I breathe out long and slow, click my safety back on. Look up at the sky. The crescent moon is a heel print on a sandbar. I hike back down to the truck.

I remember when you took me out to the Livingston place. You said, "Bad history here," and pointed at the house with a pistol I didn't know you were holding in your hand.

I stared at the green house, paled and mossed, the spray-painted words in red on the wall above the rotten porch. Those words made me afraid, and I said, "Are we going in there right now?"

You shook your head. "Nope. Just lookin'."

I glanced at the pistol, then back at the house.

Doe or buck, I know you would've pulled the trigger today. I know you would've.

You and I once found a black bear woke too early out of hibernation. It was February, and the bear was walking across a snowcrust of meadow under a late-winter rain, head down, front legs dragging.

You said to me, "You better put him down," and held out your .30-06. We were on the ridge above the bear. I was nine and I shook my head.

You held that gun between us like it was a Christmas present nobody wanted. Then you said, "You'll figure out someday that it's better to put a thing down than to let it suffer all the way through to the end. And that bear right there?" You pointed. "That bear's gonna starve to death over the next month or so."

I nodded, but I didn't reach for the gun. The rain on the snow had made a mist all around us, and I pulled my coat tighter, ducked my chin down into the collar, not wanting wet cold to get in around my throat.

You tilted your head and chewed on your upper lip. Then you shouldered the gun, slid the bolt back until it clicked, and forward again.

I turned and looked up at the tops of the trees at the edge of the clearing, pine triangles in the light gray sky, and I didn't look back even when the gun went off. Then you walked away from where I was standing, dropped down off the ridge, and a minute later I heard another gunshot. The trees didn't move above me. There was no wind, just that soft cold rain that comes at the end of winter to ice everything over, then break it apart.

"Hey," you yelled from below, "you better come down and help me skin this out."

So I turned and stepped off the ridge, my boots sliding a little on the ice, then breaking the top crust of snow, sinking through to the next layer with a sluck sluck sound.

momma's baby

I step out of the trailer with a plate full of scrambled eggs. Sit down on the steps. Late evening, the chickens are scratching and roosting, and I count only six in the porch light. I count three times and hope we haven't lost another. I get up and look under the house, out back, along the near fence. Don't find it. Sit back down to eat my scrambled eggs.

Willa must've fallen asleep watching TV because she isn't outside on the trampoline, and I can see the TV screen's blue shades coming through the front window, the scene changes cutting against the early dark.

Derlene walks out onto the porch above me. Lights a cigarette. Inhales deep and blows the smoke back out. Says, "It's getting a little weird."

I raise my eyebrows but don't say anything.

She says, "It's a little weird that Big isn't back."

"True."

Derlene smokes some more. Taps her toe against the porch post. "You think he's coming back?"

"I don't know."

"Have you heard anything?"

I take a bite of scrambled eggs. "No. But I been asking."

Derlene sniffs. Hawks a loogie and spits it out into the yard. "Hasn't anyone seen him or heard nothin'?"

I shake my head.

Derlene cherries her cigarette to the filter, squashes it against the porch rail, and shakes another cigarette out of the pack to light it. "I haven't heard shit. Even at the Flame."

"They talk about it down there?"

"Sometimes," Derlene says, "but it's all guesses. Maybe he's in jail somewhere in Washington State. Or maybe he's dead. Maybe he took off. . . ."

"Took off to where, though?"

Derlene coughs chunky. Puts a fist to her chest and taps. "Maybe he went where your daddy went."

I look away.

"He was worthless," she says. "No good for money or nothin'. Had a temp job that was solid enough to hang around your mom, and that's all."

I say, "I don't even care about that."

"You shouldn't. He was Mexican, of course, and you know what that means."

I look down at the light tan of my skin. Then out across the yard. See the outline of the banty rooster strutting. Six egg-layers now and that one rooster. I can't make out the legs of the rooster because of the darkness, but I know the rasp of his talons as they drag through the cut-grass.

I imagine talons on the insides of my wrists.

Derlene says, "Your mom always liked that. She liked that dark skin and slicked hair. She'd fall for that."

I clench my fists and look up at Derlene on the porch,

standing under the porch light. I try to picture her and my mom growing up together. People say they looked a lot alike: athletic, with wide shoulders, as wide as a man's. Pretty but big.

I try to imagine my mom now from the pictures I've seen. Wonder if she'd have Derlene's dark circles under her eyes. Wonder if she'd chain-smoke on the front porch, spew hate. Cough gunk into the yard. Drink at the Flame Bar until closing.

I'm thinking while Derlene's talking, so I miss a chunk of what she says. I start to listen again: ". . . couldn't stop talking about how muscled his back was, how he felt against her, and I kept thinking, *You'd let a Mexican get up on top of you?* Shit." Derlene drops her cigarette butt to the porch and grinds it out with the pad of her yellow slipper. "People are crazy sometimes, huh?" She's talking to herself now, more than me, and I turn and look away.

There's no light left in the yard, the sun having been dead for a full hour behind the next ridge, and only the tops of the pine trees still glowing, a single line of light along the spine to the west.

bird on a wire

In the night, Rowan comes again. This time she doesn't check JT's bed. She steps into the trailer, slides her shoes off, strips off her sweatshirt, then her jeans, and gets into my bunk. She settles there next to me, puts my hand on her hip, and I feel the smooth of her skin, the thin elastic line of her panties.

She smells different than usual, cleaner, like she washed her hair with the powdered bathroom soap from school. I wonder if she washed it in the Flame Bar's little bathroom. I picture her locking the door, leaning over the sink, and wetting her hair, pounding the soap dispenser, the gritty soap, her washing and rinsing, getting her clothes wet, then drying her hair with the industrial brown paper towels off the roll.

Rowan reaches back and pulls her hair out of the way, shifts her head on the pillow, scoots back against me, and sighs. My hand is still on her hip, my fingers in the crease at the top of her thigh, the thin material of her underwear under my fingertips, her whole body against my whole body.

She says, "Scooch in," her voice dropping off at the end like she's already falling asleep.

"Okay," I whisper, resettling myself, holding her a little tighter.

I've seen a black-and-white flicker turn its red head as its feet grip pine bark, tapping, then stopping. Tapping again. Looking straight at me with a twist of its neck. I've always wanted to hold one of those speckled birds, see its neck turn as it shines a black eye in my direction. But I don't know what I'd do if I ever had one in my hands. Would I hold on too tight? Would I crush it with my big hands? Or would I hold on too easy, afraid of hurting the bird, and then it would flap once and I'd lose my grip?

november

the wind changes

I'm doing my math homework at the kitchenette table when the door swings open.

JT hops up and sings in a twangy voice, "Brother, brother, I missed you fuckin' so." He has a black trash bag full of clothes slung over one shoulder and a pint bottle of Wild Turkey in his other hand.

He drops the trash bag and hugs me, one of those big-brother hugs where even though I'm bigger, I feel smaller. He thumps my back with the flat of his hand, and the sound echoes through my body. He smells like he drank a bottle before the pint bottle he's got in his hand. He says, "Hit it with me."

"No," I say, "I can't." I point at my math pages. The textbook.

He takes a swig. Gargles and swallows. "Why not?"

"'Cause look. I gotta do this homework."

"You're doing *homework*?" he says. "Oh, lord, fuck no." He shakes the bottle in his hand like he's about to roll a pair of dice. Then he stops and lets the liquid go steady, holds the bottle back up near my face, peeks around the side of the bottle, and smiles at me. "Come on, man. Join me and celebrate."

"JT, I really gotta get this done. I'm way, way behind in this class. I'm struggling."

JT uncaps the bottle again. Takes another swig and laughs. "No, sir. The answer is no. You're celebrating my release tonight, and that's final. You hear me?"

I look at the table. I have more than half of my math homework left to do, and for me that's at least an hour of work. I say, "I really should—"

"Celebrate with your brother? Celebrate the fact that I'm not caged up like a fuckin' zoo animal? That I can walk in or out of any goddamn door? Celebrate that I'm through with assault charges . . . menacing . . . all of that?" JT winks at me and smiles. Does a little dance that reminds me of a squirrel shaking a nut in front of its face.

I smile at the dance. Say, "Okay. Maybe a little." I take the bottle from him. "We can hang out for a while."

"That's the brother I always knew. Hit it or quit it." JT makes a pistol shape out of his hand.

I tilt the Turkey.

"That's right," JT says. "Get you some."

I hand it back, and he sits down at the table. Then he points at my homework. "Can we move these pages? And this ridiculous book?" He lifts the textbook and lets it thump down on the tabletop. "It's distracting me."

I say, "Damn you," but I slide the loose-leaf pages into the textbook and take it all to my bunk.

When I come back, JT rubs his hand over the smooth

blank tabletop. Says, "Now don't you feel a little bit better about everything?" He hands me the bottle.

A couple of swigs in, I can feel the liquor warming, my shoulders coming down. I always liked the flavor of Wild Turkey because it's what I found mixed in Coke cans in the big house when I was little. I'd steal sips then, feel the buzz come on as my coordination level dropped, the floor bucking and wiggling as I tried to keep the world straight. Football on the TV and I'd be heavy and warm in the corner of the couch, half-cans all around.

JT leans back in his chair. Says, "Jail's fucking ridiculous."

"Seems like it."

He flexes his fist. Sends shivers of muscle up his arm. "But there's time to make up workouts all day long."

I look at him, his shoulders straining the seams of his T-shirt. "You got huge in there."

"True." JT nods. "Real enough."

"How many push-ups can you do in a row now?" I ask him because I know he likes to answer that question when he's in good shape.

"New record. All the way up and all the way down," he says, "nice and slow? 177. I got fitter."

"Shit!"

He sips from the bottle. "What's your record now?"

"To be honest, I haven't really been doing much push-ups. Or at least not often."

"But when you used to work on it? Like last year, when I had you do them all the time with me. What was your best?"

"The slow version that you do? Only 43."

"That's good, though. That was good for a freshman. Real good." He slides the bottle back to me.

"Yeah, well." I take a sip off the bottle.

"You look fit, though. Been hiking a lot to fish? Is that what keeps you in shape?"

"Yep."

He nods.

We sit there and don't say anything for a minute.

JT says, "You seen much of Rowan?"

I try to look steady. Unconcerned. But I think of her skin, her kissing me that one night, her body against mine in my bed. I say, "No," and shake my head. "Not really."

"But she still looks fine?"

"It's only been 60 days."

He takes the bottle back from me. The pint's two-thirds gone now. "So you're saying a girl can't go downhill in 60 days?"

"I'm saying it's not likely."

"Shit, Little. You don't know much about women, do you?"

JT swigs on the bottle. Looks at the last few ounces. Says, "Should we go get a sixer and sit down by the fishing hole?"

I can feel the liquor in the front of my brain, burbling around like a pool of warm fish. I need to do my homework but it's too late now. I say, "Yeah, we could do that."

We leave the trailer and walk up to the Mini-Mart, duck through the door into the bright of the fluorescent lights, the wall of beer coolers, clear glass, and JT grabs two sixers, one for him and one for me.

water to drown

In the middle of the night, Rowan comes in. I'm more fighting than sleeping, struggling through the warm body-shop sleep of the drunk, the arc welding inside my body when she steps into the trailer. I open my eyes. See the outline of her standing there, blurred by the haze of my drunkenness. In the door, the yellow slant of streetlight angles behind her. She closes the door, walks toward me, stops at my bunk. I can't see her as well now, minus the outline of the lighted door, but I can hear her getting out of her boots, pulling her sweatshirt off, unzipping and sliding out of her jeans. Same as other nights.

She gets into my bunk, moves in against me, her smooth skin and a thin T-shirt. She pulls the blanket over both of us, takes my hand and puts it against the flat of her stomach. Pulls me until I'm tight against her, my body against her back, the fronts of my legs against the backs of hers. She sighs and gets quiet, relaxes, but I wake up. Even drunk, I know JT's in the trailer with us. I listen for him, wonder what will happen if he finds us like this. My body is a series of guitar strings turning at the pegs, the strings tightening,

117

pitching higher, near snapping. My head's loose drunk and hot from the Wild Turkey and beer. I'm treading water and heated. I try to keep my eyes open, Rowan's body against me, and I swim-sleep for a moment.

Then JT snorts a little, drunk snoring, loud in his bunk, and my eyes pop open again. Rowan's body goes stiff. "Hey," she whispers, "is JT home?"

"Yeah, he got home tonight."

"And you let me . . . What the fuck?"

I don't say anything.

Rowan slides from underneath the covers. Sits up quiet. Stands.

"I'm sorry," I say. My stomach tightens around the pool of alcohol in my gut. I lay there and feel the nausea flood near the top of the bank.

Rowan pulls her clothes on. Puts her feet into her boots. Leans in and whispers, "I gotta go. He'd kill us if he found us like this. *Kill* us." Rowan ties her bootlaces. Walks slowly to the door, opens it, and leaves.

I have the starting of a headache, and I sit up on the edge of my bed, stand, unsteady and swallowing to get rid of the pool of saliva around my tongue. I walk to the kitchen sink and fill a glass of water. Drink water and hope I won't throw up. Then I remember school and pray I won't be too hung-over to make it through classes.

When I'm finished with my cup of water, I hold my stomach and burp. Feel terrible. Wait for the water to settle. Wait for the nausea to pass. Lean over the sink and let my saliva drizzle into the bottom of the metal pan.

From right behind me, JT says, "Little?"

"Shit!" I jump and turn so quick that I hit my eyebrow on the faucet. I hold my eye and look at JT.

He says, "What are you doing?"

I point to the sink. "I guess I was just resting my head in there."

"You're kinda loud, don't you think? And I thought I heard the trailer door open. Did you go outside?"

"No," I say. "Sorry I was loud, though."

JT refills my cup with water and glugs it down. Holds his stomach and belches. Smiles. "Got a little shit-faced tonight, huh?"

"Yep." My eye feels wet. I take my hand away and rub my fingers together. Can't see in the dark. I say, "I think I just cut my eye."

JT can't see either. He leans in. "Really?"

"Yeah, on the faucet."

JT turns on the kitchenette light. My hand's covered in blood. I move it so he can look at the cut. "Yep," he says, "you sure did. I better get some glue." He opens the junk drawer and rummages around. Finds a tube of Super Glue. "Wash that," he says, "just a bit. Then lay down on the floor, and I'll get you fixed up."

I lean over the sink and let my eye drip into the drain. Run water and wash my hand, then my face. Push a rag to the cut.

JT grabs a dry dish towel. Hands it to me. "Now lay flat, all right?"

I lay down on the floor, and JT crouches over me. "This won't hurt—eyes never do—so just stay real still."

"Okay."

"If you don't stay still and I drip glue in your eye, that'll be a real fuckin' injury."

"I'll stay still."

He drips seam to seam. Drips and pinches. Waits at each pinch. Says, "It's under an inch long, so I can get it like this." He pinches some more. "I'm just trying not to glue my fingers to the cut, else we'd become some kinda screwed-up Siamese twins, right?"

"Right," I say. I'm staying still. Keeping the bad eye shut. Watching JT with my other eye. Laying on the floor, the room hazing and spinning, and I realize that I'm still swimming drunk. Sweating hard.

JT holds the corner of the cut. "Sleep's a little hot tonight, huh?"

"Yeah."

"I'm fuckin' pouring sweat back there."

"Me too."

"All right. This should do it." JT pinches the other corner one more time. "Just don't mess around and hit your eye on something tomorrow, okay?"

"I won't."

"Now we better crash," he says. "We've got hangovers to work on." He puts the glue back into the junk drawer. Turns the lights off. Now there's just the yellow of the one streetlight coming in the small side window.

I slide into my bunk, careful not to bump my eye.

JT starts to walk past me, then stops. "You sure you didn't open and close the trailer door before? I swear I heard that sound."

"No," I say. "Maybe you were dreaming."

"That's weird." He rubs his eyes. "I'd have bet good money on it."

He walks back to his bed. As he passes the small side window, the streetlight shines into the trailer, and I see the ripples of his muscled back, his huge shoulders, the V of his torso.

doin' my time

I feel horrible. My T-shirt is sweat-damp. I sit in the front hallway and try to finish all the problems I can before class starts, but my homework is still only two-thirds done when I turn it in at the bell. The teacher looks at the paper, then at my face. Says, "Did you really try your hardest last night?"

"Yes, ma'am."

"Are you sure? Because I said to write out the equations at the very least, even if you can't solve them."

"Oh," I say, "I'm sorry. I could do that right now if you'll let me."

She taps her desk with her red pen. "And every single time from here on out?"

"Yes, ma'am."

"Okay then. Go have a seat, finish writing out the equations, and turn this back in to me in five minutes."

As I sit at my desk and work, my stomach lurches. I burp. The girl next to me glares, then scoots her desk a few inches farther away from mine. I try to write out the last four equations without making a mistake, but the Xs and Ys and numbers keep flipping on me. I wipe my forehead and feel the sweat dripping. I put my red cover sheet over the problems, but when I focus my eyes, my stomach feels even worse. I think I might throw up. I take a deep breath and try to relax. Saliva runs in my mouth and I swallow it down. Breathe some more. Stare at the ceiling and burp again.

The girl next to me sighs and shakes her head.

I take a deep breath and finish the last equation. Then I get up, walk to the front of the room, and turn the paper in to the teacher. I say, "Thanks for the extra five minutes, ma'am."

"That's fine," she says. She points to my seat, then returns to grading the homework in front of her.

I sit back down. The rest of the students are working on the first in-class problem, and I try to write those problems down. But they're spidering around on the whiteboard at the front of the room, and I'm not sure where all the numbers and letters are supposed to go.

I rest my head on my desktop, and the Formica cools my forehead. I close my eyes and breathe. Count to ten and try to relax. My stomach clenches and releases again. I start sweating hard, first on top of my head and my face, then my whole body. Sweat everywhere. I feel a trickle of sweat work down my stomach under my T-shirt. My mouth fills with saliva again.

I raise my hand.

"Mr. McCardell?" the teacher says.

"Ma'am, can I use the bathroom?"

She frowns. "Do you really have to go?"

"Yes, ma'am."

She shakes her head no but says, "Okay. Make it quick."

I try to look calm as I stand up and walk out of the class. But as soon as the door closes behind me—as soon as I'm out in the hallway—I run.

It's not far to the bathroom, and I realize I won't make it. I get as far as the trash can by the drinking fountain, then I pitch forward and puke, hands on both sides of the can, head down inside. I throw up, dry-heave once, and throw up again. Then I retch a few more times to get the last of it.

I stand and look around. No one else is in the hall. I don't know what to do, so I pick up the trash can and carry it into the boys' bathroom. I'm not gonna empty it, because I wouldn't know where to pour it anyway, but I don't want to leave it out in the hallway. I slide the trash can into a toilet stall and close the door. Then I lean against the wall and breathe. Push my face against the tile like holding my head in snowmelt. A good cold.

I go to the sink and run the water. Wash my face, swish water around in my mouth, soap my hands.

Now that I've thrown up, I feel better. I've stopped sweating and I don't think I'll puke again. I gargle some water but it won't kill the taste. I consider putting soap in my mouth to make it feel cleaner but I don't want to.

When I get back to class, I try to breathe, try to focus and write problems off the board. None of the numbers or letters will stay put. It's like I'm watching them spin and flip on a carnival ride at the county fair. I write some equations on the page, but I'm not sure if any of them are right.

When the teacher stands up and explains each problem, I discover that all the equations I wrote down before were wrong. Not a single one correct. I rewrite them, but while I'm doing that, the class gets ahead of me, and I'm not sure what the teacher is talking about once I start listening again.

the wind changes

At lunch, I eat half of a white-bread cheese sandwich and drink two cups of water. My stomach settles most of the way. I walk into the front office and take a couple of sugar-free candies that they keep in a bowl on the front counter by the secretary. Then I walk to art class, sucking on one of the candies.

Zaylie says, "What happened to your eye?"

"I hit it on the sink."

"Really?" Zaylie smudges her drawing with her finger, trying to shade a cheekbone. "Cut it pretty bad?"

"JT had to Super Glue it."

Zaylie looks up. Touches my cut with the tip of her smudged finger. "I think it's gonna stay together . . . but that'll be a great shiner."

"Yeah?"

"For sure." Zaylie purses her lips and pulls my head to her. Kisses the cut. "All better," she says.

I like the way her lips feel on my skin, and the way she smells when she leans in close. So now I really look at her. And really looking at her like this, I see now how cute she is, see how bright her eyes are. She's small, but she doesn't look like a little girl. Not at all.

She holds an earbud out to me. Raises her eyebrows. "Thug music for a thug with a black eye?" She holds the face of her iPod toward me and there's a picture of a big, fat black man with a bunch of rings on his fingers. She says, "That's Biggie Smalls."

I take the earbud from her.

We listen to a song called "Mo Money Mo Problems." It's the first time I've ever heard it, but Zaylie knows all the words and raps along with Biggie. It's funny watching her because Zaylie is Biggie's opposite. She's not quite five feet tall, maybe 95 pounds at most. But when she raps, she raps in this sort of deep voice that isn't her normal voice at all. She gets a serious look on her face, pushes her lips out like a duck, and bobs her head back and forth.

When the song ends, Zaylie hits Pause on her iPod. "First of all," she says, "this song makes me laugh because it's not really about their problems from having more money. They don't even talk about that in the song."

"Then what's it about?"

"Well, it's really more about all three of them saying how badass they are and how they'll just steal your girl or shoot you up if you fuck with them."

"Oh, okay."

"And second of all," she says, "when you don't have *any* money, you have *real* problems. But when you're a famous rapper and you have all these nice cars and millions of dollars, what problems do you have? You used to have nothing at all, but now you have everything."

I think about the difference between the people in my town who have money and the people in my town who don't. I say, "Well, maybe now that they're rich they have a lot of people begging them to use their stuff or asking for help all the time."

"So?"

"Well, maybe they're giving away too much money. Or maybe they have so many people around them that they're sort of spread thin."

"You really think so?" Zaylie says. "You really think Biggie Smalls wasn't taking care of himself? That he wasn't getting himself a nice setup, making sure he got what he needed?"

"I mean, I don't know. I don't really know Biggie Smalls."

"Well, let me tell you, he was," Zaylie says, and she starts to draw again. *"For sure."* She squints one eye closed as she angles the side of a grease pencil.

I work on my drawing. Mrs. F's lesson today was about drawing someone in profile, and she showed us a drawing by Rembrandt van Rijn called *The Second Oriental Head* that was so good that I felt sort of overwhelmed. I try not to make art into a competition, but I know I'm never gonna draw that good even if I draw every day for the rest of my life, and I can't help noticing that Zaylie's drawings are better than mine too. But I keep drawing.

"Wait," I say, "didn't you say one time that Biggie Smalls was dead?"

"Yeah, he got shot."

"Right," I say. "So isn't getting shot a problem? I mean, he got killed, right?"

Zaylie tilts her head back and stares straight at the ceiling, the same thing she does if she's struggling with a drawing that isn't working out. "Here's the thing," she says. "People shooting at you, yes, that's a problem. But when he was hustlin' crack before that, I'm sure he was shot at then too."

"Hustlin' crack?"

"That's what he called it. And I'm sure he was shot at then too, right?"

"I don't know. Probably?"

"Clearly he had to've been. Same old problems. But what are the new ones?" Zaylie holds her index finger up and wags it back and forth, closing her eyes like there's no counter-argument she's willing to hear. She purses her lips with her eyes still closed, and—even though she's trying to argue with me—for a split second I think about kissing her.

But I don't. I smile, and when she opens her eyes, she smiles back. Then she puts her left earbud back in and starts another Biggie song: this one called "Juicy." And it begins with the line, "Dedicated to all the teachers that told me I'd never amount to nothin'." It makes me want to dedicate something to all my math teachers.

Zaylie starts rapping in her deep voice again, and I watch her for a verse, then go back to drawing my drawing.

At the end of class, Zaylie's boyfriend comes in. He's older, tall and thin, with curly hair to his shoulders and a nose ring. I was in a remedial history class with him last year, and he was always arguing with everyone in that class about how the best thing you can do for your body is to smoke weed.

I never liked him, but he seems to know Mrs. F real well. When he comes into the art room, he walks right up to her and hugs her.

I say, "Zaylie, does your boyfriend do art?"

"Matt? Yeah, he's a really good artist. He's in the advanced art class, junior/senior invites only. He does these trippy weird sculptures, crazy combo animals like mixing a jackrabbit with a tiger or something like that. That doesn't really make them sound as cool as they are, but they're pretty amazing."

Matt jokes with Mrs. F, and they both laugh, and then he turns and walks toward us. He's wearing a red T-shirt that says WEED, CALIFORNIA on it. When he gets to our table, he says, "Are you guys still drawing faces?" He looks at my drawing like it's something he found stuck to a toilet seat.

Zaylie says, "The class is called Drawing, idiot."

"Easy," Matt says. "I was only joking." He looks at my drawing and makes a little noise in the back of his throat.

I've always thought it was stupid when someone believed it was a big deal that they'd lived a year or two longer than other people. And that's the kind of guy Matt is. I think that it really wouldn't be too much trouble to break Matt in half since I have 50 or 60 pounds on him.

Matt walks around to Zaylie's side of the table. He leans down and whispers loud enough for me to hear, "Wanna go smoke with me at my truck after school?"

Zaylie shrugs. "Okay."

"Cool," he says. "See you then."

I look, and Matt kisses her while he's staring at me. Then he walks out of class.

I go back to my drawing. It's supposed to be a picture of an old woman with long hair, but the hair reminds me of gray spaghetti noodles. I say, "You like that guy?" I point at the door where Matt just left.

Zaylie's drawing straight bangs on her old woman's head even though the old woman in the picture Mrs. F gave us doesn't have any bangs. Zaylie says, "Matt can be a dick at school, but away from school he's really sweet."

I think, *That doesn't seem likely*, but I don't say it, and we both keep working on our drawings.

When I get home, JT's standing against the back fence. He says, "We got a donkey?"

"Yeah."

"When?"

"A few weeks ago." The donkey's head is down. He's not browsing or eating, just standing.

JT points. "You bought a donkey?"

"No, no. One of Big's friends brought it here. Said it was worth $1500."

"And this friend just gave it to you?"

"Yep. He said he had to pay Big for something."

JT laughs. "That's fuckin' ridiculous. Paying a debt with a donkey?"

"Willa likes it. She's ridden him."

JT reaches down and pulls a long stem of grass. Picks his teeth, then chews the end. "Willa likes everything."

The donkey looks pathetic. He's slump-necked and off-center. It seems like if he tilted a little farther to the left he'd fall over.

JT shakes his head. "It doesn't look like much of a donkey."

"Who knows? I picked up a bale of alfalfa to feed him because the man said he'd pack pretty good."

JT picks his teeth again. Bites off the frayed end of the grass stem and spits it over the fence. "Yeah?"

"That's what he said."

JT keeps chewing his stem of grass. "So where's Big to receive this donkey payment?"

I shake my head.

"You haven't heard anything?"

"I've heard some." I reach down and pull my own stem of grass. "Big was into all kinds of things last we saw him."

"And when was that?"

"Not sure." I chew on the grass. Look out at the donkey. "A while now. A real while."

"So nobody knows anything?"

"Not really. There are ideas out there. Maybe he went down the Grade. Maybe to Lewiston. Maybe he's up at Spokane?"

"You really think he might be up at Spokane?" JT shakes his head. "That doesn't sound like Big."

"Well, that's just what people're saying."

"Hmm," JT says, "but are we trying to figure this thing out or what?"

I lean on the fence post. Feel it wobble under my weight. "I guess so."

"You guess so?"

"I mean, we gotta figure out where he is or what happened or whatever."

"Right," JT says, "what happened to him. Now we're gettin' somewhere."

"So you think that's it? You think something happened to him?"

JT takes his stem of grass out of his mouth, splits it with his thumbnails, pulls it apart. "I'll tell you this. I met a lot of meth guys over the last two months. Heard a lot of stories. And none of them's good. See, where there's meth, there's all kinds of sinister. Things you wouldn't believe. Choking a man to death, then chopping him up into little pieces with a chain saw to scatter him. Or killing a man in front of his children just to take over a new territory. Or taking a guy's elderly mother to a barn and cutting off two of her fingers, then sending those to the son in an envelope." JT leans down and plucks another blade of grass.

"So you think something like that happened to Big?"

"Don't know," JT says, "but we gotta find out. Then— maybe—we gotta get even."

"Even?"

"Shit, Little. You know the rules. I might not've liked Big much. We may not've gotten along the last few years. But if someone killed family, I gotta do something about it. And you do too." JT taps me on the shoulder with his fist.

I nod, lean on the fence post again and almost go down when it buckles. I set it back upright. Tip it sideways and kick a rock against the base. Nudge another rock to the other side. Then I let it go and watch it dangle off-center, held up only by strings of barbwire.

JT spits into the donkey pen. "Family's family, right?"

"Right."

"And in the end," JT says, "that's all we got."

They called me Little because I followed you, followed you everywhere: went to work with you, watched you do odd jobs, frame an addition, run crown molding in a kitchen, split a cord of wood, install a new sink disposal, unclog a toilet for half the cost of a real plumber. You'd be in a crawl space and call for a tool, and I'd put it next to your leg for you to reach back.

That was before the new evenings came, when your mouth would twist and your lips would wet. I was in fifth grade, and I remember because I still couldn't read, the only kid in my class who couldn't make sentences out of black print on a white page, and I was sitting at the table trying to sound out words while I ate my dinner.

You got strange that year, strange acting and strange looking. Thinner and longer. You reached across the table and smacked the fork out of my mouth. I didn't know why. JT was in eighth grade, strong and fast already, the varsity football coach talking to him after each peewee game, saying he could start varsity in the ninth grade if he kept working. So when you reached across the table for me, JT stood up. He said, "Try that on me, you big fuck."

Your fight started right there, in the kitchen, the whump whump sounds of your fists, trading punches, then wrestling on your feet, and the two of you crashing through the table, splitting it straight down the middle, the crack sound of a tree crown splitting from freeze-up, and I stood and backed against the wall.

The two of you rolled once before you got to your feet again, and you pulled JT up, outside through the front door, dragging him, but JT got shots in on your ribs as you tried to club him over the head.

Then you two were outside, and I followed to the edge of the porch, the neighbor Henshaw coming around the corner of the house as you and JT were rolling in the grass. You got on top and you put in four or five solid punches, then Henshaw said, "That's enough. That's enough," and pulled you off, reaching underneath your armpits for leverage, and taking an elbow to the jaw and stumbling a little as he pulled you back.

JT and you were both cussing then, and yelling, and Henshaw was in the middle of you trying to get both of you to calm down.

I didn't say anything. I remember that Mrs. Trepp rode by in her wheelchair right then, pulled behind her lawn mower, and she didn't even turn her head at the yelling; she just kept her sunglasses facing forward as she dragged past the house.

Henshaw was talking to you both, and I turned and went back inside, cleaned the blood off the floor with the dishrag, two little pools and one long fishing line of blood cast across the floor to the wall. At the end of that line, there was a tooth, and I didn't know if it was yours or JT's. The tooth was a dogtooth, angled at its sides, broken off at the root.

Later, JT was washing his face in the trailer's kitchenette sink. His right eye was closed and his left eye was cut to a slant, shutting quick. But he smiled when he turned to me, and his teeth were all there, all in place in his mouth, not one missing, and both of his dogteeth gleamed like a new dog's before he's come into something rough to bite.

flesh and blood

I walk Willa out to the historical marker where the school bus comes on its loop. I say, "Ride the bus home today, okay?"

"Okay."

"You know my classes get out later than yours, so I can't give you a ride or else I would."

Willa nods, then says, "Did you see anything you could shoot?"

"Shoot?"

"For meat. The other day."

"Oh, no," I say. "Just a few does."

Willa has mud clumping on the sides of her tennis shoes from being with the donkey this morning. She goes there to start every day now, and sometimes I look up from cooking eggs to see her riding the donkey along the fence line. Or sometimes she's just on his back, sitting there as the donkey stands in the middle of his pen.

Willa scrapes the mud from her shoes. Uses the 4" x 4" post of the historical marker to skidge the sides of her shoe rubber. She says, "Could you shoot at one of those?"

"One of what?"

"A doe."

"Shoot a doe? No, Willa. A doe is a *female* deer."

Willa tilts her head and makes a clicking noise with her mouth.

I say, "You're only allowed to shoot males."

"Well," she says, "that's just silly."

"No, actually, that's the rule. It's the law."

"Yeah, but you don't even have a license anyway, right? And it's bow-huntin' season now."

"So?"

"So it doesn't matter what you shoot. Does it?"

"Well, I don't think—"

"No," she says. "The thing is, we need meat, right? So that's all."

The school bus pulls up. The doors open and there's a sound like a children's riot inside. When I hear all those kids yelling like that, I remember my grade school lunchroom, the smell of cafeteria food, me being wedged at a too-small table, kids bumping into me on both sides, and one of the older boys calling me a "tard" until JT jumped out of his seat to hit him across the face with his metal lunch box.

I look at Willa and wonder if she hates school as much as I did.

Willa looks up at the bus driver, then back at me. Spits through her gap-teeth onto the asphalt. "Just please shoot something for us. You promise?"

"Go to school. And ride the bus home, all right?"

"But you promise?" Willa doesn't blink.

The bus driver says, "Come on now. It ain't dallying time. You ever seen a schedule, missy?"

Willa jogs up the steps and looks back at me. "Just promise, okay?" And the look on her face is such a mix of sad and pleading and hopeful that I want to get a deer for her. I really do.

I think about that as the bus driver closes the door, puts the bus in gear, and drives off. Then I'm still thinking about it as I get in my truck and start driving to school, up over the rise through the middle of town, past the post office, the bank, the Flame Bar. My Spanish tape is going but I'm not really listening.

Willa's face is in my head as I pull off into the vacant lot before Sammy's Grocery, turn the truck back around, and head north, past my trailer up toward the Forest Service roads. Sometimes it's that easy. When I think of being in school or being in the woods, it's not much of a decision. I know I should love education or something, but the real world is a thing I can understand, a thing I can learn and come to love.

I drive up Canal, take a right at the turn, and head out on the East Fork Road to Potlatch. I park at the turnout. Pull the .30-30. Chamber the cartridges from the glove compartment, check the safety, and start hiking. I hike to the knoll, find the water spot again, and check the wind for a good drop. Then I back off. Hunker down and wait. Gun propped.

Not tired, since it's midmorning. I'm eyes wide and sights clear.

I daydream about Rowan. I think about the smell of her and the way her lips felt during that one kiss at the door of my trailer. Then I go to thinking about her body with me in bed. Her hips and her skin and that thin T-shirt being all that separated her skin from mine. I wish I'd done something one of those nights, wish I'd made a move when JT was still locked up at Orofino, wish I'd pulled Rowan into me, kissed her neck, kissed her mouth. Or maybe more.

I'm thinking about Rowan, and maybe not really looking through my sights, because I almost don't notice when a young doe comes across the gap above the first gully. I blink a couple of times. Close my eyes hard and open them once again to focus.

A larger doe appears. Good hide and well muscled. No buck, but I think of Willa's face as she got on the school bus, and I slide the safety off. I have the open sights set at a hundred yards, but this is shorter than that, an easier shot. I don't have to account for drop. I aim behind the front leg. Imagine the heart pumping, wait for the doe to stop.

She stops at water. Bends her neck to drink. I breathe in and hold it. Aim two inches left of that lead leg. Squeeze the trigger.

The bullet jiggers the doe and her forelegs buckle. She goes down face-first, like a drunken man passing out as he stumbles to his bed. I'm watching her fall, so I never see the younger doe run, but she must've skittered at the sound of the shot. When I look again, she's gone.

I click the safety on the rifle and slide over the log. Walk up to where the doe fell. By the time I get there, the pool is red-tinted. The doe's face is in the water, water to her ears, and her front legs are sprattled. I set the rifle down, take a stick and touch her open eye to make sure she's dead. After, I drag her by her hind legs, out of the water and into a pine flat.

Then I get nervous. I've never shot a doe before, and the day feels too bright, my coat and orange hat too visible, the country wide open. It's sunny, and I wish it would cloud over, turn to midday dark. I'm worried about somebody coming up on me. I drag the doe farther from the uphill path to a jumble of downed pine. Heave her over the first log. Slide her into a low, wet gap. I go back for my rifle and bring that over as well.

I pull my knife and start to cut, quick at the throat and slow over the middle, careful not to nick the bladder. I gut it but don't skin. I'll leave the doe in her skin for a couple of days as the meat cures.

I pull the doe away from her entrails, and that's when I hear it: someone whistling. I pop my head up, and there's another hunter coming up the gully trail. I can just see his bright orange hat and his shoulders. He's looking the other way, but only 200 yards from me. I take off my hat and hunker low, slide my rifle between logs and sight him in. Whisper, "Don't go to the water."

He comes over the knoll, and I see his whole body: a middle-aged man in jeans and a sweatshirt, with a compound bow, whistling and looking up into the trees. When his head pops into view, I think I recognize him, think he's one of the Johnson uncles living off 2nd Street kitty-corner through town.

He stops 100 yards from me, to the right of the water. Looks like he might take the trail in my direction.

I whisper, "Don't," as I watch him. I'm sunk as low as I can while still keeping my head up, still watching.

He's looking up through the trees, looking for something

on the hillside. He pulls a small set of binoculars out of the front pocket of his sweatshirt, looks up into the treetops high above me. I hear a woodpecker working up there, but I don't look. I keep my eyes on him.

He puts the binoculars down. Takes a deep breath and keeps hiking. Uphill and to the right, angled away from me now.

I slide the rifle down against the log. Think to myself, *What were you gonna do, Little? Shoot him?* I giggle to myself because it's not funny at all. Shake my head.

I wait for the man to get far away, then go back to work on the doe. The doe is not as big as a buck, and I know I can carry her downhill in one piece, but I hesitate. This is what I didn't think about before I pulled the trigger. I can't just carry a doe over my shoulder down this trail, not with a man behind me up the hill and maybe someone below me too. I consider cutting the doe's head off to mask her, but that'd be as big of a warning signal as no antlers. I squat above the gutted carcass and think about my options.

I can't quarter her with my knife, and I didn't bring a saw. I don't remember seeing one in the truck, but I could go look. In my head, I try to go through the truck's inventory—what all is under the seat, what I've noticed in the back—but I'm not sure if I've ever looked.

I drag sticks over the doe, cover her good, and leave her. Then I scramble over the logs to the water spot, then the trail, and start down the hillside. I hike quick, the rifle swinging on its shoulder strap.

When I get to the road and the pullout, I take the keys

out of the truck's wheel well and unlock the driver's-side door. Look underneath the seat. Find a ratchet set, a flat-head, and a rusted Phillips screwdriver. A Maglite. A John Deere baseball hat with the bill bent. I walk over to the other side, see there's an old blue tarp, one of Big's flannel shirts, a wrench, WD-40, a package of worm hooks, weights, leader and PowerBait. No saw.

I grab the tarp. Leave the rifle behind and lock the truck. Then I hike back up with the tarp under my arm. When I get to the doe, I uncover her, her eyes open and head turned. I lay the tarp and slide her on, fold her legs, roll once, and twist the end of the tarp. Then I sling the doe over my shoulder like a hundred-pound bundle of wood. Heavy but do-able. Thankful I'm as big as I am.

I start to walk with my bundle but realize that even this plan is no good. I'm carrying a tarped doe in the wide-open, the bright, midday light. There isn't a single cloud in the sky, and the sunlight is bouncing off everything like shards of col-ored glass. I hold that doe over my shoulder and look around. Even if a person can't see inside the tarp, nothing about what I'm doing looks normal. Any hunter would be curious. Any Forest Service worker. Any game warden.

I step off the trail, struggle over a log, and drag the doe under low-lying branches. I shoulder her again and hike for a few minutes where there is no trail until I find a small gully in a dark stand of trees. I set the doe down, lay her in the U of the gully, and fold the tarp corners underneath her. Then I look for branches and pinecones. Cover her as much as I can, go for more branches and cover her some more.

I hike back out to the main trail. When I get there, I

spin around slow, look at all the trees and markers, broken branches, dried tree crowns, trunk splits, and new growths. Then I hike back down to the truck.

I drive home and make a grilled-cheese sandwich, drink some water, and lay down on my bed. Decide to nap for a couple of hours, wait out the midday, and go back up at twilight. I'm tired enough and I fall right to sleep.

matchbox

It's three hours before I wake again, the day warm for fall and the trailer hot. I drink water, groggy at the sink, sweaty now, staring out the kitchenette window at the tombstones in the graveyard, cement-colored teeth jutting from the ground's jaw. I wonder where JT is. Wonder if he's looking for work somewhere. Or drinking. Out with Rowan maybe. I don't like that idea, and I shake my head, fill another glass of water, and drink that too. I look at the clock and see it's 4:09. Late enough now.

I go back outside. The sun is arcing toward the ridge to the west, making a triangle with the tops of two old-growth trees at a gap, a marker I use to indicate evening. I hop in the truck and drive back to the trail marker because I'm pretty sure no one's gonna be out bow-hunting this late. I park the truck at the pullout and hike up. I clear the tarp and heft the doe onto my shoulder. Start back down again.

As I carry the doe down the hill, the light's fading, sunset coming early in the Bitterroots, and I watch ahead, squint into the shadows, look for anyone coming up, ready to duck or take an off-branching deer trail at any time. But I see no one. I get to the truck, unlock it again, and open the passenger-side door.

In the gray of the old-growth on either side of the road, it's near dark now. I put the doe in the truck, still wrapped in the blue tarp, half sitting on the passenger seat and half where the feet go below. It looks like I've wrapped a body, a human, wedged her there in the space next to the window.

I get in on the driver's side and start the truck up, flip the lights and pull a U-turn. Drive south on the Fork Road. At the T with Canal, I see the deputy's cruiser to the right, on the creek pullout there. He flicks his lights once at me as I wait at the stop. I look over at him and consider gunning it, slide my foot to the gas pedal, but there's no outrunning a squad car, not likely in most cars, and not possible in this truck, and the deputy would know where to find me anyway even if I somehow got away. I move my foot back over to the brake, pop the shift into neutral, feel the sweat prick on my forehead as I leave the truck idling, wait at the stop sign.

The deputy whips a U-turn and slides in behind my truck. He gets out and walks up, slow. In the mirror, I see his hand on his pistol grip. "Big?" he calls out.

"No," I say. I'm yelling through the glass. "It's still Little in here. Still driving Big's truck." My window's rolled up because I didn't want the deputy thinking I was reaching for anything.

Deputy White shifts back and forth on his feet. Cranes his neck. In the dark, he can't see me, or not well enough to know who I am.

I yell again. "I'm Little. Still just Little in here."

The deputy's cruiser is off-center behind my truck, the

spotlight shining bright on my mirror. Deputy White steps to the side, lets the full light hit my mirror. I lean my face forward so he'll be able to see that it's me.

"Kill the engine," he says. "Then I need to see your hands out the window."

I turn the key. Reach and roll the window down. Turn to the side and hold my hands out.

As the deputy walks the rest of the way up, I adjust a little, shifting my weight so my big body might block his view of the passenger side. I don't want him to see the tarp or find the deer. But he stays back from the window, angles, leans forward, and looks in at my face. His hand is still on his .45, but when he sees me, he lets out a long breath. "Still no Big, huh?"

"Nope."

"We keep talking about the same things. Don't we?"

"Yeah," I say, "I guess so."

Deputy White shifts, and I hear him kick the gravel with his boot. "Have you asked around like I told you?"

"Some," I say. "But I didn't hear much."

The deputy looks off to the streetlight up Canal. Tilts his head back and sniffs. "You need to start interviewing a lot of people. Ask questions. People will talk to you because you're family. People who won't talk to me. You understand that?"

I nod.

Deputy White steps up next to the open window, and I see that he has a flashlight in his left hand. He clicks it on. Shines it into the cab. Runs it up and down the blue tarp, and his eyes get wide. "What the fuck is this? Get out of the vehicle!"

"It's not what you—"

"Shut the fuck up! And get out of the vehicle." He has his .45 in his right hand. The flashlight over the pistol barrel. He takes a couple of steps back. Shines the flashlight directly in my eyes, and I know that the pistol is behind it.

"Okay," I say, holding my hands up. "Okay. I'm getting out."

Deputy White's voice gets lower and slow. He says, "Now turn around and put your hands on the roof of the cab. Do that now."

I turn. Put my hands up on top of the truck.

He says, "Now don't you do anything sudden. I'm gonna cuff you just to figure things out, so don't you resist at all, you got that?"

"Okay."

"Whatever it is that you've done, don't get yourself shot on top of it, all right?"

"All right."

"I'm gonna cuff the left, then the right. . . ." He takes my left wrist, handcuffs it, pulls it down, then takes my right wrist.

Now that my hands are behind my back, I say, "It's not what you—"

"Shut the fuck up," he says. "Just let me do my job."

He walks me to the back of the truck, around to the passenger-side corner of the bumper. "Now sit here," he says. "You're gonna sit where I can see you while I go look under that tarp. Got it?"

"Okay."

It's hard to sit down with my wrists handcuffed behind my back, so I sort of squat and slide down the side of the truck until I can get all the way to the ground. Then I watch the deputy.

He looks unsure. Points his pistol at the passenger-side window. Looks in with the flashlight. Then he opens the door and steps back. Shines the flashlight all around the open door. Looks back at me.

He doesn't ask me any questions, so I don't say anything.

He reaches out with his flashlight hand and tugs lightly on the tarp. Pulls a little and waits. Pulls a little more. Gets a corner free and tugs on it until the bundle shifts inside the car and falls out the open door. The deer and the tarp are on the ground, and one hoof sticks out from under the blue plastic.

"Wait, this is a . . ." The deputy looks at me. "Did you shoot a deer?"

"Yes."

He laughs. Shakes his head. Squats down and peels the tarp back to uncover the whole deer. Then he stands up and sniffs. Tilts his head to the side. "Is this a doe?" He shines the flashlight head to tail.

"Yes."

"Wait," he says. "Why'd you shoot a doe?"

"For Willa."

"For who?"

"For my cousin. She's the ten-year-old girl who lives next door to me. You've seen her?"

"Yeah," he says, "I've seen her. And she's the one who asked you to shoot it?"

"Willa said they'd been out of meat for a while. She said

boy or girl deer doesn't matter if you're hungry. So I shot her whatever I saw next."

Deputy White pulls one of the doe's legs up. Opens the deer and sees where I gutted her. "You realize this is illegal, right?"

"Yes."

"And you know you can get in a lot of trouble for this."

"Yes, sir."

The deputy stands again. Sniffs. "Poaching's a big deal." He reholsters his pistol. Puts his hands on his hips. "Poaching's a real big deal. You understand me?"

"Yes, sir."

"And this isn't gonna be good for you." The deputy flips the tarp back over the deer with the toe of his boot. "So there's one brother just out of jail and the other brother about to head in."

I look at him. Wonder if I'd go to adult jail or juvie since I'm only 16. But I don't ask.

The deputy says, "So where do we go from here? I could take you in to the game warden myself, or down to County, or we could call someone up here." He takes a few steps and stands out by the front of the truck. From where I'm sitting, the streetlight behind him, I can see only his outline, his elbows out, his thumbs hooked in his utility belt. He stands there a long time looking out across the road. No cars come by.

After a few minutes, he walks back to where I'm sitting. "Get up," he says.

I have to roll to my knees because of the handcuffs. The deputy reaches down under my arms and pulls me up. He doesn't unlock the cuffs and he doesn't put me in the cruiser. We stand there without speaking, and I can't tell what the deputy's thinking.

A couple of times I almost ask if I'm going to jail, but I don't.

Deputy White says, "You understand debt, right?"

"Sir?"

He says, "When you owe somebody but you don't have what it takes to pay it off?"

"Yeah, I think so."

"Good," he says. "See, I've got a lot of charges I need to wipe from the books. And the only way to do that is to find Big. But everyone in this town is about as much help as a copper dollar. You know what I'm saying?"

"Yeah, I think so."

"But you're family. You," he says, and taps my chest. "So you can learn things I can't."

I don't say anything because for once he wasn't asking a question.

"You don't have a license, you don't have a tag, and you shot a doe. That's three strikes. Idaho judges have been doling out prison time for poachers lately along with money fines that you could never afford. Plus lifetime hunting bans. So, I gotta ask you, do you ever want to hunt again?"

"Yes, sir."

"And are you interested in serving time at this juncture?"

I shake my head.

"Then today's your lucky day, Mr. Little McCardell, because I'm not interested in taking you in just yet. Instead, you're gonna help me out." He grabs my shirtsleeve and walks me over by the doe. It's kinda weird how he's pulling me around and I'm letting him even though he's six inches shorter than me. Smaller built and not too strong. But I don't really have another option.

"Kneel here," he says. He grips under my armpit to help me kneel down. "And is this the rifle you used today?" He points to the Henry's that's fixed to the gun rack.

"Yeah."

"Okay then." He pulls it out. Puts it on the ground between me and the doe.

Then Deputy White gets his phone out. Says, "I'm gonna take a few pictures here, and just a tip: you won't wanna be smiling if a judge sees these later." I look up at the camera, straight-faced, and he presses the button a few times before he puts his phone away.

When he swings his flashlight in another direction, it shifts from light to dark. There's no moon yet. I look up and see the stars beginning to prick through the sky's blue, blue turning dark as bruising.

Deputy White walks back to his cruiser, does something for a minute, then comes back to where I'm still kneeling by the doe. He leans down and picks up the rifle. Puts it on the gun rack in the truck. "Four weeks," he says. "You find me Big in the next four weeks, or you're going in for this. Full charges. You got that?"

"Yes."

"Are you sure? Because I'm not fuckin' around, and I seen what you done."

I'm still on my knees, looking at the doe once again spot-lighted by the deputy's flashlight. I say, "What if I can't find him? What if he's . . ."

"Either way, just find him. Alive or dead. Either way."

"But if I can't find out what happened?"

"For me, that won't be good enough." The deputy pulls me to a standing position, turns me around, and uncuffs me. "If you don't find Big—in one form or another—then you're going in for sure." He starts to walk back to his cruiser, then stops. "As for that deer there, you better eat every last bit of it. No wastin'. You hear?"

I'm rubbing my wrist where the cuffs dug in. I look at the doe laying on its side by my feet. Say, "Yes, sir."

don't think twice, it's all right

When I get home, I carry the doe to the shed and hang it by its rear hooves inside. Put shovels, rakes, and three 4" x 4"s in front to hide it. Then I stand in the doorway and try to breathe, try to relax, try to believe that everything's going to work out with the deputy, that I'll be able to give him enough information to avoid the poaching charges.

The corrugated tin shed frames the early-night sky out in front of me, the stars like fish eggs on the bottom of a big, dark river. Looking up, I imagine giant salmon spawning bright white eggs, finning the river above me.

I look to the north, the graves beginning, the first few plots at the west end—gravestone pale—stones becoming fence posts or stumps or nothing at all as the dark cuts their color.

I lean to the left to maybe see the outline of the donkey, but I can't see anything there, and I accidentally put my face against the side of the hanging doe. I pull back. She doesn't smell like a male deer—no muskiness to her—but there's still a wild smell, an animal smell in her fur, and I reach out and pet the doe, stroke with the fur's grain, then against it, feel the cowlick swirl behind the shoulder, and my finger touches the incut of the bullet's puncture.

I don't know what to do about the deputy.

Four weeks.

If Willa eats something she likes, she eats louder, makes big breathing noises, chewing noises, smacks her lips. Picks her food up and eats it with her hands, or piles food onto her fork with her fingers.

When I cook backstrap and eggs and bring two plates over to the house porch, Willa hops off the trampoline and comes running. She sits down, and as soon as I put a plate in her lap, she goes to work. "Venison," she says with her mouth full, "oh my goodness."

"I'm glad you like it."

"Like it?" Willa makes a small happy noise in the back of her throat and keeps eating. Getting caught by the deputy makes it harder for me to enjoy it, but watching Willa makes me smile.

I say, "How was school today?"

Willa's shoulders jerk up and down but she keeps eating.

I've heaped our plates, and we both eat without talking for a couple of minutes. Then I hear a gas engine far off. Look up and see Mrs. Trepp again. See her lawn mower out in front of her, those thin, strong hands clutching the handle.

The ropes in her forearms. Her giant sunglasses covering her everyday glasses. It's colder out this evening, and she has a hat on, a red stocking cap with a white puffball on top.

Willa points with her fork. "Do you see her? She looks like she's a friend of Santa Claus."

"Willa, she probably wears whatever she's got. She's just a lady tryin' to get by."

As I say that, Mrs. Trepp comes over the Orofino Bridge, her lawn mower running hard, last turn before she passes us.

Willa takes another bite. Says, "I just had a thought . . ." But she stops talking as Mrs. Trepp pulls closer to our property behind her mower. Then something strange happens. As she motors past, Mrs. Trepp turns her head and stares straight at us, at me and Willa, or seems to behind those shades. She doesn't wave or smile or do anything other than look at us, but even that look is shocking. I've never seen her look at us before. Not once.

She seems to stare straight at us, her mower running in front of her, and then she's past us and she turns her head back to face the road. We watch her drag up the hill into the main part of town, then disappear over the rise.

When she's gone, I say, "What was that?"

Willa's holding her fork in the air, a forkful of food, but she's not eating it. She says, "I don't know."

"So does she recognize us now?"

"Maybe," she says. "Do you think she's always recognized us?"

"Or do you think she saw something that night when . . . ?"

Willa shakes her head. "I really don't know."

We both eat for a minute.

Then I remember that Willa was saying something before. "Hey, what were you gonna say before that all started?"

"Uh . . ." Willa takes a bite of eggs. Chews and thinks. "What?"

"Before she looked at us like that. What were you starting to say?"

"Oh, right. I was gonna ask, when Mrs. Trepp gets into town in Weippe, or wherever else she goes, does she put her lawn mower away?"

"What do you mean?"

"I mean, does she hide it?" Willa says. "So no one else steals it? Does she hide it in the bushes or something?"

"I wouldn't have any idea."

"Like if she's going to the store, does she put it in a parking spot? Or does she just leave it outside the front doors? 'Cause even on a four-wheeler, we park it in a parking space. You know?"

"Yeah," I say. "But I have no idea."

Willa forks a little piece of venison into her mouth. Says, "I hope she leaves it in a parking spot, right in the center between the lines. That'd be perfect."

"She might," I say. "She's an odd lady."

"Or"—Willa forks a piece of meat and holds it up in the air, tapping it against the air like she's ringing an invisible bell—"maybe she's not odd. Maybe she just needs to go get food like the rest of us. Maybe she never could afford a truck or an ATV, but she had a lawn mower at her house, and that's all there was to it." Willa chomps down on that bite of venison and smiles.

"Maybe so," I say. Sometimes I think Willa understands more than I give her credit for.

Willa scrapes the last of her eggs to the side of her plate and forks them into her mouth. "Hey, Little," she says, "what does a momma lion say to her cubs before they eat?"

"I don't know. What does she say?"

Willa holds up one of her hands like it's a claw and bares her teeth. "The momma lion says, 'Shall we prey?'" And with that, Willa laughs so hard that she tilts over to the side and drops her fork down the porch steps.

You used to take me wood collecting on the old logging sites east, or out along the Judge Town Road south, the tangle of clear-cut slash across the hillside. We'd run our Homelite saws on the steeps, drop pine rounds to finish later with the hydraulic splitter.

I'd watch you work the cut, and I'd do what you did, your whole routine. You'd run your chain saw dry for five seconds, then two pumps on the oil bulb, ten seconds of full gas, then turn it off. Hike to the uphill side of a downed log. You'd get low and settle your feet, right and left, before starting the saw again, the saw balanced against the wood. Then you'd cut the rounds, angle in, then down, then away, finishing the cut like pushing a smaller kid down on the playground.

I imitated all that. Worked till I sweated. We'd stack a full cord in the bed, heap until the suspension sagged.

That was before Madison gave you the Grade territory, the full run to Orofino, before you restored your Chevy Silverado to stock, plus a six-inch lift, before you could afford the flat-black Z28 with the yellow center stripe, before people were always coming to the house owing you money. Before you lost weight and got twitchy. Before I was afraid of you.

get in line, brother

I'm at the table studying my *Idiot's Guide to Learning Spanish*. Practicing basic phrases.

Hasta mañana.

Hasta luego.

A tiempo.

JT comes in. He has his shirt off. He smells bad but looks solid, like he just did a set of 100 push-ups. The veins in his arms lay like pink paracord on his skin. He flips the cover of my book and reads the front. Says, "Whoa, Little, you trying to raise a ghost?"

"Huh?"

"I said, are you trying to raise a fuckin' ghost from these pages?"

I flip the book back open. Go back to reading.

JT walks to the sink and pours a big cup of water. Drinks it all, then shakes his head. "Shit, Little. He's a dead man, or as good as dead. To us anyway. And he sure as hell isn't coming back around here."

"Who are you talking about?"

JT wipes his sweaty forehead with the back of his wrist. Says, "You know damn well who I'm talking about."

"Dad?"

JT points at me. "Don't call him that. Don't ever call him that. You wanna call him something real, you just say Jésus Gómez. At least that was his real name."

I look at JT. See the veins rise in his neck. See the way his shoulder muscles twitch.

JT turns back to the sink. Looks out the little kitchenette window. Beyond him, there are grave markers I can't see from where I'm sitting.

"Anyway," he says, "that fucker's never coming back."

"I know."

JT pours another cup of water. Takes a sip. "So if you know, then why the book?" He looks at me. Raises his eyebrows.

I shrug.

"Figures," he says.

"What does that mean?"

"It means, you were always soft."

I glare at JT. "Soft?"

"Babied." JT puts his head in the sink and dumps the rest of the water over the back of his head, lets it run down into the drain.

I say, "What the hell are you talking about? Who babied me?"

JT dries his neck with the dish towel. Dries it slow, like he has all the time in the world, like we're not even having a conversation. "I babied you," he says, "a little bit. But mostly Big did."

"You really think that?"

JT holds his hands up. Smiles. Doesn't say anything at all. I say again, "You really think that?"

JT washes his water cup out with his fingertips. No soap. Puts it on the drying rack upside down. "I'd say the proof's in the now. Who's tougher? Let's think about it. You or me?"

"Fuck you, JT. You're older."

JT smiles and dries his hands with the towel. "Yeah, but you're taller. Bigger than me now, right? And even so, do you think there'd ever be a day when you could take me?" He shakes his head. Smiles again. "Not a chance. Not a single fuckin' chance in hell. And you know it." He winks and throws the dish towel onto the counter. Then he walks past me down the hall to his bed. Gets in and groans a long, slow sigh.

time and time again

After school the next day, I go to the shed. The deer's cured and I've only pulled backstrap, so I lay out the tarp on the floor of the trailer, haul the deer in, and carve up the rest. Saw and cut. Roll wax paper and seal the seams with strips of masking tape. When I'm finished, I put half the meat in paper bags with handles to carry to the deep freeze in the big house.

Derlene's there, playing solitaire at the table. She looks up. "What do you want?"

"Just need to put something in here."

She takes a drink from a mug. Flips three cards from the stack. "This ain't your house, Little."

"I know. This is for Willa." I open the freezer. Move plastic-bagged leftovers around to make room.

"Well, don't mess anything up in there."

"I won't." I stack the venison packages between an empty Hot Pockets box and a freezer-burned loaf of white bread. Close the freezer. Stand and fold the paper bag.

Derlene moves a king stack over to a blank space. Looks up from her cards. "What's all that anyway?"

"Meat."

Derlene takes a sip of her drink and smiles. "So you stole it or something?"

"No," I say. "And it doesn't matter. Like I said, it's for Willa."

"Kinda pissy tonight, ain't you?" she says. "What, do you think we can't take care of her? Think she needs your help?"

I shake my head no. But we both know what I really think.

Derlene says, "Let me ask you something: Who pays the taxes on this property, the property *you* live on?"

"Big?"

"Maybe," she says, and wags her finger above the top of her mug. "Maybe he used to. But not no more. Lucky had to pay the taxes the other day. He had to use his unemployment money on *that*. Now tell me that's not fuckin' total and compete ridiculousness."

"Huh?" I say.

Derlene flips three cards and moves a queen. Squints at the flip. Says, "Tell me something: What happened to Big?"

I shrug.

Derlene looks at me now. Picks a card off the table. Holds it up, then turns it so I can see what it is, a one-eyed jack. "I think you're lying," she says, and she shakes the card in the air. "You were always stuck to Big like glue. So where the fuck is he?"

When I walk outside, JT's behind the house, smoking a joint.

I say, "Where'd you get that?"

JT blows smoke into the air. Smiles and says, "I got magic hands."

"So you got it from Derlene?"

He nods.

"Did you sneak in?"

"Stole it from her purse in the living room while you two were having that nice little chat." JT's staring in the direction of the graveyard, where the first oak tree overhangs the west-side plots. He says, "You seem to be going over the past a lot lately."

"Not really."

"So no more than usual?"

I don't know what to tell him. It's been a long time since I've told JT how I feel about anything. "Maybe?"

"You know . . ." JT inhales deep. Holds his smoke a few seconds. Then exhales. Shakes his head. "None of that shit ever messed with me."

"None of what shit?"

"The past." He takes another drag. Taps the end-ash off the joint. "The past didn't fuck me up at all. I'm good. See? Real good."

I want to say "What fucks a person up more than the past?" but I don't ask. JT doesn't look at me and I don't look at him. We both stare out into the graveyard, the taller gravestones tilting a little as if nothing in this town can keep straight.

JT smokes.

We hear tires, and turn. A jacked-up Ford Ranger pulls into the yard between the house and the trailer. The driver and the two guys in the back were former football teammates of JT's in high school. JT says, "That's my ride. A bunch of us are hanging out at a house in Judge Town tonight. Wanna come with?"

"No," I say. "Thanks, though."

JT starts walking toward the truck. Turns and smiles at me, walking backward. He says, "Gotta study your little math sheets again?"

"Right."

JT hops up into the bed of the truck. One of the guys hands him a Busch Light tall can, and JT yells, "Get all those Xs and Ys in the right place, Little, you hear? That shit's super important."

I flip him off, and he smiles and pops the top of his beer can. Guzzles the first third.

The driver starts to roll the truck. On the back bumper, there's a sticker that reads:

CANADIAN WOLVES:
SMOKE A PACK A DAY

I make a pistol motion at JT and pull the trigger.

He catches the bullet in his hand and blows me a kiss like a pageant girl, laughs, and waves with his wrist turning as the truck fishtails onto the asphalt.

edged in black

Back in September, Willa's eye was blue to yellow, and every day she wanted to talk about it. "Hey, I gotta say something."

"No, Willa. We made a deal, remember."

"But you know what I feel like?"

I shook my head.

Willa pressed her index finger where the bruise was mushy. The swelling was so thick that her finger mark took a couple of seconds to disappear. She said, "I feel like my heart's full of birds."

"It's gonna be okay." I hugged her. "This is the only way. This is it."

"They're big black birds and they gotta get out. You know what I'm saying?"

"This is the only way, Willa. And we're going to stick with it, because this is what we've got."

Willa was so much shorter than me that her face was pressed against my ribs. She looked up at me and said, "I'm not sure, though."

"This is it," I said. "We were there then—you and me—and that's it. Okay?"

Willa had her eyes closed now and tears were leaking out of the sides. She stepped back and turned in the other direction. I couldn't see her face but I knew she was crying harder. She said, "I just don't know."

"You need to let me have it, okay, Willa? It's mine now, and that's just the way it's going to be. It's mine from here on out."

Willa made her hands into a little cup, like she was holding something, a liquid maybe, something that might spill. Then she put her lips to her hands, as if to drink.

out among the stars

I'm not doing homework. I'm studying my Spanish words. Hoping a few of them stick. So far, I try to memorize simple things, phrases and nouns. Colors and numbers. *"Verde,"* I say. "Green." Then, *"Azul."* I close my eyes. Remember and say, "Blue."

There's a knock on the trailer door. I open it and see Rowan, her smile a warped juniper fence. She has a Sprite bottle in her hand. "Care to share?" she says, and holds the bottle out to me. Leans against the trailer.

I take the bottle, the liquid light brown, not Sprite. I uncap it and smell the opening. Wince a little. "What is that?"

"It's Trick Mix. I scored it from a few different places."

I put the cap back on. Say, "It smells pretty bad."

"Really?" She leans against the side of the trailer. Says, "Then I'd have to tell you to man up, Mr. Little. And can I come in or what?"

I step back and watch Rowan struggle on the steps. Her balance is three-legged chair.

I sit down at the table, and she clunks down across from me.

I say, "You want me to make you some food?"

Rowan's eyeliner is streaked to her left ear, like a thin bruise. She says, "I might be past that."

"Do you want water then?" I fill a cup.

"I guess I could cut my liquor with a little water." She points to the bottle. "You should catch up while I slow down." She nudges the Sprite bottle closer to me.

JT couldn't get me to drink tonight, but Rowan can. I look at her face and am willing to do anything. I uncap the Sprite again, hold my breath, and take a sip of the mixture. Swallow it. Try not to make a face but fail anyway.

Rowan giggles. Sips her water. "You like it that much, huh?"

"It's delicious." I take another sip. Shake my head.

"You're never gonna get anywhere sipping like that." Rowan pushes herself to a standing position, goes to the cupboard, and pulls JT's moose antler shot glass. Slaps it down on the table. Pours a shot for me. "Here. Hit that."

I pick up the shot glass and take a deep breath. Then I knock it back, and my stomach clenches. Trick Mix is like iodine, Dr Pepper, and rubbing alcohol put in a blender. I breathe low and slow, drop my head. "Holy shit," I say. "What the . . ."

Rowan says, "One, two, buckle your shoe," and refills the shot glass for me.

Three more shots and the alcohol hits me like a sledge on a fence spike. "Oh, damn," I say, and stand up. Wobble a little.

Rowan laughs. "Trick Mix has got you for sure now. That's about how much I've had. Not much but Trick Mix makes it enough, right?"

I spread my feet wider. Wobble some more. "Feels like I'm sad-dancing to music that isn't even playing."

"Sad-dancing?" Rowan says. "Don't dance alone, baby."

Then she's up, and we're dancing together, her long arms wrapped around my waist and her head tucked just below my chin. My world is spinning, but it's spinning with Rowan inside it, her thin frame in my arms, and when she looks up with her Cleopatra eyes, I have to kiss her.

We're kissing then, lapping at each other with our medicine mouths, and my breath tastes like her breath, a Trick Mix bite. I keep telling myself that this is Rowan, Rowan against me, Rowan's chest against my chest, Rowan's hips against my hips, Rowan's mouth against my mouth, and our bodies dancing to a music that isn't even playing.

We dance past the trailer door and I think for a second about reaching for the lock and locking it, but then we're past the door, and there's no going back anymore, and Rowan takes off her shirt, and peels off mine as well, and we sort of sway for a moment above my bunk, dancing and kissing before we tumble sideways into what would've been my bunk but I'm too tall, and I hit my head on the board above and stop. Rowan falls into bed, but I stagger backward against the wall.

Rowan stands back up, next to me now, and says, "I'm so sorry. Are you okay?" and she pulls my head down and kisses my scalp, and she ducks my head low, below the board above my bunk, and she holds my head still as we slide sideways into bed. I'm laying on my back and she's on top of me, kissing my head all over, and she's in her bra, her small round breasts in front of my eyes as she cradles my head.

"Does it hurt?" she says.

"No."

"You hit it hard, though. Do you feel dizzy?"

"Yeah," I say, "but not from that."

She slides down and kisses me on the mouth. "I'll make it better," she says. "This will make everything better."

She reaches down and unzips my jeans, kisses my chest, my stomach, moves farther. I'm on my back in my bed that is no longer my bed, and suddenly it's like that meteor shower I saw last summer when there was nothing happening in the moonless night, nothing at all across the star-flecked sky, until all of a sudden there were burning lines of light, one, two, then three, then countless, every few seconds, blazing against the black expanse, bright white tracers and flashes, lines of burning meteor light, bursting arcs, so many glowing tracers that I couldn't believe the stars above my head, and this night, Rowan in all her wonder.

In the morning, I turn over acid-mouthed, post–Trick Mix hazed, to reach for Rowan, to pull her closer to me, but she's already gone. I open my eyes to see the empty half of the bunk, none of her clothes on the floor, nothing of hers to show that she was ever here.

I sit up and the blood rushes my head. My brain is a rusty hinge. I put my feet on the floor, slow, my head in my hands. There's a low noise, and I look to my right to see JT's arm hanging off the end of his bed. He's sleeping upside down, snoring a little, his feet on his pillow. I see the tattoo on his bare shoulder. Look at my right shoulder and see the same tattoo:

BROTHERS

I worry about when he got here. Wonder if he saw Rowan or walked right past us in the dark. Wonder what time Rowan left the trailer, and what JT would've done to me if he'd caught me with Rowan. But even thinking about that, even with my headache now, I think of Rowan in my bed last night. Hold my head and smile. I think about us dancing and kissing our way through the trailer, how I bumped my head on the board above my bunk and the feeling of her bra scraping against my face as she kissed my hair, my scalp, the way her naked skin felt against my chest, the way everything was.

I lay back down. Feel my head pumping, my brain cells slow-crushing, like there's too much pressure in the air. My mouth tastes as if I've never had a drink of water in my life. My tongue sticks to the insides of my teeth.

While I'm laying there, I remember that it's Wednesday, a school day. But I'm not going to school. I'm gonna drink some water and go back to sleep.

Afternoon. Deputy White drives his cruiser into the yard. Pops the door and steps out. He doesn't call for Big this time. Instead, he says, "Little? JT?"

I'm back next to the shed where he doesn't see me. I'm unspooling barbwire to fix a break in the donkey's run, and I can see the deputy from under the side roof, the wood cover. I step out from behind a half-cord of stovewood. Say, "JT's not here. He's been gone since late morning."

"Oh," he says. "Okay."

"What do you need?"

"Well, I wanted to talk to both of you, but I guess one'll have to do."

I'm holding a framing hammer in one hand, a long flathead screwdriver in the other, the combo to pop staples and rerun the line. The deputy looks at the tools. He blinks. Says, "We found Big's Camaro. The stateys did."

I scrape a smear of paint off the hammer's handle with the screwdriver. Say, "Where?"

"Out by Judge Town. Out at a lab."

"A meth lab?"

"Yep."

I keep scraping at the paint. "You sure it was his?"

"No doubt," he says. "We matched up the VIN."

"Okay then. So is he maybe out there?"

"Well, we don't know. The thing is, we didn't find a trace of Big. Nothing. And that's a little weird."

I scrape another mark of paint off the handle of the hammer.

The deputy shifts on his feet. "So I'm sorry to tell you but we're opening a criminal investigation."

I look up. "What does that mean?"

"It means we think something happened to Big. That's what. State police and all." Deputy White hooks his thumbs in his utility belt. "Up until now, I've been trying to find him regarding other charges. But now . . ."

I say, "It's probably nothing. Like I've said, Big's run off and come back before."

"You keep saying that," the deputy says, "but remember that you only have three and a half more weeks. Right? I'll be focusing on Judge Town now. Where the car was left. And you better ask around there too because you still owe me some information. We made a trade."

I stop chipping paint. Regrip the hammer.

Deputy White points at me. "You're running out of time. Don't you forget that. All right?"

I nod and say, "I won't."

"Good. Now I've given you a lead, and you better follow up. This is clannish country out here. People don't talk to the law. So you do your part for me. You hear?"

"Yeah," I say, "I got it."

comes around

Thursday. Art class. I always get the sheets of paper, and Zaylie always gets the grease pencils or charcoal. Then Mrs. F walks around and hands out different types of erasers and smudge paper stumps. But when I get to our table with the paper for me and Zaylie, there aren't any pencils on the tabletop. Zaylie never picked them up. Her hair's pulled forward over her face. She's moving her head to a beat I can't hear.

"Hey," I say.

Zaylie doesn't say anything. She doesn't clear her hair away from her face.

I stand there for a minute and look at her. Then I go to Mrs. F's desk for our pencils, pick up two 9Bs from the jar, return to our table, sit down, and slide a pencil toward Zaylie. She takes it and hands me one of her earbuds. I put it in.

Tupac again. The middle of a song that repeats a chorus:

*Keep ya head up, ooooh, child, things are gonna
  get easier
Oooooh, child, things are gonna get brighter*

When the song ends, Zaylie hits Replay and we listen to it again. After she starts the song for the third time, I turn to her and try to see her face. But she's still hunched down, her hair hanging forward, her left hand covering her face as well.

I nudge her shoulder. Say, "You all right?"

"Yeah," she says. "I'm fine."

We draw some more. Zaylie plays the song for the fourth, then the fifth time.

I tap the table. "Are you sure?"

"Yeah," she says. "I'm fuckin' great."

"Zaylie?"

She shakes her head but doesn't say anything.

"Zaylie, what's going on?"

She shakes her head. "Fuck Matt."

I nod. "He *is* an asshole."

She doesn't correct me this time. Doesn't stick up for him. She swipes her hair to the side, and I can see how much she's been crying. Her swollen eyes.

"What'd he do?"

Zaylie lays her pencil flat on the table and spins it once. "He slept with that bitch Julie."

"Julie . . . The one with the three nose rings?"

"Yep."

"Really? That girl? How'd you find out?"

"His friends joked about it in front of me, and I could just tell from Matt's face that it was true. He tried to deny it, but it was obvious."

"Shit."

"Yeah, well." Zaylie shrugs. Picks up her pencil and starts drawing again.

I know she's trying to act tough about it. I say, "Just so you know, you're way prettier than that girl."

Zaylie sniffs and tucks her hair behind her ear. "You mean, I'm way shorter than that girl? Too small?"

"No, I said 'prettier.' And that girl's stupid too. She thinks nose rings make her cool, or tough, or . . . I don't even know what. She also has that stupid tattoo on her forearm."

"I know." Zaylie wipes her eyes on her sleeve. "A tattoo of bacon and eggs? I guess it's supposed to be ironic, like she's so cool that she can have a stupid tattoo."

"Or," I say, "she's so *stupid* that she can have a *stupid* tattoo."

Zaylie giggles at that. Says, "Can we listen to that song again? Do you care?"

"No, that's fine." I adjust my earbud and wait for Tupac to start up once again.

Matt walks into class late in the period. This time he doesn't go and talk to Mrs. F before coming over to our table. He walks right up to Zaylie. "Listen," he says, "you gotta talk to me. People talk this stuff through."

Zaylie looks up.

I look at Matt. He stands there in a green shirt that says LEGALIZE IT.

"No," Zaylie says, "I don't have to talk to you."

"You know what?" Matt waves his hands in the air like he's swiping at mosquitoes. "You shouldn't believe everything you hear."

"So you're saying it's not true?"

"Of course it's not true. They were *joking*. It was a fucking joke. Couldn't you tell?"

Zaylie says, "Then why'd you look at him like that? Why'd you look so panicked?"

Matt rubs his eyes. " 'Cause it was a bad joke. It was stupid, and I don't like stupid jokes."

"Hey, you two." Mrs. F calls from her desk, points at Matt and Zaylie. "That's too loud for class. You two need to talk after the period's over."

"Okay," Zaylie says. "Matt was just leaving."

"No," he says. "I wasn't just leaving. I'm not leaving until we talk."

"Well," Zaylie says, and stands up. "I've gotta get more art pencils so I can do more *art*. Little, do you want some too?" She starts to step around the back of my chair.

I stand up to get out of her way, and I say, "Yeah, sure," but I'm so big that I have to get out from behind the table to let her by.

Matt's in my way, though. He's right there, at the gap between the tables, in front of us, blocking me. I say, "Excuse me," and try to slide past him, but he won't move. So I say, "Hey, man, can you move for a second?" I'm wedged between Matt and Zaylie, and between the two tables.

Matt reaches across me and puts his hand on Zaylie's shoulder. "Listen . . . ," he says, and sort of shakes her shoulder. "You need to accept the truth."

Zaylie brushes his hand off, and his arm bumps into me. Zaylie holds up one finger. "Don't touch me."

I'm right in the middle of them, feeling like the most awkward person in the world. "Hey, guys, I—"

"Look," Matt says, and leans across my body again, this

time with both of his arms grabbing Zaylie's shoulders. One of his arms is touching me.

I sit down on the table behind me, on top of some other kid's drawing. "Hey!" the kid says.

Mrs. F is up and coming around the back of her desk.

Zaylie starts to turn and go the other way, but Matt spins her around to face him. He says, "You have to talk to me right now. You don't have a choice."

Zaylie says, "Get your hands off me!"

And that's when I stand up and grab his T-shirt. Twist the fabric in my fists.

"Hey!" Matt says, looking like a hunter backed against a wall by a moose, not sure which way to go. He grabs my wrists with his skinny little hands, but he can't make me let go of him.

I say, "She said she doesn't wanna talk right now." I'm holding his T-shirt tight and backing him up.

Matt's face turns red. "Hey, you can't—"

Suddenly Mrs. F is next to me, saying, "Little. Let go!"

So I do let go and I shove him pretty hard, and he stumbles backward ten feet or so, trips and hits his head on a pottery kiln. He doesn't hit it hard enough to get knocked out or anything like that, but he lays on the floor and holds the back of his head.

I say, "I'm sorry, Mrs. F. Zaylie just kept telling him no, and he kept running into me, and he was grabbing at her, and I—"

"I saw everything," she says. "Don't worry."

The whole class is standing at their desks, everyone looking at me.

"Uh," I say, and turn to Zaylie. But she's already throwing her stuff into her backpack. "Hey, Zaylie?"

She slings her schoolbag over her shoulder, grabs her iPod and earbuds, and runs out of the room. I start to follow her, but Mrs. F steps in front of me. "Let her go. Let her get some space, okay?"

I look around the room, everyone still standing.

Then I look at Matt. He's on his hands and knees on the floor, looking up at me, wondering if he should stand while I'm still there.

Mrs. F says to me, "Stay here," and she goes over to where Matt is. "Are you okay, Matt?" She bends down and puts a hand on his back.

Matt nods a little.

"Are you sure?"

He nods again.

"All right." Mrs. F stands and holds her hands up. Looks at the class. "I'm going to walk Little down to the office now. Will someone walk with Matt in a few minutes, once he gets back on his feet?"

A girl raises her hand to volunteer.

"Thank you," Mrs. F says. Then she turns to me. "Are you ready? We better go to the office and let them know what happened."

As we walk down the hall, I don't know what to say. Mrs. F is my favorite teacher ever, and I love her class, and I want to apologize somehow, to say something that'll make everything a little better. I say, "Mrs. F, I'm just really—"

"I know." Mrs. F smiles at me.

"I'm sorry, though. I shouldn't have done that."

"In my class, or not at all?"

"In your class, of course. I mean, I guess I'm not sorry I pushed him."

"So he's not a good guy?"

"No," I say, "I don't think so."

"Well"—she smiles again—"I trust your judgment. But, unfortunately, the principal won't. So you'll be gone for a few days. Just say you're sorry, okay? Say you were defending a girl, but you were wrong to hurt him. Say it was an accident that he hit his head on the kiln. And no matter what, stay calm, all right?"

"All right," I say, and I do feel calm. The strange thing is, I never felt uncalm, even when I was backing Matt up, even when I was pushing him, and I wonder if that's how JT feels when he does something in a fight.

roll call

Suspended. I wake up early anyway because I'm used to it. Eat breakfast. Go out and listen to my Spanish tapes in the truck for a while, run the heater to keep warm. Then I go and lie on the trampoline in my jacket and stare at the late-fall clouds, make shapes out of cirrus, watch my breath huff in the air, wonder where Rowan's been the last couple of days.

After a little while, I walk up into the cemetery and look at the work list. See what plots need plant removal and which headstones have cracks, work for three and a half hours and log my time in the notebook. Then I pick up the cash in the envelope for my previous hours of work and walk back to the trailer to hide it in the wall.

On the way through the yard, I notice that there's another chicken missing. I count and recount, look under the trailer and porch, but she's gone, one of the good layers, a Rhode Island Red. I search all over for the carcass, up by the Baptist church, through the near section of the cemetery, in the donkey's pen, but the hen is gone. Not mauled and left around or half-eaten, but just vanished, coyote snatched maybe, and now there are only five chickens left. I hunt eggs in the grass, but there are only three eggs to be found.

I was eight years old. We were in a ranch home near Weippe, and I'd stayed quiet since you said, "Dammit to fuckin' hell!" and threw your iron cat's paw clattering on the floor.

You were doing a bathroom renovation for a friend of a friend, and every time you tore something apart you found a new problem. PVC where metal piping should've been. The subfloor tacked at an angle in the corner. The wax seal long blown at the base of the toilet, a circle of brown rot under the linoleum.

I held your tools and stayed quiet. Sometimes you let me pop a countertop or break through a sheet of drywall when we did a job like this, and I was hoping you'd let me pry with the Estwing Handy Bar.

You said, "Mexicans, for sure . . . no fuckin' doubt. We're looking at their work here, just all garbled to fuck." You took a deep breath and put your hands on your hips. "See here, Little, you know what I mean, right?"

I nodded even though I didn't.

You looked at me and made a clicking noise with your

tongue and your teeth. You said, "All I'm saying is *most* Mexicans are worthless. Just sayin' *most*, not *all*. Right?"

You nodded then, so I nodded.

I knew that nodding was the right answer, and I was holding your tools in that small space, the two of us closed in that bathroom together.

You picked up your cat's paw. Leaned over and spit Red Man leaf tobacco in the toilet. "That's all I'm saying. If a man wants to grow up to be a good Mexican, he could. That'd be his choice for sure."

new cut road

On the second day of my suspension, I work again, this time a full day, seven o'clock to three o'clock. I repair 15 cracked headstones. Clear four plots. Listen to Spanish in the truck while I eat my cheese sandwich for lunch.

Not long after I get back to the trailer in the afternoon—while I'm running a flake of alfalfa up to the donkey—a silver Toyota Corolla pulls into the yard. There's heavy bass thumping inside the car, rap music blaring from behind the tinted windshield. The engine cuts and I wait to see who it is. The door opens and Zaylie gets out. "Hey," she says.

"Oh, hey."

"I hope you don't mind," she says, "but I got your address from Mr. Polchowski. He said you'd be fine with me visiting you during your confinement."

"Yeah, that's fine."

Zaylie twists her hair with her index finger. Says, "I just wanted to say thank you for sticking up for me."

I flip the alfalfa flake over the donkey's fence. Walk on back to Zaylie. "No problem."

"Really, though, thank you. And I'm sorry you got suspended for it."

"It's all right. My classes were already messed up."

"Now you're gonna be further behind," she says. "Can I make it up to you? I can cook spaghetti, and *SVU* reruns are on tonight. Then a new one later."

"What's *SVU*?"

"You know, *SVU*. The show."

"No," I say. "What's that?"

Zaylie gets a weird smile on her face like she can't tell if I'm kidding or not. "You've never seen *Law & Order: Special Victims Unit*?"

"No."

"Oh, wow. That's fuckin' crazy. Sad, actually. It's one of the greatest shows of all time."

"Oh."

"No," she says. "Not 'Oh.' This is important. You've gotta see *SVU*. It's new on Wednesdays, but there's reruns all the time."

I shake my head. "I don't have a TV."

"Wait, are you messing with me?" Zaylie rubs her eyes like she's trying to wake up from a deep sleep. Then she pulls her hair back and holds it at the back of her head. "Little, are you kidding me?"

"No. My brother threw it and it broke. That was four or five months ago. Back in the summer."

"Your brother? You mean the football player?"

"Yeah."

Zaylie finds a rubber band and pulls it over her fist, loops it three times to finish her ponytail. "He just threw your television?"

"Yeah."

"That's fucked up. I'm sorry."

I shrug. "It's just a TV."

"Did you just shrug your shoulders?" Zaylie shakes her head. "Are you pretending that losing your TV isn't that big of a deal?"

"Not really. I mean—"

"Losing a television is a big deal, a *real* big deal. You don't have to watch it all the time, but you have to watch television. At least sometimes. For sure."

"What am I supposed to do? Go to my aunt and uncle's? Hold their beers for them while we all watch?"

"If you have to. But ooh, I have an idea." Zaylie raises her hand in an exaggerated way like she's in class. "See, you should could come over to my house right now, watch *SVU*, and eat the spaghetti I'm gonna cook for you."

"Sounds good," I say. "Let me wash my hands and change my shirt."

"Okay." Zaylie points to her car. "I'll just listen to some thug jams while you do whatever you need to do." She opens the car door, leans in, and turns the key. Rap comes on loud. Zaylie yells over the music. "'My Favorite Mutiny'! The Coup!"

I have no idea what she's talking about. I smile and nod.

"Go get your stuff," she yells. "I'll wait here." She closes her eyes and starts dancing, leaning on her open car door, the music blaring, and she looks cute dancing like that, moving her hips as she leans against the car.

I go inside the trailer. Wash my hands and face. Brush

my teeth. Change my T-shirt and put on fresh deodorant. Smell myself.

When I walk back outside, I see Derlene's on the other side of the Corolla.

Zaylie has her hand to her ear. "What'd you say?"

Derlene's holding a Natty Ice in one hand, a cigarette in the other. She says, "I said, 'Turn that fuckin' shit off.'"

"Oh!" Zaylie laughs. Yells back at Derlene, "I'll turn it off if you want me to. It's your yard. But let's not call it shit because that's Talib Kweli."

"Excuse me?" Derlene takes a glug of beer. Swallows.

Zaylie turns the music off. "I said"—Zaylie smiles—"It's not shit."

"Listen." Derlene points with her cigarette. "If you wanna sass me like a little bitch, then you can just—"

"Whoa, whoa . . . ," I say, stepping between them. "Derlene, you don't even know what you're talking about. And Zaylie? Let's go."

Zaylie gets in on the driver's side, and I walk around to the passenger's door.

Derlene's standing there by my side of the car, smoking and glaring as I get in. When Zaylie backs the car up, Derlene throws her half-full beer against the car windshield. It clanks and sprays but the glass doesn't crack.

"That's the last fuckin' straw." Zaylie slams on the brake and undoes her seat belt.

"No." I put my hand on her shoulder. "Let's just go. Derlene's always like this and it didn't even break the windshield."

Zaylie looks at me and says, "Fine." She whips the wheel

and pulls the car onto the road. Then she lets off the gas and glares as she slow-rolls past the house.

I say, "Well, now you've met my lovely aunt Derlene."

"She's great," Zaylie says. "I fuckin' love that woman."

"Right," I say. "If you two got to know each other, you'd be best friends for sure."

Zaylie laughs and turns the car radio back on. Scrolls her iPod and starts another rap song I've never heard before.

Zaylie's house is one of the good three-bedroom places in the section of Weippe where everyone owns two cars and there are no broken-down vehicles parked in the yards. Her house is stick-built, not manufactured, and it's new-paint blue with a red door, and a porch that goes all the way across the front.

I say, "This is a nice place."

"My dad let me paint the door myself. Do you like it?"

"Yeah."

As we step up onto the porch, Zaylie says, "My parents are gone until late tonight. They have an after-work meeting. They work at the same company, and there's some sorta volunteering thing they have to go to."

We walk in, and I see knickknacks everywhere, a shelf in the living room filled with Coca-Cola collector items, and another with Boise State Broncos cups, Bronco plates, Bronco vases, shot glasses, and a bottle opener, all orange and blue. A higher shelf on the opposite wall has Betty Boop figurines crowded to spilling.

Zaylie says, "My mom likes to collect things. Can you tell?" She makes a face and sighs real loud.

I look around. I've never been in a house like this: clean, no dust on the shelves, no dishes on the floor, no dirty laundry on the couch.

Zaylie puts her keys and purse down on the dining room table. Says, "Does your mom live in your trailer with you?"

I shake my head.

"In the house then?"

"No. My mom's been gone since I was a baby."

"Gone?"

I nod.

"You mean *gone* gone?"

"Yeah."

"Oh, shit. I'm sorry. I didn't mean . . ." Zaylie puts her hand on my arm.

I say, "I don't even remember it."

Zaylie makes a face and looks like she's trying to think of what to say next. She bites on one side of her lip, then on the other.

"Really," I say, "that was so long ago. Don't worry about it."

"Okay . . . ," Zaylie says, and lets her hand drop.

I say, "We should eat."

"All right . . ." Zaylie walks into the kitchen and pulls a large metal pot out of the cupboard. "Do you like spaghetti? I mean, I'll warn you that my spaghetti's pretty amazing. You might not be able to stop eating once you start."

"That sounds good, then."

Zaylie fills the pot with water. Puts it on the stove and turns the burner to high. "So who does your cooking for you?"

"Me."

"You cook everything?"

I nod.

"So we should cook this together since you're a kitchen man?"

"Okay. What do you need me to do?"

"How 'bout"—Zaylie points at the sink—"go over and wash your hands, then get the vegetables out of the crisper drawer. You can wash and chop veggies, and I'll cook the meat and the noodles. Deal?"

"Deal."

It's fun cooking with Zaylie. She puts on music, and not rap this time. It's some other kind of music that I don't know anything about, but it's happy sounding. She says, "Do you know who this is?"

"No." I shake my head.

"Are you kidding me?" Zaylie has a spatula in her hand and she whips it around. "This right here"—she points at the stereo with the spatula—"is Bob Marley. 'No Woman No Cry'? 'Three Little Birds'? 'Redemption Song'?"

I shake my head and go back to chopping bell peppers.

"You're hopeless," Zaylie says. "Were you raised by wolves on the moon?" She's pointing at me with the spatula.

I pretend to be afraid. "Go easy with that thing."

"I'm not gonna hurt you with this"—she jabs at me—"but I *am* gonna educate you. It's important. You don't know music, you don't know TV . . . Wait," she says, and covers her mouth. "What *do* you know?"

"Nothing, apparently," I say, and stop chopping. Smile at her.

"Yep, that's what I'm worried about," Zaylie says. "Without me, you could go an entire life without pop culture. And without pop culture . . . you could become *irrelevant*." She sets the spatula down and steps up next to me. Pulls my head down to her height and kisses the side of my face. "Start listening and watching," she says, then picks her spatula back up. "I don't want you to be disconnected. That could be dangerous."

I shake my head and go back to chopping vegetables.

Zaylie stirs the hamburger in the frying pan. Shakes salt over the top. Pepper after. "But seriously," she says, "if you don't watch TV or listen to music, what do you do? What do you *like* to do?"

"Fishing and hunting mostly. Being in the woods, or just by the river."

"Seriously?"

"Yeah. That's what I love." I make a circle in the air with my knife. "All this country around here. It's real pretty."

"Okay." Zaylie nods slow, then a little faster. "Okay."

We eat on the couch after Zaylie makes a big deal of introducing me to the television, saying things like "*THIS* is a television. And *THIS* is a television remote."

The spaghetti is good. I haven't eaten anything like it in a long, long time, and as soon as I finish my first bowl I go for another.

"Eat a third," Zaylie calls to me as I walk into the kitchen. "We made enough to feed the whole school."

We watch an *SVU* episode. It starts with a woman who's been raped by the same man for 15 years and ends with the main police detective setting out cross-country to examine old, forgotten rape kits.

Zaylie says, "Isn't this show awesome?"

"Um, it's okay."

"No, no." Zaylie covers my mouth with her hand. "Don't even talk like that about *SVU*. You can't say it's 'okay' because that's a horrible fucking lie. *SVU* is absolutely the best show on television. No question."

"Okay," I say, through her fingers. "All right, it's pretty good."

"You just don't understand it yet. But you will. There's another episode on now, and I'm not saying we *have* to watch it, but we probably should. Don't you think?"

Zaylie keeps my mouth covered, and I hold my hands up like someone's pointing a gun at me.

"Good," she says, "then it's all decided. I'll make us some peppermint tea, and you tell me what happens at the start of the show."

I narrate from the couch while she starts the water. I say, "They're investigating the rape of a young girl—"

"How old?" Zaylie says from the kitchen.

"How old what?"

"How old is the girl?"

"Not sure yet . . ." I try to describe the girl.

Zaylie pops her head around the corner. "Ooh, I know this one. It's messed up."

"Really?" I say.

"Oh, yeah. Liv is gonna go undercover in a prison. You'll see. Orange jumpsuit and everything." Zaylie ducks back into the kitchen. Yells, "This tea's almost ready. Just keep telling me what's going on, all right?"

"All right," I laugh, "but that makes no sense since you already know the episode."

"I like to hear the details."

The show goes to a commercial, and Zaylie walks in with our peppermint tea. We sip and watch the rest of the episode and the main detective lady does go undercover in a prison and almost gets raped herself.

Zaylie takes my tea mug from me and sets both of our mugs on the coffee table. She says, "Isn't this the best show?" and she slides over onto my lap, just like that. I put my arms around her. She's so small sitting on my lap, and I realize she can't weigh much more than 100 pounds. She's less than half my size.

But she smells good. Her shampoo is a faint fruit smell, and she's wearing some kind of perfume too, not much but a little, and I sort of want to lean in and smell her, and I would if it wouldn't seem too weird.

Zaylie says, "Thanks for coming over tonight," and she puts her arms around my neck. Tilts her head and leans in. I can feel the smooth skin of her cheek against my cheek. She kisses me there on the side of my face again, just like she did in the kitchen. I pull my head back a little, and she kisses me on the mouth. We kiss for a minute, our mouths opening. Her breath tinted by peppermint tea.

We kiss and she holds my face, runs her fingers through my hair.

I still have my arms around her. I don't know what to do with my hands.

After a minute, Zaylie pulls back. She says, "I've been wanting to kiss you for a while. I love the face you make when you're focused on drawing in class. It's really cute."

I say, "I'm not good at drawing."

"You're fine. And anyway, that doesn't matter. I like watching you focus. I like that look you get." Zaylie kisses me again, this time harder. We bump noses. Her tooth scrapes against my lip. She has her arms around my neck again and she holds me a little tighter.

She feels good on my lap and I like kissing her, but I still don't know what to do with my hands. I sort of grab her hips and pull her in.

She stops and rests her head on my shoulder. Says, "Would you do something for me?"

"Okay."

"But it's kind of weird," she says. "Sort of weird. Not too weird, though. Is that okay?"

"I guess?"

"I mean, maybe it's not that weird. So I'll just say it. Would you go into my room with me and hold me? Just hold me in bed? I'm not trying to . . . you know, not that I don't want you to do more or anything . . . I just . . . would you lay with me in there?"

"Okay."

Zaylie gets off my lap and stands up. Takes my hand and pulls me to my feet.

I follow her into her room. I don't really know what she's

thinking. It makes me think of those outdated cans on the bargain shelf at Sammy's Grocery where the labels have all fallen off and everything's just marked with an orange 25-cents sticker, and it's impossible to know what's going on inside each can. There could be anything in there, and I have no idea.

Zaylie's room is painted bright red. She pulls my face down and kisses me again. Just once. Then she peels her long-sleeve shirt off, unbuttons her jeans, slides them down, and stands there for a minute in her white bra and white underwear. There's lace around the edges, and I can't help staring.

Zaylie looks good in her bra. Really good.

She gets into bed and says, "Come here," and holds her arms open.

I unlace my boots. Slide my feet out. Take off my T-shirt and my jeans. Then I get into bed with her. She pulls the covers over us and scooches up against me. She doesn't start kissing me again, so I just put my arm around her and she rests her head on me. She presses close, her skin against my skin, and says, "This feels nice." She drapes her arm across my chest. "Thank you."

Her skin feels so good, and I want to start kissing her again. I imagine doing a few things, undoing her bra and peeling off her underwear, and it's hard not to at least try, but she seems happy the way we are, laying here like this, and I try not to think too much.

We lie there for a while. I close my eyes but don't fall asleep.

Then, out of a long silence, Zaylie says, "You know, Matt's rich."

"What?"

"Yeah, like *rich* rich. Like *real* rich."

I say, "But I thought—"

"That he wears shitty clothes and smokes weed all the time like a piece of white trash?"

"Yeah."

"I know. But that's just a façade. His family has serious money. One of those ridiculous houses near the Grade above the Clearwater. They have a four-car garage and a speedboat."

I laugh, thinking about expensive speedboats and long North Idaho winters.

Zaylie laughs too.

We lay there a little while longer, then Zaylie drums her fingers on my chest. Pops her head up. "I better take you home before my parents get here. They get super weird about boys." She kisses me quick on the cheek and slides out of bed.

"Wouldn't most parents be weird about this?" I point at Zaylie's bra.

She's pulling on her jeans, and she stops, halfway. Looks at herself. "Yeah," she says, "I guess."

I roll over and get up. Go for my boots and clothes.

Zaylie grabs her shirt and walks out to the living room.

When I come into the kitchen, Zaylie's washing my mug, my plate, and my fork in the sink. She rinses and dries them, puts them away in the cupboard. "See?" she says, and points at the couch and the table by the TV. "Only one person's eaten dinner here, right? Only one person's been here all night."

don't go near the water

After Zaylie drops me off at my place, I stand in the yard and stare up at the sky. The stars look like silver nails hammered through a dark ceiling. I'm staring, looking at the patterns laid out, when I hear an odd bump inside the trailer. I go to the door. Put my hand on the handle and hear something else. I'm not sure what it is.

I open the door, step up and in, and stop. Down the hall, in JT's bed, in the small light of the back window, I can see the outline of JT above someone, a girl. Her small whining sounds as his big body moves up and down, his grunting like an animal in a pen, his pushing, his rising and falling, and I stand there listening to it for a moment, watching the little that I can see, which is not much in that light.

They keep going, and I keep standing there, my feet stuck as pitch to bark, until I hear Rowan's whisper, just enough of her voice to know that it's her, and JT stops for a moment, and then Rowan turns over underneath him, her long limbs unmistakable even in the half-light of the small window, and JT starts again above her, and I can't watch or listen any longer.

I shut the door. Step out into the yard. Feel like the air has thinned, like the night has expanded away from me and even the air isn't dense enough to breathe well. I look up and see the cherry of Derlene's cigarette on the big-house porch, and I have to walk away before she says anything to me because tonight I wouldn't take it from her.

I walk around the town for an hour, go down Main Street to Carle, then west past the community center and park, over the Orofino, past the Pierce Tire Shop, and up by the Catholic church into the back-road loop. There's no moon above me and no clouds, the Milky Way a cream smudge across the drawing of the sky. I sit down at the edge of a clearing, the ground wet but I don't care.

I try to forget what I saw. Forget what I heard. I lay back and close my eyes, lay on the wet ground and try to fall asleep. But it's cold and my mind keeps flashing images of JT's bed, and I get nowhere near sleep before I start to shiver. Then I get up and walk again, make my way home slow, loop south through the bottom of town, down Third to Moscrip and up past City Hall before going back north on Main Street. When I get to the trailer, I listen hard at the door before I turn the handle.

When I come into the trailer, I hear them both snoring the back-flat gurgle of drunken sleep. In the glint of light from the small window, I can see the naked sheen of Rowan's chest, the dips and the rises. I stand and stare for a long time wondering what JT ever did to win a girl like Rowan.

But I know exactly what it was. What it's always been.

JT was 15 and I was 12. He was only a sophomore that fall but already on the varsity football team and starting both offense and defense. He'd be second-team All-League at corner and Honorable Mention at wide receiver at the end of that season.

We'd go down to the ballfield on Sundays in October, and he'd have me throw the football in all sorts of directions. He'd practice adjusting to the ball in the air. He'd say, "Now throw it over my other shoulder." Or, "Throw it to me this time but throw it right as I come out of my break, and throw it real low. Make me dive for it either way. Surprise me."

We'd do this for an hour or more, until my arm got tired. JT was never tired, though. He could never get enough of football, never practice enough, never play enough.

We were walking down Main Street one day after practicing. It wasn't warm, but JT was sweaty from sprinting and he had his shirt off. We were walking along the sidewalk, and a car of older girls drove by us real slow in a flat-black Dodge

Charger. The girl in the passenger-side window leaned out. "Hey, good-looking," she yelled at JT.

JT nodded at her but didn't say anything.

The girl said, "You keep looking fine, all right?" Then the other girl, the driver, dropped the pedal and spun out the wheels, gunning the car into the flats, and the girl who was leaning out the window screamed and slid back into the car. We watched it go down the road a quarter-mile, then arc the slow bank out of town south toward Weippe.

We walked along the block on the sidewalk, heading toward Sammy's, and JT didn't say anything. He had the football in his hands and he'd spin it, regrip it, then spin it again.

I said, "Do you know her?"

"Maybe," JT said. "Yeah, I know her."

"She's real pretty."

"So?" he said.

"Well, did you see her? Did you see her hair and all that?"

"Yeah."

"So," I said, "you shoulda talked to her or something. Not just stayed quiet like that."

JT smirked and shook his head. Didn't say anything. He just kept spinning that football in his hand as we walked down the block. Finally, he said, "If you wanna get a girl, you gotta not care at all. That's the truth."

"Really?" I looked at his face to see if he was messing with me. But he didn't smile or squint up one eye like he did when he was playing a trick. I said, "Don't you have to

207

treat them right and all that stuff? Write them notes and give them flowers?"

"No," JT said. He didn't explain more than that.

"No?"

"No," he said again. "You don't. That's just movie shit. That's all."

"But I thought . . ."

"Nope," he said. "Think about it this way. Think 'bout how Big treats us."

"What?"

"Think about it. Think how Big treats us like we're trash, like we're worthless unless we're helping him with something. But what do we do? We do everything he says."

"That doesn't make any sense," I said. "First of all, we aren't girls. And second, we don't want him to . . . well, you know. Plus he's bigger and older than us."

JT cocked the football back at his shoulder like he might throw it into the street. But he didn't throw it. He said, "So?"

"So?" I said. "So he doesn't have to treat us like that. If that's how it has to be with girls, why does Big treat us like that?"

"No, you don't understand," JT said, and he spun that football in his hand once more. "If you want to control something, if you want a person to do what you say, then you have to treat them real bad. Treat them like shit. And that way they'll know who's boss. You understand? Big always lets us know who's boss, and I let everyone else around me know just the same. See?"

We kept walking down the street, and I thought about what JT was saying. But there was something that didn't make sense to me. "Wait," I said. "What if you don't want to control someone?"

JT shoved the football into my stomach, and I grabbed it and looked up at his face.

"Fuck you," JT said, and smiled at me. "That's just little-kid talk, *Little*. So from now on, you just try to be a grown-up, okay?"

drifter

The shower stall in the trailer is built for a man of five-five, not six-five. I have to bend my knees and duck down low to get my head wet. When I duck, my elbows and butt touch the side walls and I sort of smear down awkwardly. JT's six-three and thinner than me, and even he can't fit in the shower too good.

I keep yellow Dawn dish soap in the shower stall, and I scrub to my elbows to cut any poison oak oil from the last two days of work in the cemetery. When I'm washing the soap off my right arm, that's when I see the black spot in the crook of my elbow. Feel the little lump of a burrowed tick. I jet the water straight on, soak the spot, and hope he backs out, but he's head-deep-to-latch, so I have to wait. I finish my shower and get out. Dry off and wrap my towel around my waist. Pad into the kitchen.

I sit down at the table, reach over to the drawer for a lighter and a pair of tweezers, and set those on the tabletop. Scooch forward and rewrap my towel. Then I take the tweezers in my left hand, fumbling a little because I'm not good with that hand.

Rowan gets up. I turn and see her standing naked next to

JT's bed, her back to me, her naked body long and thin, and I stare at her as she reaches across the bed for her underwear. I remember her with JT last night, and I get a weird feeling in my stomach like swallowing hot sauce without any food. I'm still staring at Rowan when she reaches for her T-shirt on the floor, and I look away so I don't get caught.

I'm turned back to the table and I hear her walk up the hallway behind me. She comes into the kitchen wearing only that T-shirt and underwear, and that underwear is lacy black panties, see-through in back, and I stare again as she walks to the sink and gets a drink of water. She gulps a glass, then turns around and says, "Morning, Mr. Stares-a-Lot."

"Good morning."

"What're the tweezers for?" She points. "Got a splinter?"

"No. They're for a tick." I lean and show her the crook of my arm.

She twists her mouth. Leans on the table to look. "You want help with it?"

"Probably. My left hand's near worthless."

"Okay then." Rowan pulls her hair behind her head, out of the way, tucks it into the back of her T-shirt. Then she takes the tweezers and sits down in the chair next to mine. As she leans forward to examine the tick, I can see down the loose collar of her T-shirt.

Rowan spreads the skin on my arm with her fingertips, tilts her head one way, then the other. "It's pretty buried in there. I might have to use a match."

Rowan's breath is sour.

"Yep," I say, and lean back a little, out of breath-shot.

Rowan goes to the kitchenette junk drawer and comes

back with a book of matches, lights one, and lets it burn for a few seconds. Then she blows it out and puts the smoking end against the butt of the tick. Says, "A couple of these should . . ." and lights another match.

That second match gets the tick moving. It wriggles, its back two legs doing a little work now, and Rowan says, "I can pull . . . those jaws won't be so clamped now."

I nod but keep my arm still.

Rowan focuses like she's bubbling a Scantron test in school, and I remember math classes with her, watching her face as she worked, her focus as I stared at her from the next desk over. She wipes her nose with the back of her hand. Goes to pulling at the tick with the tweezers.

I say, "Don't tear it up. I got an infection once from that."

"Excuse me, cowboy." Rowan stops and looks steady at me. "But this ain't my first rodeo."

She picks at the tick, pulls little by little, regripping the tick with each pull, getting more of the body. The tick's back legs are wiggling all around, then its mid-legs. She keeps pulling. Says, "Almost got it now."

Her hair smells good when she's hunched over the tick. I lean in, can't help myself, and I get a whiff of her scalp, smell the earth in her skin.

"Right here," Rowan says, and finishes pulling the tick. "Look at this guy." She holds him up, a little teardrop, black, thin legs like hairs moving on either side of the tweezers. Rowan says, "May you never bite again, Mr. Tick," and clamps the tweezers shut, a bright drop of red spangling her forefinger.

"Thanks, Rowan. Thanks for pulling it."

"No problem," she says. She gets up and washes the tweezers in the sink. I look at her see-through panties again, her naked legs below, try not to but I don't know where else to look and that's all I want to look at anyway. I shake my head when I think about her and JT again, and I close my eyes.

While she's washing the tweezers, Rowan says, "Should we go to school today?" and looks at me with a dead face. Then she laughs so hard that she has to lean on the counter.

I say, "That's why I took a shower."

"I was kidding," Rowan says, and looks over her shoulder. "I'm thinking, maybe . . . fuck school forever?"

"But are you still gonna graduate?"

"No." She shakes her head. "I don't think so. I haven't been to school in two weeks, and I missed a week before that too. I'm not passing any of my classes anyway."

"But school's easy for you. You could talk to your teachers. Figure something out?" I hear myself sounding like Mr. Polchowski, trying to give good advice.

"No, it doesn't matter," Rowan says. "I'll do my GED or something."

"Then what? What do you do all day?"

"I do things. Side jobs. Nothing to really talk about. Plus I read and hang out at the Flame."

"And you're just gonna keep doing . . . this?"

"This?" Rowan dries the tweezers on a dishrag but stares at me the whole time. "Am I bothering you, Little?"

She's staring so hard that I have to look away. "No, I just . . ." I pick at the hole in my arm where the tick was. The hole is dark from blood, almost black. I say, "It's just that you're only a junior. You know?"

Rowan makes a little clicking noise with her mouth. Puts her hands on her hips. "I'm young and fucked up. I'm the American dream."

JT groans from his bed. Rolls to the edge of his mattress, sits up, and groans louder. Then he clears his throat like an airplane engine. Stands and shuffles out to the kitchenette. Says, "It's nice to hear you two talking so *fuckin'* loud early in the morning."

Rowan says, "Good morning to you too, Mr. Sunshine."

JT shakes his head. Slides past her and gets a glass off the drying rack. Fills it with water and drinks most of it. "Little, have we got any aspirin here?"

I point to the cupboard.

He turns and opens it. Gets the aspirin bottle out, pops the top, and shakes three into his palm. "Damn," he says, and swallows the aspirin dry.

Rowan smiles. "A little hungover?"

JT looks like he wants to keep his eyes closed for the rest of his life. He puts his hand on Rowan's ass. "We don't have anything to do today, do we, baby?"

I look at Rowan. Look at JT's hand. Say, "We gotta go to school. Rowan, I could give you a ride."

"No," Rowan says. She kisses the side of JT's face. "We're gonna be outlaws today. Maybe we'll rob Sammy's Grocery and run. Maybe hit up the bank."

"Fine by me," JT says, but his eyes are closed, and it looks like the only place he's running to is back to bed.

I say, "I better eat something before school," and I open the fridge to get some eggs, but we're all out and I'll have to go hunt some outside. The truth is, I don't feel all that hungry seeing JT and Rowan together like this.

it could be

Zaylie puts her hand on my leg in art class while we listen to music and draw. I think about Rowan then, and I don't know how to feel about anything.

I guess Rowan's with JT again? I don't know, and maybe I'm trying to be something with her that I'm not. Maybe I'm like one of those scrub jays that spends all his time making the redtail hawk sound, and it seems like he's forgotten that he's a different kind of bird, a bird that has more to do than imitation.

Matt comes into the classroom late in the period, but Mrs. F says, "No, no. No!" and points to the door. Matt goes back out, but he waits in the hallway for Zaylie.

I don't want any part of this Matt and Zaylie thing. She isn't holding my hand as we come out of class and she's a step in front of me, so I cut right to the doors, push through the exit, and then I'm out in the open like I'm flying through trees and I've found a gap.

this old house

When I get home from school, Willa's on the trampoline, but she isn't jumping. She's sitting on the springs with her legs dangling over the edge.

"Are you okay?" I say.

"Yeah."

"Are you sure?"

She makes a face as serious as homework. "I'm just a little scared."

"Scared of what?"

"Well," she says, "some kids at school found out that we live right down from the Livingston place."

"Yeah," I say, "but what?"

"And they said I'd be too chicken to go there."

"Well, that's stupid," I say. "Don't listen to them."

"But I am chicken about it. It's true."

I smile at her. "Everyone's chicken about that place. They say it's haunted. And I know adults who won't go there."

"Well, I'm a *teeny* bit chicken," Willa says, "but I'm not *too* chicken. I could go there, you know."

"I know you could."

"If I wanted to, I really could."

"Yeah," I say, "I know."

Willa squints and looks straight at me. "What exactly happened there?"

The Livingston place is where Emma Livingston went crazy and killed her three children before shooting herself. But I don't want to tell that story to Willa, so I say, "I think someone was killed there."

"Well, yeah," Willa says, "everyone knows that. And it was kids, right?"

"I don't know. People've been telling different versions of the story for a long time."

"I think maybe in this case the worst story is true."

I shrug. "Some stories are true, and some aren't."

Willa reaches down and pulls a wide stem of grass, licks it and presses it between her thumbs. Then she blows a long, squeaky note. "I guess," she says, "but I sorta feel like this one is true. And some of the kids at school dared me to go up and steal something from there."

"From the Livingston place?"

"Yeah, and they said I'm a bright yellow chicken if I don't."

"Well, don't listen to them. They're just being kids."

"Hey," Willa says, "I'm just being a kid too. This is what kids do." She blows another squeaky note on her grass stem.

"So you're saying you really wanna go up there?"

Willa throws her wet piece of grass to the side. Picks a new one. "Would you go with me?"

"I could," I say. "I went up there with JT one time."

"Really? What'd it look like?"

"Just an old house. Bad-built. Run-down. It was locked up pretty good, but you could tell people had squatted and trashed the place."

Willa nods. Licks her new piece of grass and places it careful between her thumbs. She says, "Did it feel haunted?"

"I don't know. I was younger, so yeah, it probably did."

Willa blows a new squeaky note, higher-pitched than the last. She says, "I bet it's super haunted. I bet ghosts come out all over the place after dark."

"We're not going there after dark."

"Why, is it too scary?"

"No, but people sometimes squat there. After dark, I'm not sure who you'd run into."

Willa says, "We could go there right now, though, right?"

"I guess."

"Really?" Willa hops to her feet. "Thanks." She hugs me. "And we gotta bring something back to prove that we went, okay?"

It's less than a half-mile to that old house through the cemetery and up a path, but it's afternoon in the late fall, and it gets darker as we walk, like we really are walking toward something terrible. It doesn't help that we pass graves along the way. Willa doesn't speak, and after a while, she reaches out and takes ahold of my hand.

The trail to the house is overgrown from lack of use. A few times I have to step on blackberry vines to pin them down for Willa. She steps on top of them, and we continue.

Willa says, "Want me to tell a joke so this doesn't feel so scary?"

"Okay."

"Let me think . . . it's gotta be a good one." She's holding on to my hand pretty tight, and when I look at her face, her eyebrows are scrunched down serious. "Okay," she says, "I've got one."

"Go for it."

"So," she says, "why are there fences around cemeteries?"

"I don't know, Willa. Why?"

"Because people are dying to get in." Willa giggles so hard that she lets go of my hand. Then she grabs it again. "Did you get the joke?"

"Yeah, I got it."

"That's hilarious, right?"

I smile but I don't say anything because right then the trees open up in front of us where the land was cleared long ago. We're at the edge of the yard, the grass three feet tall and poison oak growths iron red and oily all along the north side of the clearing.

We stop and look.

The house is a sickly green color like the six inches of moss on the roof have bled color down onto the rest of the structure. The windows are knocked out and some of them have plywood over them. One board reads BLOOD SMELL in red spray paint. Another says CHILDREN.

Willa says, "This is real creepy."

"Yep."

"Do you think . . ."

I look at her, but she doesn't finish her question. She's staring at the house, blinking quick so she doesn't keep her eyes closed for very long, as if keeping her eyes closed might allow something to attack her before she can open them again.

She says, "We gotta get something."

"What?"

"Something," she says. "From the house. I need to take something to school with me tomorrow to show I was here."

"Okay, what should we get?"

"I don't know. Let's go up on the porch and look around." Willa pulls me forward.

I step slow, careful, watching where my feet go so they don't break a stick or make a loud noise. The only sounds around that place are the wind gusts in the treetops above the clearing. But then a sentinel crow starts squawking from above us—*cruaack cruaack*—him calling from high on a branch, his crow's head tilting back and forth on its black swivel. Most big clearings in these mountains have warden crows, but it doesn't make me feel any better about the sound of it.

Willa and I wind around a big poison oak patch, through the grass, and step up onto the first porch step. The step creaks under my weight, groans like an old man getting up out of a chair, and I say, "Willa, I don't trust this porch. This house is pretty old, and it was never well built."

"You can't leave me here." Willa grips my hand tighter.

"I'm not trying to leave you. I'm just saying that this porch might break under my weight. I'm at least 230."

"The inside might be stronger," Willa says. "Hardwood floors, right?"

"I don't know about that."

"Well, we can look in that one window, right?" She points to a window that doesn't have plywood across it.

"Okay."

We shuffle forward. I test each porch board before fully weighting it, and every one groans under my full weight, but none break. When we get to the window, we look in. The living room holds an old couch, sunken in the middle, and two chairs. A lamp is laying on the floor, snapped in two, its shade torn. Someone a long time ago stacked wood near the fireplace, broke up a desk and put that on the woodpile too. There's also a mattress, not a bed, but a double mattress sticking partway out from behind the couch. The dust in the room looks thick but it's hard to tell. The window's grime-covered, and even rubbing it doesn't make it clearer, so it's hard to tell if everything inside is covered in dust or if the window is just real dirty.

"We can't see the next room from here," Willa says. "So let's go around."

We follow the wraparound porch. Get to a side door. And there we find something weird: a new doorknob, bright gold-colored. Shiny. Not more than a few months old.

Willa says, "Do you see that?"

"Yeah, that's weird."

"What do you think?"

"Well, it's pretty new." I look down and see there's still wood shavings on the porch from someone drilling the lockhole. Also boot marks. I say, "I think we better get out of here."

"Right now?"

"Yeah. There are cookers up here. People make meth in any space they can get hold of. And if somebody comes back while we're here . . ."

"Okay," she says, "we should go. But help me grab this." She's working at a small, broken window to the right of the door, pulling on a glass shard that's stuck in the window-sill. She wiggles it back and forth.

I help her. Wiggle and pull, and the shard comes free. Through the window, I can see the setup. Pots and burners. Antihistab packets, white fuel, starting fluid, gasoline anti-freeze, and empty Pepsi two-liters in a pile next to tubing. Some of the material's covered with a tarp, but it's obvious what everything is. "Yeah," I say, "we better go now." I hand the piece of glass to Willa, and she hops off the porch.

I step down onto the lower porch step and it breaks. My leg goes through the rotten wood. It's not far to the ground underneath, but my ankle rolls. I pull my leg free of the hole, hop on one foot out into the meadow, and sit down next to a bright red patch of poison oak.

Willa says, "Are you okay? Was that your ankle?"

"Yeah," I say. Rub my ankle. Move it a little.

"Is it okay?"

"Just rolled up a bit. It'll be all right."

Out back of the house, a Forest Service road comes from the woods' side. A long time ago, rangers went up that road and dropped a dozen trees across it with a chain saw, making it impassable for vehicles. And no one ever opened it again because of the murder. The Forest Service didn't want people driving up there, and everyone accepted that.

But from where I'm sitting in the meadow, holding my ankle, I can see straight down that road to the turn, and I can see that someone's cut two of the old trees into sections and pushed them off into the side ditch. There are tire marks, broken saplings up the middle of the road, fresh chain saw marks on the nearest tree chunks.

I say, "That isn't good. Look. People have been here. They changed that doorknob out and opened the road too. It wasn't like this last time I came out."

"Who's been here?"

"I don't know."

"Bad people?" Willa says.

"Probably. That was a setup we saw."

"What kind of a setup?"

"Drugs." I roll onto my knees. Willa tries to help me get to my feet but it's no use. I'm way too big for her to help me.

"You can do it," she says. She pulls on the sleeve of my shirt.

I push and hop on one foot. Try to weight my ankle full, but it's no good, like I've hammered a 16-penny nail into the joint and it's all bound up. I weight it halfway, limp, and hop along.

Willa says, "You got it?"

"Yeah, it's only an ankle," I say, "and it doesn't hurt too bad." I limp back through the meadow, Willa holding my hand now to support me.

The light's dying with the evening, the dark of the trail out in front of us. Willa's holding her shard of glass in one

223

hand, leading me along with the other. The temperature's dropped, and I think for the first time that it might freeze tonight. Willa shivers but doesn't complain.

I hop and limp behind her. Say, "You gonna take that piece of glass with you to school tomorrow?"

"For sure," she says. "I'll tell all the kids we came here today."

"Will they believe you?"

Willa says, "If I have this old piece of glass they will. See how thin it is? Only old glass gets thin like this." She lets go of my hand to run her fingers along the tapered end of the shard.

"How do you know about that?"

"Not sure." Willa shrugs. "Hey, wanna hear another joke? Could help you as you limp?"

"Okay."

"So here goes: Knock, knock."

"Who's there?"

Willa looks back at me. "Harry."

"Harry who?" I say.

"Harry up, man. It's getting cold out here."

after all

Coming through the cemetery, we pass white-gray gravestones dyed black by shadows. Willa trips on a low stone and falls down in front of me. Gets back up quick and says, "I'm fine."

We keep walking.

She says, "Do you think it's weird that we live on the edge of a graveyard?"

"A little bit."

"I think it's pretty weird. Where our house sits now has to be a spot that most people didn't ever want."

"I'm sure that's true," I say. "Probably made it cheaper, though."

We get to one of the oldest grave plots, one that's surrounded by wrought iron. I fixed the joints on the corners once.

Willa taps on an iron candle holder. Says, "Do you think there's something after?"

"After?" I say.

"Yeah, after you die. Like you go somewhere or something?"

"Like heaven or hell?"

"Sure."

I don't spend a lot of time thinking about that. I guess I never have. I say, "I really wouldn't know."

"Well, no one knows," Willa says. "But what do you think?"

"Maybe? Maybe not?" I steady myself by holding the wrought iron. Roll my ankle a little to loosen it. The sprain's not too bad since I can move it.

Willa leans down close to the top of the candle holder, puts her face against the opening. She says, "Where do you think Big is right now?"

"I don't know. That's something else I really couldn't say."

She stands up again. Sniffs the air and looks around. "Maybe he's in hell, huh?"

She starts walking again and I follow her.

god's hands

JT's gone again. I have no idea where. There's a knock on the trailer door, and I open it. The deputy's standing at the step, his cruiser lit up behind him. "Checking in," he says.

"All right."

He says, "So what do you have for me?"

I just took Willa to the big house and walked back over to my trailer. I haven't been home for three minutes. My boots are off but I haven't put ice on my ankle yet. I'm not in the mood to talk to the deputy. I say, "I don't know anything new. And maybe I won't ever."

"No, no. You better find something out," he says. "Have you been talking to people at all? Have you been asking around?"

"I talked to someone today."

"And?"

"And," I say, "she said maybe Big's in hell."

The deputy crosses his arms and shakes his head. "What's wrong with you?" he says. "Do you think this is funny?"

"No."

"Then don't mess around with me. Either you give me a

lead—you find me some information—or you're going in on that poaching charge. You got that?"

"Yeah."

"Are you sure? Because you only have three weeks left now."

"All right," I say.

I just want to sit down. My ankle's swelling and it needs some ice. I don't want to think about this stuff right now.

"Three weeks is all," the deputy says again. "I'll be back to check on you again soon." He turns and walks to his cruiser, and I close my door before he drives off.

I get a bag of frozen peas and sit down at the kitchenette table, put the peas on my ankle. My Spanish book is still sitting there, so I open it and read words that are similar in English and Spanish.

There's another knock, and this time I don't get up. I yell, "It's still open, Deputy."

The door opens, but it's Rowan. "Deputy?" she says.

"Sorry. I thought you were someone else."

"As in the law?"

"Right."

She laughs. Says, "I'm pretty law-like."

I shift the bag of peas on my ankle. The cold feels good.

Rowan sits down across from me. "What's wrong with your ankle?"

"Rolled it, but it's fine. It just needs a little ice."

She smiles. "You're having a funny month: split eye, tick in your arm, a rolled ankle."

"Funny's not really how I'd describe things right now."

Rowan says, "The other option's shooting yourself, right?"

I smile, but she doesn't.

There's something different about Rowan tonight. I don't know what it is at first and then I figure it out: she's sober. Shaky. I look at her face and see that she's started to cry. She leans forward and puts her hands flat on the table, her fingers spread wide. She turns and wipes one side of her face on her shoulder. She doesn't choke or sob. She just cries a little, quiet.

I say, "You and JT, huh? You two are back together?"

She wipes the other side of her face on her other shoulder. "No."

"You're not? 'Cause it seemed like . . ."

"I don't know. Maybe? Does that make you mad?"

"I just thought that after we . . . you know." But I feel guilty talking like that. I think of Zaylie and I know I'm no better than anybody.

Rowan nods. Wipes a tear away with the back of her hand. "There's things you don't know about me. There's things about my life that make it more complicated than you're thinking."

"Like what?"

"Like things I can't tell you. Most of them not good. Some of them so fucked up that you don't even want to hear about them."

"Well, maybe I do, though. Maybe I'd want to know."

"No," she says, "you really don't." And the way she says it, I know she won't tell me. When Rowan doesn't want to say something, she won't, no matter what.

She stands up. "You always make me food when I come here, so let me make you something for once." She sniffles and wipes her face on her sleeve again. "Since your ankle's rolled up and all that."

"You don't have to make me food. My ankle's not that bad."

"Just let me make you something. What do you want?" She opens the fridge. Leans in. "You've got bread and butter and cheese in here. So maybe grilled cheese?"

"Okay. That sounds pretty good."

Rowan cooks, and I sit and ice my ankle. Rowan sings while she cooks, a low, slow song that I've never heard before. Then another song sorta like the first one. They sound like something you'd hear in church in a movie. I like listening to her voice, and I lean my head back and close my eyes. The frozen peas make my foot go numb and my ankle doesn't hurt anymore after that.

After Rowan finishes the second song, I say, "You like to sing?"

"I do."

"Every kind of song or do you have favorites?"

"Everyone has favorites," she says. "Me, I like old songs, songs my grandpa used to sing in the truck when he took me on rodeo trips when I was little."

"Did he pass away or is he still around?"

"My grandpa?" Rowan says, and puts my grilled-cheese sandwich down in front of me. "My grandpa's closer to God now."

six years before

You took me steelhead fishing on the North Fork of the Clearwater. Winter morning when I was ten. You had me wear a
down coat under your FrogWear that I had to roll up at the
ankles and wrists to make it fit me. There were sandwiches
in the cooler. A thermos of Baileys and Captain Morgan, plus
Folgers. You drove us at 6 am dark in December. The cab of
the truck smelled like mint Copenhagen as we passed the
drop-down level of the fallow fields above the Grade.

You played old country—Hank Williams, Merle Haggard,
Johnny Cash—as we dip-ducked the Grade to the Idaho 12,
then northwest along the river. I tried to catch the day-
break, but the country was too steep, and the sunrise snuck
behind us as something more gray than gold.

Off the dam road, early light, and you backed the truck
trailer down the ramp, looked over your shoulder to sight
the boat into the water. Then we got out and walked back. I
watched you ease the boat off the trailer, jerk the bowline,
and beach the bow on the river sand. You pulled a WD-40 can
from inside the boat and said, "Start with this on your hands
and rub. Kill the human scent." You sprayed your palms and

rubbed. Then handed me the can. "Something in it's fishy," you said. "I never knew what." You spit Copenhagen into the gravel. Toed the brown.

When you rigged the rods, I watched your huge fingers tie the ten-pound test. Set bobbers and swivels above the leaders. You said, "We'll run Michael Jacksons today. White head on a black body." You smiled and held up a plug for me to see.

I didn't get the joke, didn't know anything about steelheading or Michael Jackson, so I stayed quiet and smiled when you smiled. Watched everything you did like I was learning church rules.

You rowed us upriver, underneath the power lines, and I fished over the top of you. Fished the edge of each hole as you told me stories. Great fishermen you knew, weird animal stories, boating accidents. Little boys who caught 20-pound Chinook on four-pound fly lines. Complainers who wrecked whole days with their whining. And a story about a man with hands so bad that he could barely hold a pole. You said, "I wanted to duct-tape his rod into his hands, so if he fell out of the boat and drowned, at least I'd get a good rod back when we recovered the body." You laughed and shook your head. Unscrewed the cap on your thermos. Took a few sips of your Irish coffee.

The hooks were barbless because of the native run, so it was harder to hook a fish when it struck. I didn't time two strikes well, and the fish spit the hooks. Then there was nothing. I cast for hours, hoping for another strike, watching the pink indicator bob as it drifted, waiting for any dip, hoping to impress you, hoping to make you proud of me.

In the afternoon, you finally hooked a fish and handed me the pole. Said, "I'll work the net when the time comes." Then you sat down and coached me while you drank more Irish coffee and I fought the fish.

The fish zagged downriver, cut out of the eddy into the current. The reel hummed, and you said, "Now tighten that drag."

I screwed it down a turn. Felt the rod bend in half. "Now loosen," you said.

I fought that fish to the boat three times over 15 minutes. But he was a large fish, red-sided, long in the river, and he shied at the net each time you dipped. So I let the drag go again and made the fish work and turn back upriver to us. Then you netted him nose-first and pulled him out of the water.

I was used to rainbow trout in Orofino or up on Deer Creek, the reservoir, and I'd never seen a trout over two pounds. You said, "That's at least 20 right there. Maybe 21?" You took the hook out with your needle-nose. Said, "Hold him up and feel him." I tried but he slipped. I tried again but he was heavy and wet.

"Don't lose him overboard," you said. "Here, sit down."

I did what you told me, sitting on the board across the bow. Then you put the fish in my lap. "Now hook a thumb through its gills."

I hooked, and put my other hand under its back. "Like this?" I stood and held it.

"That's it," you said. "Got you a big ol' fish. Cheers." You held your thermos cup above your head. Tipped a drip on the fish's head in salute. Then you shot the rest and refilled. "Now let's clip that adipose."

"The what?"

"Right there. If we cut this fin, it'll look like a hatchery fish." You took a pair of shears from your tackle box, duct-taped handles. You slid them along the back and clipped the fin. Said, "Now drop that hog in this garbage bag. We'll clean it at home. Let the animals run at the muck."

I put our fish in the bag and rolled it like you showed me.

We went back to fishing, but we didn't catch anything else, and you drifted us down to the boat ramp. After you went and got the truck, you winched the boat back onto the trailer and told me to eat a sandwich.

"Do you want one too?" I asked.

"No, no." You waved me off. Sipped from your thermos cup. "Not hungry, really." It was early afternoon. Beginning to snow. You hooked the bra onto the front of the boat to protect it from the gravel mix on the roads. Bungee-corded the sides. Put the rods in the back of the pickup.

When we drove up the Grade, it was snowing hard. The truck was swerving, and I could feel the pull of the trailer, side to side. You were slurring the ends of your words, or running them long. You said, "You done rill goooood." Then, "Good tension on the fisshh," the ending of *fish* sounding like you were trying to shush a baby in a crib.

I knew better than to ask if you were okay to drive, so I just said, "Thanks for taking me today," and I watched the road, ready to pull the wheel if you drifted across the center line or turned into a ditch. All around us, the snow dropped hard and heavy onto the winter stubble, the white layer evening things out, turning the world to one shade, the land reset to a smooth flat white.

I think about you and that dog sometimes. Try to picture you young but it's so hard to see you as anything but big and tall.

I know you were 11, barely older than Willa is now. And I guess you loved that dog since you talked about it for 60 years after.

You said your daddy drank turpentine, and I've heard of that. Heard of mouthwash fifths. Kerosene. Cough syrup or vanilla bottles. You said he'd come in from the shed, stumbly from the paint thinner. Turn with the hammer in his hand. Left-handed but it didn't make him creative.

The tumor was the thing. It was four inches across and raised on the left side of the dog's head, growing fast. The dog was a black Lab mix, some pit too, but a dog so sweet it grew up sleeping in your bed and chasing red squirrels in summer.

I picture you looking like Willa, bald-headed because of lice shaves, but still looking like her some: a serious face all the time except when you're laughing.

I picture you like Willa, so even now, even after everything, I don't wish that one terrible day on you.

Your daddy handed you the .32, grabbed you by the hair the way you grabbed JT by the hair, the way JT grabs Rowan by the hair.

He said, "You're gonna put it down."

When I say, "Hey, be gentle," it's just because I'm not as tough as any of you.

never walk alone

In the morning—before school—I find another gutted-out chicken. Count four still living in the yard, the hens scratching for worms. After I toss the carcass, I search for eggs and find only two, both behind the trailer step, and I cook those, then get dressed.

When I come out of the trailer again, Willa's jumping on the trampoline. It's a cold morning, not cold enough for frost, but wet cold, and her hands and face are bright pink. I say, "Are you freezing?"

Willa stops jumping. Looks past me.

I turn and see Mrs. Trepp at the far turn of the 11, dragging along in her wheelchair, behind her lawn mower, gloves on and that Santa hat on her head.

Willa and I wait and watch. Mrs. Trepp rumbles toward us, doesn't seem to notice us at all, and looks like she's about to pass us again and pull over the hill into the middle of town, but then she turns a little, lets go of the gas lever on the lawn mower, the engine dies, and she rolls a few feet with her momentum, then stops in the gravel on our side of the road.

Willa hops off the trampoline and stands next to me. Doesn't say anything.

Mrs. Trepp turns and looks at us through those huge sunglasses that she wears. She says, "Come here."

"Us?"

"Yes, you," she says. "Come over here."

We start walking toward her. Willa takes my hand.

Mrs. Trepp says, "You've nothing to be scared of."

I nod, and Willa doesn't say anything.

Mrs. Trepp reaches into her coat pocket, struggles with something, her hand a little shaky.

Willa grips my hand tight. Says, "We don't want any trouble."

Mrs. Trepp stops wiggling her hand in her pocket. Smiles at us. "Trouble?"

Willa nods.

Mrs. Trepp fishes around in her pocket a little more, then pulls out her hand. Her fist is clenched, and she reaches, holding something.

I put out my hand.

"Here," she says, and drops two things into my palm. Two cellophane-wrapped candies.

"Candy?"

"Root beer barrels. They're my addiction. I suck on two of them on the way to the store, and two on the way back. Those two are my return barrels."

I say, "Then are you sure you don't want them?" But Willa's already grabbed one.

"No, no." Mrs. Trepp smiles. "You know, I used to know your momma when she was a girl."

"Derlene?" Willa says. She's already unwrapped the root beer barrel and popped it into her mouth. She makes a sucking sound through her teeth.

Mrs. Trepp shakes her head. "No, I did know her too, but I meant your momma." She turns her sunglasses in my direction.

I'm unwrapping my root beer barrel, but I stop. "You knew my mom?"

"I used to give her root beer barrels just like this. But that was a long, long time ago. 20 years? 30? I'm not even sure."

I hold that root beer barrel between my index finger and thumb.

"Go on now," Mrs. Trepp says. "Try it. 'Cause they're real good."

I pop the root beer barrel into my mouth, and the sugar releases onto my tongue.

"See?" Mrs. Trepp says.

I nod.

Mrs. Trepp sniffs and adjusts her sunglasses. "Yep. I knew your momma, and this girl here reminds me a little bit of her." She points at Willa.

Willa looks up at me. She has that root beer barrel tucked in her cheek, and she's smiling.

"Well," Mrs. Trepp says, "I gotta go now, but you two have a real nice day."

Willa says, "You have a real nice day too, okay?"

I say, "Thanks, ma'am," but I'm not really sure if I'm saying thanks for the candy or thanks for telling me that my mom was a little like Willa.

Mrs. Trepp doesn't say anything else. I don't know how she's able to do what she does next—because she's pretty old—but she grabs the handle of the mower hard, on the right side, at the corner of the handle, and the whole mower rotates on its rear right wheel and turns sideways. Then she bends over and reaches down, grips the starter handle on the pull cord and rips it once. Hard. The engine turns over and catches, slow at first, then speeding up.

Mrs. Trepp rotates the mower forward again and gives us a little wave. Then she engages the self-propelling gear, and the mower jerks. She grabs tight with both hands, and the mower pulls her back onto the road, and she doesn't look back.

Willa's school bus passes Mrs. Trepp at the start of the hill, in front of the Mini-Mart, and I say, "Go grab your school stuff, okay?"

"Okay," Willa says, and runs into the house.

I watch Mrs. Trepp a little longer, until she crests the hill and passes over the top, then I go back to my trailer to grab my books.

At school later, Room 2 with Mr. Polchowski. "Little," he says, "things aren't good. I did a grade check with all of your teachers, and your grades are in bad shape." He shakes his head. Sighs and retightens his ponytail. "Your attendance is the worst it's ever been. So what's going on?"

I don't know where to start. I can't tell about Big being gone. He wouldn't understand. I can't explain Rowan and Zaylie. Or how Rowan is maybe my brother's girlfriend and not mine anyway, but I don't know. I can't tell about the deputy showing up at my trailer, or about maybe getting charged with poaching in less than three weeks now. But that's all I'm thinking about. Plus Mrs. Trepp this morning.

I say, "I've just got a lot going on right now, and it's just . . ." but I don't know how to explain anything.

"Yeah?" he says, and his face looks so serious.

"I'm sorry," I say. "I'm just really messing up right now."

"Okay," he says, "that's pretty honest. We can work with that. So let's see . . . I think math might be the biggest problem area. What if we just work on math every day during this period for a couple of weeks? All right?"

"All right."

"Good. And just to be straight with you, your grade is a 44 percent right now, 16 percent under passing. So if that doesn't change soon, it'll be too late to get you back to a passing grade. So you've got to really focus now."

"All right."

"I'll run to the restroom and be right back. You go ahead and crack that textbook, start reading the example, and we'll get going."

When he comes back, we work on math together for the rest of the period. It goes okay, and I start to understand some of it again. If math was always like this, if it was one-on-one, going at my own pace, getting to ask questions anytime I got confused, and going over things slow anytime things didn't make sense, I think I could do it. Maybe.

In the afternoon, Zaylie's waiting for me when I come into art class. She pulls my face down to hers and kisses me. "Good to see you," she says.

I say, "Good to see you too."

"You wanna come over again tomorrow night? I could come pick you up at say, six o'clock?"

"Sure," I say. "But you don't have to pick me up. I have a truck."

"Okay then. Six it is," she says. "My house."

The bell rings, and people start shuffling to their desks.

Zaylie says, "And that's the signal for us to draw like the brilliant, world-class artists that we are. You get the paper. I'll get the soft pencils."

The whole time we draw, Zaylie's left hand is resting on the inside of my thigh under our table. I keep thinking about Rowan but I try hard not to.

After school, I pull more Canada thistle for Mr. Reynolds at the cemetery. It's getting dark earlier in the evening now, and I stop working at dusk. He left an envelope taped under the box for me, and I open it and find $60 inside. I stuff that in the pocket of my coat, record my two and a half new hours in the notebook, then walk home through the graveyard.

JT and Rowan are drinking Natty Ice at the table when I come in. Playing draw poker for pennies. There's a large pile of pennies in the middle of the table.

Rowan pooches her lips out to make a duck face. Says, "You too scared to stay in, Mr. Jay-Tay? Gonna fold up again like a five-dollar camp chair?" She swigs her beer. Rattles the last ounce in the bottom of the can. Slow-drips the foam into her mouth. Then she sets her can down and whispers, "Come on, scaredy-cat. Make a move."

"Gimme time," JT says. "Time, time, time. Maybe I *will* stay and maybe I *won't* stay. We'll just have to see." He looks at his cards, then the pile, then his cards again.

"Well, you better ante up quick." Rowan fakes like she's gonna throw her cards down.

"No, no, wait!" JT says. "Hold on now. Let me think."

I set my schoolbag down next to the last kitchenette chair. Take my coat off. Sit and untie my bootlaces. Slide my boots off and stretch my feet, up and down. My one ankle is real tight still, swollen a little, so I get back up to grab ice from the freezer.

Just as I sit back down and settle the ice on my ankle, we all hear a car horn honking out in the yard. I take the ice off my ankle, stand up, and look out the kitchenette window. See the front end of a white Chevy Silverado next to the trampoline.

JT says, "Who is it?"

"Hey," I say, "isn't that your daddy's truck?"

Rowan sets her cards down. Comes to the window next to me and looks out. "Oh, shit," she says. "That's not good."

JT says, "He's here for real?"

"Yeah. My daddy."

JT's still holding his cards in front of him. Still sitting.

I say, "Maybe it won't be too bad."

Rowan looks at JT. Shakes her head.

JT drops his cards and stands up. "Better go out and meet the man on the field, right?" He slides his feet into his boots. Doesn't lace them. Opens the trailer door and steps out.

I say, "Go easy now." Rowan and I follow him. I'm in my socks.

It's cold out. We can all see our breath in the air. It's going to freeze for sure tonight.

Rowan's daddy is out of his truck already. He's shaking

his index finger at JT, walking up to him. He puts his finger in JT's face. Says, "You slimy motherfucker, you—"

"Whoa, whoa," JT says. "It doesn't have to be like this."

"After what you did to her? What you went in for?"

"Over and done with," JT says. "Got some time to think things through. Got some time to change myself a bit. Haven't hit her since. Not even close."

"People don't change in two months. That was just a starter stint for you."

"Still over and done with," JT says. "I did the 60, and Rowan and I have moved on."

Rowan's daddy sniffs, then spits in the grass. "Look at her. You see how young she is? She's only a junior in high school." He points at Rowan. "And you, young lady, you get in that truck right now."

Rowan stays where she is, standing next to me. She doesn't say anything.

Her daddy says, "I mean it, girl. You better get in that truck."

I look at Rowan's face and it reminds me of a full oil pan, dark and blank. Not a ripple across it.

"Listen here," JT says, "let's just all relax a little bit. You know what I'm saying?"

"No, motherfucker, I don't know what you're saying. And I'm warning you." Rowan's daddy raises that index finger again, puts it in JT's face. Rowan's daddy is a well-built guy, strong arms and tall, a workaday man his whole life, but him warning JT is like me threatening a rain cloud not to drop any water. There isn't shit he can do even if he thinks he can.

I say, "Let's just relax now," and I take a step forward. "Let's just settle this down and talk calm." I mean to put my big body between him and JT.

But JT says to him, "We all know you haven't been a saint yourself, have you now?" He looks over his shoulder at Rowan as he says this, and I wish he hadn't opened his mouth.

It's too late then. I'm in my socks on the wet grass and I take a step to get in between them, but Rowan's daddy says, "What did you say to me?"

I try to wedge between them but the gap's disappeared. They're face-to-face now, same heights, shorter than me but the same as each other.

"You know what I said." JT looks right at him. "You heard me pretty good, didn't you?"

And that's when Rowan's daddy swings. I'm standing on his left side, and he swings with his right hand.

As strong as he is, he hasn't spent enough time fighting, and not against anyone like JT. He swings big and round, his fist coming back first and making a long arc on its way to wherever he meant it to go.

Most people step back when they're swung at but that was never JT's style. He steps in, straight in, and that big, round punch from Rowan's daddy just sort of goes past the back of JT's head and it ends up that his shoulder is closer to JT's face than his fist.

JT swings low and short, puts a couple of body shots in on Rowan's daddy right away, and I can tell that they take it out of him. The older man's hands go down and his arms straighten out, and he looks almost like he's trying to pretend he's a bird with straight, long wings. His arms flap at his sides.

JT grabs two fistfuls of work shirt at the collar and drives Rowan's daddy back against the front of the white Silverado pickup, then he props him up and hits him once—hard—in the throat. And it's over just like that. Rowan's daddy drops down to his knees on the grass, and I know he's trying to find air, but it looks more like he's checking the ground to find a hole he can throw up in. He sorta crawls around like that.

Rowan yells, "Daddy! Oh, shit!" and goes and tries to help him up. But he still can't get air to pass in or out. It's like JT's wrapped binder twine around his neck and pulled it tight, knotted it, and Rowan's daddy keeps crawling and making that little sound in his throat like he's saying, "Hear, hear, hear, hear," real short and quick, and then he slumps down and lays on his side on the ground.

Rowan looks up at JT. "Did you kill him?"

"No," JT says. "He'll be fine. He just needs time to work it through. I've hit men in the throat before and they never die. So he'll come around. You'll see."

But the way Rowan's dad is laying there, it does look like he could die. His face is all dark and tight, and it doesn't look like he'll ever be able to breathe again.

"Dammit," Rowan says, and gets down on one knee, her hand resting on her daddy's shoulder.

JT walks around the side of the pickup and opens the driver's-side door. He reaches under the seat until he finds a pistol, a semiautomatic .45. He pops the clip. Empties the cartridges into his hand. Then he clears the chamber. He puts all the live rounds in his pocket. Stashes the gun back underneath the seat. Says, "I wonder if there's another clip under here somewhere," and he feels around until he finds that one too.

After a few more seconds, Rowan's daddy takes a big, gasping breath. He's still laying on his side near the truck's bumper. He doesn't look good, but he's breathing now, taking breaths in and out, and I watch his chest rise and fall.

JT walks over to him and leans down. "You better get going now. This'll teach you to come here and throw a punch at me. And if you come back with a gun, I'll bury you. You got that? It's not a threat. It's a promise. So you just stay away."

Rowan's daddy doesn't say anything. I'm not sure he can talk just yet, and even if he could, he probably wouldn't say anything to JT right now. JT made it pretty clear who the bigger dog is.

"Let's go," Rowan says. "We better get you out of here, Daddy."

JT looks at Rowan. "You're leaving too?"

She nods.

I say, "Let's get him up into his truck, all right?"

JT shakes his head and folds his arms. "I'm not helping him with shit."

So Rowan and I prop her daddy up to a sitting position. Each of us gets an arm under one of his armpits, then we lift him to his feet. He shuffles like a drunk person, but we walk him over to his truck.

Rowan says, "Now take ahold of that steering wheel and pull yourself up and in, okay?"

Her daddy doesn't say anything but he pulls up on the steering wheel and we push as he pulls. We get him settled into his driver's seat.

Rowan says, "Now scoot over." We start pushing him again, and he falls to his side, still breathing ragged. "Get over on that passenger side so I can drive you, all right?" Rowan closes that door and jogs around to the passenger side. Pulls her daddy a little farther toward that far door.

JT says to Rowan, "Are you even gonna kiss me goodbye?"

Rowan shakes her head and runs back around the truck again. Hops up. Scoots the bench seat forward a little, then pulls the driver's door shut.

I wave but JT doesn't.

Rowan starts the truck and pops it into gear. Pulls it through the turnaround, looping past the trampoline in the middle of the yard, then up onto the road.

"Fuckin' crazy people," JT says. "What're you gonna do about it, you know?"

one piece at a time

At school the next day, I see Rowan in the hall before third period lets out. She's leaning against a locker, wearing big, wide sunglasses even though it's 42 degrees out and raining. Her lip is split, puffed to half an inch, and dark as chokecherry.

"Hey, you all right?" I lean in and try to see her eyes behind those sunglasses.

"Oh, yeah," she says, and sucks saliva off her fat lip. "I'm doing great."

When she turns a little, I can see the start of her double black eyes. "Shit, Rowan, I'm sorry."

"Yeah, it was a great night last night. One of the better ones. Hope tonight's just as good, ya know?"

I can't remember the last time I saw Rowan at school. I say, "And you're here today?"

Rowan drools a little off her smashed lip. Spits on the floor next to her locker. "Wouldn't miss it for anything. This place is fuckin' wonderful."

She pulls me into a shadow behind an open door to an empty room. Rowan's back is against the wall and my body is blocking everything in the hallway. But there's no one around.

"What are we . . ."

"Shh," she says, and pours something from a baggie onto the back of her hand. She lifts it to her nose. Snorts it. Pours another small pile on the same spot and holds it up to my nose.

"No, I'm good."

She holds her hand there for me to reconsider. Her hand starts to shake. Then she shrugs and snorts that pile too.

"Rowan, you . . ."

The bell rings, and classes let out. The hallway gets crazy, people weaving all around us.

"Um," I say, "want me to walk you to class?"

"Sure," she says, and takes my hand, pulls me into the middle of the swarm.

Two months ago, this would've been the highlight of my year—holding Rowan's hand, walking down the hallway at school—but now I'm nervous, feel awkward, look for Zaylie in every group of girls we pass. I don't want to explain what Rowan is to me, or talk to Zaylie about what we're doing, or if we're even doing anything. I don't want to have a conversation about dating or anything. But Rowan keeps holding my hand, her fingers laced in mine, and we weave through people to her next class.

We don't pass Zaylie, or I don't think we pass her. I don't see her. She must be in the other hallway or already in class before we pass by.

I let go of Rowan's hand at her lab door. Say, "Do your best, I guess. Right?"

Rowan points to the table covered in single burners and beakers. "Ironically, we're going to do chemical reactions."

She smiles and her lip cracks open. A little spot of blood blooms there.

Inside the class, I see kids putting on goggles, taking beakers from a rack, walking around with worksheets in their hands.

Rowan hugs me. "Wish me luck, 'cause I don't know any of the chemical structures or properties for this lab work."

"Good luck?"

Rowan smiles. Leans in and touches her nose to my nose. That close, I can only see her sunglasses. She doesn't kiss me. She's holding both of my hands now, and the bell rings. Rowan lets go of me and walks into her chemistry class. I turn and head down the hall, late to my class.

The rest of the school day's okay, gets better as it goes along, and finally it's nice to be in art class with Zaylie. We draw from a picture of an old military veteran sitting in a wheelchair. He's sort of smiling, and it's a challenge to get his smile right. When Zaylie finishes her drawing, she laughs out loud and shows it to me. "This is one of the worst drawings I've ever done."

Mine's equally bad, with the wheelchair's wheels all lopsided, and we both laugh so hard that Mrs. F has to ask us to be quiet.

After school, I follow Zaylie in my truck as she drives to Weippe. At her house, she turns on reruns of *Law and Order: SVU* and makes us celery sticks with peanut butter and more peppermint tea. We sit on the couch and snack. Zaylie puts her feet in my lap as we watch two episodes. More rape and murder. The second show starts with an amputated leg that leads the detectives into something called "the body modification world." It's a disgusting episode, real creepy, and I keep checking Zaylie's face to see if she looks as disturbed as I feel, but she doesn't cringe at anything.

After that show, she says, "You're starting to like *SVU*, huh?"

"Actually"—I shake my head—"I don't know if I do."

"You're just messing with me, right? Wait, are you serious?" Zaylie's face looks focused, straight, like she's trying to decide about going all in at the World Series of Poker.

I laugh. "You're really into this show, aren't you?"

Zaylie slides over onto my lap. "Yeah, so?" She kisses me, soft at first, then more serious. She's so intense, and I really do like her. But we're kissing, and I feel bad because I keep thinking about Rowan's split lip today, her black eye, and last night. I keep wondering exactly what happened when Rowan got home, and I wish I'd protected her somehow, gone home with her, or not let her go home at all.

Zaylie and I are kissing. Her tongue is grazing the tip of my tongue, and her breath is sweet and bright from the peppermint tea, and I wonder if my breath is as good as hers. We start to kiss harder, and her body is against me, and she feels good on my lap, feels like she fits there.

Zaylie peels off her shirt. She's wearing a different bra from the other day, pink and lacy, and she looks amazing in it.

"Wow," I say. "You look *really* good."

"Oh, you like this bra on me?" Zaylie smiles and pulls my face closer to her body.

I kiss the swell of her breasts, just above the lace. I hold her rib cage in my hands, kiss across her chest.

She sucks in air. Leans down and kisses me hard on the mouth.

We're both breathing harder now, sort of gasping and kissing at each other, and it's hard to describe the way Zaylie kisses, but it's as good as hot food after you've been hungry and cold and working outside all day in the rain, and I don't want to stop kissing her now, and my mind shuts down, and there's only Zaylie, nothing else.

Then she stops.

Pulls back.

Looks at the clock on top of the TV and says, "Oh, shit. It's almost seven o'clock. My parents are gonna be home *really fucking* soon. You've got to get out of here." She stands up and grabs her shirt. Puts it back on. "Damn," she says.

I want to stay where I am—stay here, keep kissing Zaylie, go to her bedroom together, take our clothes off—but I stand up because she's pulling me to my feet. "Quick now. Come on. Sorry, I know I keep rushing you out of here." She runs around the couch, checking the floor. "Did you bring anything else? Is any of this stuff yours? They'll kill me if they know a boy was here."

"Really?"

Zaylie stops and stares at me, makes a serious face. "Yeah, I'd be done. My parents would probably lock me in my room until I'm 30 just to be sure."

"To be sure of what?"

Zaylie laughs. Pushes me toward the door with both hands. "To be sure that you don't violate my innocence. You know?"

"That makes me sound horrible."

"Right, of course," she says. "And I wouldn't mind if you *did* violate my innocence—clearly—but my parents don't have to know that." She opens the door and pushes me out. "See you at school?" She stands on her toes on the step and kisses me again. "Thanks for hanging out tonight."

"Sure."

"Now go," she says. "Get the hell out of here." She pushes me again, and I turn and jog to my truck, my sore ankle hobbling me a little. I know I don't have to jog, but Zaylie's rushing, and that makes me rush too.

land of dreams

It's a cold Saturday, but JT's shirtless on the baseball diamond's outfield grass. I'm watching from the foul pole and he doesn't see me. He has four beer cans making a square for cone drills, each about ten yards apart. He sets up a forward sprint, angling backpedal, a lateral shuffle, a forward sprint, then a switch. He runs his first set, rep after rep through the sprints until he's gasping for air. Then he drops and does a set of 50 push-ups. After the push-ups, he walks to a corner beer, cracks it, and glugs it down. Then he grabs some infield sand, pours it into the top of the empty can, and sets it back up as a cone again. Then he rests for a minute before he starts the next set.

JT doesn't see me during his first two sets. Then he looks up. "Little?"

"Just watching."

He raises his eyebrows. "Wanna do a set with me?"

I shake my head. I used to do these things with him. We used to do little challenges all the time, jump-lunges or pull-up contests. 40-yard sprint repeats. And it's probably why I'm still pretty strong now, but I don't love working out the way JT does. He enjoys that kind of pushing hard, that burning in his muscles. I'd rather be fishing a creek all evening or hiking a ridge with a rifle in my hands.

JT says, "At least do a few sets of push-ups with me. Keep that upper body in shape."

So I do three sets of 20 push-ups while he goes through another set of his cones and 50 push-ups. Then he cracks his third beer. Downs that one too.

I sit on the grass after my push-ups. Say, "Is the beer part of your drills?"

JT shrugs. "Makes it more fun, right?"

"And what are you working out for, anyway?"

"Football," he says. "I can still play."

With his shirt off and his built-up jail body, I believe him. He could still hurt someone on the field. He could still hurt someone anywhere.

I say, "Do you think you'll get another shot?"

"I hope so. Somewhere. Two community colleges sent me letters this week."

"And you might play for one of them?"

"If nothing else. But I'm still hoping for Boise State. I'm gonna send a YouTube link out, maybe to a few places, then we'll see. Also Coach said he could help."

"Yeah?"

He nods and smiles. Pours sand in the third beer can. "Coach always loved me," he says, then gets down in a crouch to start his final set of cones.

I wave and walk back across the outfield and the road, back to the trailer to make some food.

time and time

I eat, and JT doesn't come back. I go outside and look at the field, and he's not there. He must've gone for more beer. Headed to the Flame or somewhere else that might serve him even though he's underage.

It gets dark.

I keep thinking Rowan might show up, but she doesn't. I should do my math homework, but I can't make myself. I try to study Spanish also, but I can't concentrate on anything in a book. I keep thinking about too many things.

My ankle's sore, and I use that as an excuse. I work on loosening it, hold my leg out straight, roll my foot around a little, hear it pop as it turns. I stand up and stretch my Achilles for a while, then turn my foot to the inside and hold that for a minute too, trying to get some range of motion back. It pops again, loud, but even that doesn't hurt too bad.

I'm standing next to the table where my homework's splayed out, but I don't sit back down. I don't want to.

◇ ◇ ◇

258

I shouldn't do this—I know it—but I drive up Shanghai Road, watch the green mile markers on the right, pull the truck over at the spot. Then I hike the deer trail in the dark. Move quick. Over the little ridge and through the three tree gaps that I marked back in September.

Last summer, your cheeks sank. Teeth chattering though it wasn't cold. Telling the same story five times and I watched your mouth moving, wondered where two more of your teeth had gone since the last time I'd seen you a few days before. Now there was a new gap across the front left.

"Hear that?" you said.

And when I said, "No," you held your shaky finger up like you were giving the sky one more chance to reconsider its options.

I didn't want anything to do with Judge Town, the shacks, manufactured double-wides cut in half and sealed off with Visqueen, tin siding, tilt doors, fifth wheels on 8" x 8" blocks, broken-down cars, and backyard garbage heaps ready for burning. I didn't like the gallon-size off-brand ziplocks and yellow-powder bundles either.

You told me to stuff duffel bags, four of them, and load up the trunk of your Camaro, so I did. You said, "You're comin' on this one."

I tilted my head like a dog waiting for a better answer.

But you said, "I gotta have you on this. No other way to do it," and we got in your car.

You turned the key but kept your foot on the brake and sniffed a spoon. Held one out for me and said, "Hit one for courage?" but I looked out the window and kept looking too, over the road and the baseball diamond until you put the spoon away, reached across to my side of the car, opened the glove compartment and got out both pistols. You slid the snub-nose .357 Magnum into my lap.

I looked back at you then.

You said, "Better keep that in your front belt. Easier to pull."

"Am I gonna have to use it?"

"Hope not. But you never know what a man's gonna have to do. Isn't that right?"

We drove over the rise, and the evening splashed pink across the bottom of the clouds.

You said, "You're almost six and a half feet tall now. That and a pistol makes you a lot to handle in a room full of people."

I popped the cylinder—all five loaded—and clicked it back in place. Set the gun on my thigh.

You drove the long-banked turn out of town. All your fingers were twitching on the steering wheel, tapping at it like we were listening to some kind of fast music. But there was no music playing.

We fishtailed onto the Judge Town split, and you laughed at it. "They'll think twice before they cross me tonight. Both of us there makes it real complicated."

I didn't like that night, didn't like the room or the man at the table with the yellow beard, the stain in his mustache from his cigarettes. I didn't like the two guys who stood on either side of me as we walked in, and I stood against the wall to know what was behind me. There were seven other people in the room. It's strange to know nobody's name and to leave it at that.

When we left, the warm night opened up to us with the smell of late dew as the gravel crunched beneath our boots. "Don't look back," you said. "They want us to look back. They want us scared of them. So don't let them have that pleasure."

after all

I skip school on Monday because I need to clear my head. I drive out to Deer Creek Reservoir, north up the 11 toward the old logging village of Headquarters, where the Camas Prairie Railroad used to end its line back when the mills were still running. That was when Pierce had 1,000 people living in town instead of 350, back when two out of three houses weren't abandoned or for sale.

I see a horse up ahead. I slow the truck to a stop and realize it isn't a horse. It's a Shiras moose, a big female, no antlers, head dipping down, walking toward me in my lane on the highway. As she gets close, she ambles to the yellow line, still walking, not running, no more fear of the truck than if it was a single mosquito humming there on the asphalt. I sit in the idling truck and watch her pass, and the moose doesn't turn her head as she slides by my driver's-side window, three feet from me, moving on behind now. I watch her travel 100 feet in the mirror, 200, then off the road through a gully and up a hillside.

I sit in the truck, idling on the highway, and don't drive for another minute. I sit and wonder at the moose, no other cars or trucks passing either way, just the empty highway like a river running dark through the green hills, my truck a drift boat on the black-asphalt water.

Sometimes I think about how we're all spread out along here, in these dead North Idaho towns, old US Forest Service and Potlatch logging sites, and everyone young hoping to leave as soon as possible because there's a world out there that's supposed to be better than this, a world that's moved into the 21st century, a world with cell phone coverage and Internet and better cars, a world with colleges and fancy restaurants and jobs people go to every day, wearing silk ties and expensive suits. But I don't know if I ever want to leave. I like this land where there are more deer than people, where moose walk the highway, where trees are taking back the old cuts.

Sometimes I feel like I'm 60 years old, not 16. My body's strong, but this country has worked on me, this region's water, its wind, its seasons, its heat and cold. I'm stuck where I grew. There are fishing poles in the back of this truck right now, the same fishing poles I learned on when I was five years old. And I'll fish with them today at Deer Creek.

all i do is drive

It's Tuesday—a school day—and I don't have any of my homework done in the three classes where they check homework before lunch. I look for Rowan in the halls but I don't see her. Check for Zaylie and don't see her either.

I'm walking past Room 2 during lunch, and Mr. Polchowski steps out. Says, "Hey," and stops me.

"Hey."

Mr. Polchowski tightens his ponytail. Says, "I'm worried about you. Haven't seen you enough lately."

"I know. I'll work on it."

"How about you come in this period? Right now. Come in and do some work with me, and we'll try to catch you up a bit before you go to any more classes."

"All right," I say. "I can do that. But I'll have to come right back. I gotta run to my truck for something."

"I'll be here," he says. "See you in five minutes, then?"

"Okay. Five minutes."

But I don't go back. At my truck, I look at all my schoolbooks on the passenger seat and I get overwhelmed. That math textbook is almost three inches thick just sitting there, closed, and I start to think of all the pages I haven't looked at, all the equations I don't know. I think about my skipped class days, skipped homework, missing quizzes, blank worksheets. And when I think about all of it, I realize there's more things I don't know than things I do.

I walk around to the driver's side and hop in. Turn the ignition and hear my *Complete Idiot's Guide to Learning Spanish* cassette come on.

But before I pop the truck into drive, the passenger-side door opens and Zaylie hops up. "Sorry," she says, "I followed you because I have to tell you something. I need to explain something."

I wasn't expecting her to show up right then, and I don't say anything other than "Oh."

She says, "I have to tell you why I always kick you out so quick at my house. Why I never want you to meet my parents and all that." She takes a big breath and starts nodding at what she's about to say. Then she blurts it out. "See— basically—I'm LDS."

"You're what?"

"LDS. Mormon," she says. "That's our church."

"All right," I say.

Zaylie has her hair pulled to the side with a barrette, her bright green eyes shimmering. She looks small and worried. But pretty too. "So," she says, "my parents want me to live a life that isn't what they call 'polluted' by violent TV, or by music that has cussing in it, or by boys who aren't LDS. You know?"

I nod like I understand, like I know how it would be if I ever had parents or rules or anything like that.

"The thing is," she says, "I've looked online, and LDS doesn't mean the same thing everywhere. There's really cool LDS in other places, people who live interesting lives. But we're Intermountain, see?"

I don't see.

She went on. "I've looked online, and we're the paranoid ones, the extremists, the Intermountain LDS. That's my family. And the problem's what they want for me. See, I don't like any of the LDS boys here. None of them. They're boring to me. And I can't imagine a life without Tupac or *SVU*. You know?"

I don't know. I don't understand how she feels. But I like how Zaylie is, how intense she is. The serious face she makes when she talks about something she cares about. I say, "It's good that you're thinking your own things, right?"

"No, it's not good," she says. "My parents don't trust me. They're always checking up on me. Did you know that I own two iPods? One with Shawn Mendes and Taylor Swift on it? And that's the one that I keep on my pillow at home. My mom scrolls through and listens to all the lyrics on it, and the other day she erased a Jordan Pruitt song because it talked about 'making out with no strings attached.' She said the song was too suggestive. And that was Jordan Pruitt."

"I don't know what that means."

"What it means? It means that my parents are ridiculous. Jordan Pruitt is from the Disney Channel. She's so young in the mind that it's painful. She wouldn't know the real world if it hit her in the back of the head with a broken beer bottle."

"Oh," I say.

"No, you don't understand. I'm gonna be 16 in a week. I'm a sophomore in high school. I'm living in a small town in Idaho and I gotta get *the fuck* out of here." Zaylie takes a deep breath.

I say, "You know what's weird? I was just thinking about this yesterday, how the rest of the world is supposed to be better than this."

"Yeah?"

"But what if it isn't? What if this is good right here?"

Zaylie shakes her head. "You live in a trailer with no adults. You get to do whatever you want, every day. So your opinion on this doesn't really count to me."

"Yeah, but—"

"I'm sorry," she says, "and I'm sure you've got something going on that's fucked up too. I'm sure everybody does, and all that. It's just that sometimes I feel like I have a plastic bag over my head and my parents keep tightening the drawstrings around my throat. Either I'm gonna suffocate right here or I'm gonna have to rip that bag to pieces and start throwing punches. You know?"

I nod, and I don't try to explain what I was thinking about the moose and all that. I don't think Zaylie would hear it right now.

She pulls her phone out and looks at the screen to check the time. "Dammit. We've gotta go back to class now or we're gonna be late. Lunch is pretty much over."

"Actually," I say, "I don't think I'm gonna go back to class today. Sorry. But I'm gonna miss art."

"See?" Zaylie says. "That's what I'm talking about. If I skipped a class? One single class period? Shit!" She opens the door and slides out. "I guess I'll see you when I see you." She slams the door and walks away. Doesn't look back as she stomps into the school building.

I don't know what that would feel like, to have parents checking up on me, parents knowing if I skipped a class or not. I feel bad about leaving Mr. Polchowski waiting for me at his room right now. I feel bad when I waste his time like this, but I don't really know how it feels to be Zaylie. I mostly get to do what I want with school. I'm still in school just because I've decided to be there, because I want to finish for me.

I wonder if Zaylie's more mad at me or if she's just mad about a lot of things. It seems like it should rain right now, or that dark clouds should roll in, but instead the afternoon sun slides out from behind a puffy ball of cumulus and nearly blinds me with its brightness. The sunlight shines directly through the front windshield as I pop the truck into drive, and when I angle around a U-turn and head north onto the road to Pierce, the sunlight warms the back of my neck, shines bright behind me like I'm escaping something. But whatever it is that I'm escaping, it has reach, and it follows me home.

personal jesus

I fish the creek low, in the shallow drops as it comes into town, and catch a couple of tiny trout, not big enough to eat. So I throw them back.

Willa's sitting on the trailer's step when I get home. I step out of the truck. Walk up to her. See that she's been crying. "What's wrong?" I say.

"I got suspended," she says.

"Suspended?"

She picks at a long splinter on the step. Says, "From school."

"How?" I say. "What'd you do?"

"Nothing, really. I was just showing that piece of glass at recess. I was yelling at this kid Jeremiah because he wasn't listening to me, and the recess lady came over and saw me yelling at him with a piece of glass in my hand." Willa starts to cry again. "She said I was trying to cut him with the glass."

"But that's not true."

"I know," Willa says. "I tried to explain. I tried real hard. They called home but nobody picked it up, so they kept me in the office until the end of the day and told me to ride the bus home and not come back to school tomorrow."

"Did they say how many days you're supposed to stay out?"

"Till next week. Till Monday."

"But that's way too long."

"Right," she says, "and it was over something they got wrong too. That wasn't even what I was trying to do."

I sit down next to her on the trailer step and put my arm around her. "I'm sorry."

She tries to shrug my arm off. "School's stupid anyways. And I hate it."

I keep my arm draped over her shoulders but I hold her a little lighter. Lean back against the trailer door. "You've done a good job this year, and you've gotta keep trying. Remember our deal?" Even as I say it I feel a little guilty.

"Yeah. I remember."

"Well," I say, "what's the deal?"

"You want me to say it to you?"

"Yeah."

She sniffs. "We won't quit for anything."

"Right. That's our deal, you and me. We're not quitting school. We're sticking it out even if it gets hard. Okay?"

I know I'm being a hypocrite, and I feel bad about it, like I'm tricking Willa. But I don't know what else to say.

Willa rubs her face with her hands. "But what am I supposed to do all week?"

"I don't know."

"No, for real, Little. What am I supposed to do?"

"Let me see . . ." I hug her again, and this time she doesn't shrug me off. "Maybe some reading and math? Do an hour of each every day?"

"Okay," she says, "that's not too much."

"No, you can do it. And I'll check that you do." I lift her chin so I can see her face. "And if you do those two hours first, you can be outside the rest of the day. You can be with the donkey, collect eggs, climb trees, and all that."

Willa smiles. "All right."

"Now let's go eat some food," I say. "I'll see what I have."

"It's the second." Willa smiles.

"It's the second what?"

"It's the second of the month," she says, and fishes in her pocket. She pulls out some food stamps. "I stole half of them from her purse."

"You got half?"

"Yep."

"Nice," I say. "Good work."

"Yep, before she could trade 'em, I stole 'em. So what should we buy? Pumpkin pie? Ice cream? Bacon?" She stands up. "We better go to the store right now."

As we walk to the truck, I say, "Tell me a joke, okay?"

"No, I really don't feel like jokes right now. But maybe after some bacon and ice cream," she says. "After bacon and ice cream, everything's always a little bit better."

girl power

I can't skip school on Wednesday because Willa's at home watching me go and come back. She'd know if I went at the wrong time or drove in the wrong direction. Before I leave, I write out what she has to do for her reading and math.

"Our deal," Willa says, and holds out her pinkie to me.

We lock pinkies, and I say, "Have a good day here, all right?"

"All right."

Then I drive to school. Pay attention all morning. Take notes. Just for Willa. Just so I won't be such a hypocrite. But I still hate everything other than art class. That's just the way it is for me.

As I try to draw a picture of JT that isn't working out, I say, "Zaylie, what are you listening to today?"

Zaylie holds out one earbud. "Girl power."

I put the earbud in and hear nothing. Raise my eyebrows.

Zaylie smiles like a coyote. "You ready? I fast-forwarded and paused. This is Nikki Minaj's feature section in 'Monster.' The only time she ever fully throws down."

"Throws down?"

"Yeah, throws down for real. It's like she's knifing somebody in a bathtub."

"Okay . . ."

Zaylie giggles and hits Play. And it *is* serious. This rapper girl is talking about killing and sucking blood. She says she's a "motherfuckin' monster." It makes me smile, and Zaylie sees my smile. "See," she says, "girl power's the greatest."

Zaylie plays the feature three more times like she always does. For Zaylie, if a song's good once, it's better the fourth or fifth time in a row.

We're both drawing, and I'm starting to memorize the words when Zaylie stops the music. "Now," she says, "you're ready for M.I.A."

Like everything else she introduces to me, I don't know what she's talking about.

Zaylie does a little dance to no music at all. "Oh, you'll like this. Trust me. She's a terrorist."

"What?"

"Maya. She's so dangerous, we can't even have her on tour in the US."

"Are you making that up?"

Zaylie purses her lips and closes her eyes, and if we weren't in class right now, I would just lean in and kiss her. She has so much attitude. I wait until she opens her eyes again, then I look back down at my paper. Shake my head.

"What?" Zaylie says.

"Nothing," I say. "You're just funny."

We draw and listen to M.I.A. saying that all she wants to do is take our money.

At the end of class, Zaylie says, "After today, you might be ready for Jane Doe's feature with Black Star, 'Twice Inna Lifetime.' Maybe tomorrow."

" 'Twice in a Lifetime'?"

"I said, you *might* be ready. Might be. Maybe."

that night

Up off a Forest Service road. I dug the hole deep. Went through loam, dirt, six inches of clay, and a layer of round rock after. The hole had to be big, and I worked until my palms blistered to the first creases of my fingers.

It was at least to my chest when I knew it was deep enough. I had to chop a step into the side wall to climb out without slipping. Covered in mud and clay. Hands red as rust. I wiped my nose on the back of my wrist and smeared mud across my face.

Then I went to the bushes.

i promise you

Friday night, I'm asleep when Rowan comes. I see her outline in the doorway when I open my eyes. She's pulled the door but she's still standing outside, leaning against the metal doorjamb. It's raining, and she's standing in the drizzle.

"Rowan?" I sit up. "Are you okay?"

"Mmm," she says.

I stand and walk over to the door. "You wanna come in?"

She nods. Her eyes close halfway.

"Are you all right?"

I flip the light on behind me. Reach out and grab Rowan under her arm. Pull her up into the trailer. She's soaking wet. So drunk she can barely stand. I set her down in one of the kitchenette chairs, then go back and shut the trailer door. Lock it. Grab a towel at the shower stall.

Rowan mumbles, "I have s'thin' for you."

"What?"

"Here." She tries to unzip her coat a couple of times and misses the zipper. Then she gets it and pulls it down. Reaches inside her coat to a pocket on the left side. Fumbles around for a minute.

"What are you . . . ?"

She pulls something out of her pocket and hands it to me. "Here," she says again.

It's a white plastic grocery bag rolled up a few times around whatever's inside, then taped with a long run of black electrical tape. "What is this?"

Rowan shrugs, her head lolling forward.

"Rowan?"

She blinks hard and sniffs. Opens her eyes wide.

I pick at the tape. Get a corner loose and unwind it until it comes free from the plastic. Then I unroll the bag. See a stack of money in the bottom, the bills covered in powder. I pull them out, all 20s, almost half an inch thick. "What are you . . ." I start to count it, get halfway through, and realize that it's about $2,000.

Rowan's eyes are closing again.

"What is this?" I shake the money in front of her face.

She points. " 'S'money."

"Yeah, I know it's money. A lot of money. But what's it from?"

She shakes her head.

"And the powder?"

She giggles. "Tha's crank, Young Little."

"Oh, shit. What'd you do?"

But her eyes are closing again, and her skin looks pale, her chin falling to her chest.

I set the money on the table. Then think about how much money it is and picture JT coming in, finding it sitting there on the table, so I pry the pressboard slat back and put it into the wall with my other money. Stuff it down and tap the nail back into place.

When I turn around, Rowan's eyes are open again. She's slumped and her head's tilted to the side. Her eyes are open and she's smiling. "Shhh," she says, "secret." She leans a little farther and starts to fall out of her chair.

I catch her. "How much did you drink tonight?"

She doesn't answer me. Closes her eyes again.

"I think you gotta eat something. Drink some milk, maybe? Get something else in your stomach."

I take a cup to the fridge and fill it with milk. Turn back to the table and kneel down in front of Rowan. She's asleep now. Passed out. I shake her. "Rowan! Wake up! You gotta drink some of this."

Her eyes open and she nods. Then she starts to fall asleep again and I shake her some more. Push her upright. "Rowan!"

Her eyes go wide and she takes a deep breath. "I not . . ."

I put the cup to her lips, tilt it, and some of the milk goes in her mouth, some on the front of her coat. "Swallow that, okay?"

She swallows some. Spills some.

I tilt her chin up and pour some more milk into her mouth. She swallows again. I have to wake her a few times, but we keep working on the milk until the cup is empty. Then I go to the sink and get a dish towel, wet it, and come back to clean up Rowan's mess. "Could you eat something if I made it for you?"

She shakes her head.

"Anything? Just a little bit?"

She puts her head on the table. Closes her eyes again. "I'ma puke."

"No, no." I lift her, carry her to the bathroom, and set her down in the doorway because the bathroom is way too small to fit both of us. I shove her inside and get her arms propped up on the seat of the toilet, realize that one side of her hair has fallen into the toilet bowl. I pull it back out but it's dripping wet and I have to wring it out. Then I hold all her hair back, both her rain-dampened hair and her sopping toilet hair.

Rowan starts retching, heaves a couple of times, then vomits into the toilet. All the milk comes up plus whatever else.

I say, "It's all right. Get it out."

I remember the first time I drank. I was ten. JT stole a six-pack of talls from Uncle Lucky. JT was 13. We sat in the graveyard and drank three tall cans each. After two of them, my stomach felt like it was going to burst, but JT and I were laughing together, telling stories, and I wanted to laugh like that with him forever. So I cracked the third and kept sipping until it was gone.

I remember laying on my side on the graveyard grass, the graves shifting back and forth like the roll of a rapid as the water comes over an underwater rock. And when I tried to stand up, someone had jellied my legs and I ran sideways until an oak tree knocked me down.

Back in the trailer, JT leaned me over the toilet and said, "It's all right. Just get it out."

I didn't even remember puking for the first time. Or when we went back inside the trailer. Or how it got to be nighttime so sudden.

Rowan's whole body goes rigid. She heaves and throws up over and over.

"Keep going," I say again, but I don't know how much more she has in her.

She reaches a finger into her mouth and gags herself. Throws up a little more, not much. She leans to the side and rests her face in the vomit that's on her sweatshirt sleeve. Mumbles, "Oh, shhh . . ."

"It's okay," I say. "I can help you clean up too."

She waves her finger around in the air, then sticks it back into her mouth. Gags herself once more.

I say, "It's gotta be mostly out now."

She dry-heaves a few times, but she's finished. She gasps and leans sideways, wet vomit slicking her chin.

"Let's see. We gotta . . ." but I don't know what to do. Her clothes are damp from the rain. Her hair is damp on one side, wet on the other from the toilet. She has vomit all over the front of her, down her sleeve, on the side of her face and under her nose. I go to the kitchen sink and get a rag. Put soap on it and warm water. Walk back to the bathroom and start to scrub Rowan's shoulder and arm. But the vomit just rubs into the sweatshirt's fabric. I wipe her face, but there's no way to really clean her up this way.

I say, "I'm gonna have to get you in the shower. Okay?"

Rowan sniffs and opens her eyes. Doesn't say anything.

Then she closes her eyes again and slumps into the space between the toilet and the wall. It's a small gap there. She's wedged, but I pull her out, drag her into the hallway. She's so listless I imagine for a moment that she's dead, and the thought scares me enough that I shake her until she moans.

I peel off her sweatshirt, pull her vomit-soaked shirt over her head, lean her back against the wall. Then I unlace her boots, slide those off, and peel her socks. I struggle with her jeans, damp from the rain, and then I realize it doesn't matter. They're already wet. So I leave them on.

I go to start the shower. The stall is so small that there's no way I could get in with Rowan and close the door behind us. I'll have to be half in and half out, getting water everywhere. I strip off my shirt. Lay a towel down outside the shower on the floor, hoping it catches most of the extra water. Then I turn the shower head so it's spraying against the far wall.

I lift Rowan under the armpits, drag her into the shower stall. Say, "Wake up, Rowan. Stand up and try to help me." She plants her feet, but she doesn't do anything else.

I put shampoo in her armpits, in her hair, and wash around her mouth, her chin, her throat, anywhere there was vomit. She leans heavy on me, and I hold her in place with one arm while scrubbing her with the other, and it's like trying to hold a big fish above the water without hooking the gills.

I almost have all the soap washed out of Rowan's hair when I hear a sound. Because of the running water, I can't hear what it is at first and I'm not sure until the pounding starts. I turn the shower off.

JT's voice: "Hey, Little, you accidentally locked the door. Let me in, man."

I'm half in and half out of the shower. Dripping wet. No shirt on.

Rowan's in her jeans and bra.

She's leaning against the wall of the shower, my arm around her back, my hand in her far armpit. I see a huge clump of white soapy bubbles in the back of her hair, so I turn her around, flip the water back on for a few seconds and direct it on that spot. Then I flip the water off again.

JT yells, "Seriously, what the fuck, man? Open this *fuckin'* door!"

I pull Rowan out of the shower stall. Lower her dripping wet to the floor. Go get a couple of towels, pull Rowan back up and wrap her in one. Then I walk her to the kitchenette, set her in a chair, and lean her head onto the table. She's pretty much passed out and she doesn't move when I let go of her.

I jog back to my bunk, towel off for five seconds, then put on a new T-shirt.

I go to the door and unlock it. Pull it open.

JT holds up his hands. "Are you kidding me? What the fuck was that?"

"Long story, man. Rowan got real drunk and showed up here . . . I guess she was looking for you?"

"What?" JT steps into the trailer. Sees the shower stall open, the water on the floor, the wet towels. Turns and sees Rowan at the kitchenette table, her arms and head resting on the tabletop, her upper body wrapped in a towel. Her jeans dripping wet.

"What the hell's going on?"

"Like I said, she got real drunk. I think she has alcohol poisoning or something."

"Why is she in a towel?"

"What?"

He grabs a handful of my hair. "You better fuckin' answer me right now. I said why is she in a towel?"

"JT, listen to me! She has alcohol poisoning. She was puking in the bathroom and I was standing there trying to help her."

JT still has my hair twisted in his fist so my head's turned at an odd angle. He says, "Are you lying to me?"

"What the fuck, man? Go smell her vomit-drunk breath, and then tell me if I'm lying."

JT lets go of my hair, and we both turn and look at Rowan. She's slumped in the kitchenette chair, her eyes closed, her head still resting on the table.

JT leans in close to her. Says, "Are you drunk for real?"

Rowan doesn't open her eyes.

JT grabs her hair and lifts her head. He says, "Are you drunk for real?"

I say, "Let go of her hair! What the fuck, man? She's passed out!"

JT keeps hold of her hair and points at me with his other hand. "You do *not* tell me what to do with her, or with anything else. No one gets to tell me what to do, ever. Got that?"

"Let go! You hear me? Look at her face. She's fuckin' passed out and you're pulling her head around by her hair."

JT leans in close to Rowan's face. Her eyes are closed, lips slack, her tongue coming out the side of her mouth. JT lets go of her hair, and her head drops against the tabletop with a clunk.

"Dammit," I say, and push him.

JT gets in my face. "Don't push me. And don't ever fuckin' tell me what to do."

"I was helping her."

"Shut up." JT's face is close to mine. I can smell the beer on his breath. For a second I think he might hit me, and I try not to be intimidated. But I can't help it. I'm afraid of him, afraid of what he could do to me. I clench my stomach just in case he hits me with one of those quick low body shots I've seen him throw before. I try to be ready with my hands even though I don't think there's any chance I could beat him if he hit me first.

But JT doesn't hit me. Instead, he says, "I'm gonna let this one go. I'm gonna put some sweats and a T-shirt on Rowan, and I want you not to watch. You got that?"

That doesn't make any sense since I've already seen her in her bra and I just helped her shower, but I say, "Okay. I'll keep my back turned."

JT walks past me and mumbles, "This is a fucked-up situation." He opens one of his clothes drawers in the back of the trailer, gets something out, then returns to the table for Rowan, carries her to his bed, and lays her down. "Now don't look," he says.

"Yeah, I heard you." I turn my back and stand there next to my bunk. Wait while JT dresses her.

She keeps mumbling something, and I hear my name a few times, but the rest of what she says doesn't make sense. JT doesn't say anything in return.

I say, "When you set her up to sleep after, put her on her side so if she pukes she won't choke."

"I'm not a fuckin' idiot," JT says. "And she's not the first drunk person I've been around."

"Just saying."

"Yeah, well, you don't have to. You've already done enough tonight, don't you think?"

I shake my head, and I want to tell him what I really think about him right now, but I don't.

JT says, "Will you turn those bright kitchen lights off? We're fuckin' going to sleep back here."

So I know he's done dressing her.

I turn the lights off, go into the bathroom to take a piss, and walk back to my bunk. I get in bed and pull the covers over myself. Then I lay in bed and can't sleep. I keep thinking about JT and Rowan, and how I never even hear them talk about anything. The only thing I've ever known about them was sloppy kissing and drunk games, and the bedtime sounds I'll never get out of my brain no matter how long I live.

But if Rowan and I were together, we'd be more than her and JT ever could be. Way more. Without a doubt.

I was walking a draw. Eleven years old. Moving through the trees in the bright sunlight, just me alone, and I was carrying my 10/22 but not really planning to shoot anything, just walking and carrying the rifle because I liked to hike gun-heavy.

A coyote came out in front of me. It didn't cross the road. It ran up the edge of the Forest Service line, padding along the side of the road on the soft shoulder, and I guess the wind was in my face because the coyote didn't notice me until we were only 20 feet apart. I'd stopped and raised the gun. Cartridge already chambered and the safety off. But I didn't pull the trigger. Not yet.

The coyote stopped. Lifted his head. Shifted one way, then the other. I saw the missing hair along his flank, a patch of mange, a line of gray, and underneath, his thin ribs, his hungry frame, his shoulders short on rabbit.

He dropped his nose to the ground. Tried to smell me better. Looked confused and shifted his feet as I fingered the trigger. Grooved it. Wondered if a single bullet would kill him, only a .22 but maybe a good shot. I held the bead on his head, just above his eyes.

He waited on me.

That was the strange thing. He waited for me to make a decision and he looked directly at the gun. At me. He let me choose, even if that choice wasn't going to be good for him. He waited and waited, and I held my gun until it shook.

Sometimes I feel like that coyote.

this side of the law

Zaylie and I are sharing earbuds in art class on Monday. Listening to Tupac's "California Love." I say, "You think California's really all that great?"

Zaylie says, "It's gotta be better than Idaho, right?"

"I don't know. Seems like there's shittiness everywhere." I'm trying to shade a drawing of Mrs. F, hiding the drawing with my hand so she won't see what I'm doing as she walks around the room to give students feedback.

Zaylie nods a little. "You might be right," she says. "It might be some kind of crappy in California."

Zaylie's drawing me today. We're all supposed to pick someone in the classroom without telling them. And because they don't know they're being drawn, they're not going to stay still and model for the artist. Mrs. F said that this way there's more of a *feeling* of a person than a perfect image. I'm not supposed to know who's drawing me—if anyone— but Zaylie said at the start of the class, "I'm drawing you," so I know.

She keeps staring at my face, narrowing her eyes, looking at her paper, then back at me.

She picks up her iPod and starts "California Love" again.

I say, "I'm not saying everything's gotta be bad in California. Some of it might be good too. There's probably both. Like everywhere."

"Of course," Zaylie says. She looks at me, tilts her head, clicks her mouth, and goes back to her drawing.

I look down at my paper. I'm trying to shade the left side of Mrs. F's nose but it just makes her nose look wide, like a cucumber cut in half and pasted to her face. I erase the whole nose and start over again.

Zaylie says, "The clubs sound pretty cool there. You know? Have you ever been to one?"

"A club?"

"Yeah."

"No," I say. "I've never been anywhere like that."

"Me neither."

"My grandpa used to drive down the Grade to go to a strip club, but I don't think that's the same thing."

"No," Zaylie says, "not strip clubs. I think Tupac means dancing clubs. I read that he liked to dance."

"Sure," I say, "but I can't picture that."

"Well, haven't you ever seen those on TV? Like in a show like *SVU* or something? There are clubs in that show sometimes."

"Zaylie, my *SVU* experience is limited to hanging out with you."

"Right," she says, and flicks me on the forearm. "And we should do that some more."

"Okay," I say, and look down at my drawing. Start to draw a new nose for Mrs. F.

"Really, though," Zaylie says, "we should hang out more. And I'm sorry about the other day, about getting in your truck and all that, about being so pissed."

"It's all right."

"No, it's not. You've got your things too, I'm sure. I don't have a rough life or anything. I shouldn't complain about it."

"It's okay," I say. "Really." The thing is, I do understand. Everyone's got their own stuff. And I don't know what it would be like to have parents always telling me what to do.

"So can we hang out after school maybe?"

"Yeah, I think so."

"Cool." Zaylie flips her drawing of me so I can see it. And it's pretty good. It sort of looks like me.

I say, "Wanna see mine? It's not done, and it's not good, but . . ." I turn it around. By accident, I've made Mrs. F look 20 years older, way fatter, with weird blotches on her face.

Zaylie covers her mouth, her eyes wide. She says, "Do *not* show that to her. It is *not* flattering. And if she asks, say it's someone else. Just say you didn't understand the assignment and drew someone you used to know in town."

"Okay, I guess I just don't have a gift for drawing women."

"No," Zaylie says, "not trying to be too harsh here, but you do *not* have that gift."

Zaylie and I go to her locker after school, then out to her car. She says, "I'll drive you there so we can ride together. Then I can drive you back to your truck later." She holds out a stick of Wrigley's Big Red. "Gum?"

"Thanks."

We chew gum and drive. Listen to yet another rapper I've never heard of.

When we get to Zaylie's street in Weippe, and almost to her house, she stops the car. Pops it into park. Her house is maybe 100 feet up the street. I look sideways at the houses around us and wonder why we stopped. Then I look up at Zaylie's house. There's a Clearwater County sheriff's cruiser out in front.

I say, "That's not good."

"No, it's fine," she says. "My uncle's a deputy."

"Oh, and he hangs out at your house?"

"Sometimes. He's probably hanging out with my dad." Zaylie puts her hand back on the gear selector. Says, "You're not a fan of the police, are you?"

"No, I mean, whatever." I try to act like I don't care either way.

"And you're not a very good liar." Zaylie pops the car into reverse. Backs into a driveway. Pulls forward and drives back the way we came. "I'm sorry," she says, "my dad's home early. We can't hang out. I'll take you back to your truck, then I better get home. He'll wonder what took me that long but it'll be okay. I'll say I had to meet with teachers after school."

When we get back to the Timberline parking lot, to my truck, Zaylie says, "Sorry," again.

"It's fine. Really."

Zaylie climbs out of her seat and gets onto my lap. "Thanks for understanding," she says, and slides her knees on either side of my legs. We're wedged into her small car, my head near the ceiling and Zaylie taking up the space between me and the dashboard. Zaylie unbuttons the top three buttons of her shirt, and I can see the lace along the edge of her bra. She kisses me and I put my arms around her. She feels little but strong. Her tongue tastes like Big Red chewing gum, cinnamon, bright flavoring. She kisses me hard and opens her mouth, licks the tip of my tongue with her tongue.

Zaylie rubs her body against mine, her shirt open, the faint smell of her perfume on her collarbones. She breathes heavy into my ear. Kisses down the side of my face and neck. Then she stops. Takes a deep breath. Pops the door open and gets out. "Sorry, soldier. I've gotta boot you now." She's standing on the gravel, and she pulls my hand to get me moving. I take a deep breath and shake my head, climb awkward out of her little Corolla. Stand up next to the car, and Zaylie hugs me, more than a foot shorter than me. She wraps her arms around me, then pulls back and takes hold of the roof of her car with one hand, uses the inside of the car as a step-up, and leans out to me, now almost the same height. She kisses me again. "We'll hang out soon?" she says.

"Yeah, that sounds good."

"Maybe do a little more next time?" Zaylie winks and buttons up her shirt.

I like Zaylie, like how unpredictable she is, her smile, and the way she switches from one thing to the next so quickly that I can barely keep up.

down in the valley

Late Monday evening, dark outside. I'm doing my math homework in the trailer, at the table, and it's going okay. I've looked at 17 problems so far and I've done six on my own, only left 11 to do at school in Room 2. Better than average. Now I'm working on a problem asking for X that doesn't seem to have an answer, and I think of what Mr. Polchowski always says and I try to solve it two different ways, but neither way works. I tap my pencil against the paper and start to stare off, and that's when I see it: the particleboard loose. I blink a couple of times before I realize what I'm looking at. Then I get up and walk to the wall.

The particleboard is peeled back, the nail dangling in its hole. I pry the board a little farther open, look inside, and don't see my money. Reach down and find two ziplock bags. Full. I pull them out and set them on the kitchenette table, and in the light, I see the yellow. I open one and smell it. Close it again. Say, "Fuck."

Then I wait.

When I hear him outside, I stand up. He opens the door, and I step into the door gap and push him out onto the grass.

He stumbles backward into the streetlight's shadow. I yell, "What the fuck, JT?"

"What?"

I step up to him in the dark. "Are you stashing in our trailer? Dealing? And you fuckin' stole my money too!"

JT puts his hand up. "What the hell are you talking about?"

"I found the baggies."

He squares up, the way I've seen him turn before. "Little, I'm warning you. You stay out of my stuff."

"Your stuff? No, this was with *my* stuff. And where the fuck is my money?"

"I don't know what you're talking about."

"Don't lie to me, JT. My money . . . in the wall."

JT leans his head back and looks up at the night sky like I'm annoying him, like I'm a worried kid and he's the grown adult who understands things better than I do. And that does it for me.

I swing at him. I aim right at his chin, but I don't hit him straight-on like I want to because he reacts and steps forward a little bit like he always does, and the punch goes past his chin, catches him along the side of his shaved head. I put a lot into that punch, but I don't get enough of JT to make him go down or even to knock him back. My punch just sort of skims him.

I try to keep my hands up and my elbows inside and go to work on him after that—like I've seen him do to so many other people—but he's fighting by the same rules, stronger than me and more experienced too. I get a couple of shots in, but nothing solid, and JT works his head inside on me and he pounds me up in the ribs. The third or fourth shot on my left side makes me drop my hands, and JT lines up a straight right and punches me in the middle of my chest, on my sternum. And that does it.

I go to my knees. Then the ground. Try to breathe. But even laying on my side on the grass, trying to pull air in, it's like I have a cement pyramid block resting on my chest. I stay there and gasp, suck at air and choke.

I lay sideways, look at the yellow shine of the streetlight coming through the dark grass, more black than green. I open my mouth wide and try to pull more air into my lungs but the pressure on my chest keeps my lungs half-closed.

JT puts his hand on my back. "Just relax," he says, "relax, and you'll be able to breathe soon enough."

I stay down and wait. Lie there and look at the blades of grass near my face. Take shallow breaths through my open mouth until I can get deeper breaths past my spasming chest. My eyes water and I try not to cry.

Then the pressure stops and I'm able to fill my lungs. It doesn't feel good, but I can breathe again. I roll to my knees. Press my forehead to the ground, the cool of the grass and the mud against my head, and I take bigger breaths, try to make my chest move all the way in and out.

"I'm stashing," JT says, "but not in the wall. And I don't know shit about your money."

"Whatever," I say, my forehead still pressed against the ground.

"It's the truth," he says. "Are you sure your money's gone?"

"Yeah."

"How much was it?"

I'm rubbing my chest now, trying to rub the stiffness out. Still struggling a little with big breaths, but breathing a lot better. I say, "Gonna pretend you don't know?"

"Listen," he says, "I'm telling you I don't know shit about it. So just tell me what it was and we'll figure things out from there."

"Almost $3,000."

"Saving up for that plot of land?" JT kneels next to me. "Those five acres you showed me last summer?"

"Yeah."

JT puts his hand on my back again. "$3,000's a lot of money. Who might have it?"

"You."

"Shit, Little. You're not hearing me."

"No, I'm not. And go look at what you left behind in the trailer."

"I didn't take anything, but all right, fine. I'll go look." He stands up, and I hear him walk over to the trailer. Hear the door squeak open, then shut.

I roll back onto my side, then onto my back. Lay flat on the grass. Hold my chest and stare at the sky. There are small gaps in between clouds. Scattered stars I don't recognize. It's always weird to me that I can't recognize part of a constellation without seeing it in full, how the whole sky can confuse me on a cloudy night.

JT comes back out of the trailer holding the two ziplocks. "This is a shit ton of yellow crank. What the fuck?"

"Yep."

"How'd it get there?"

"JT . . ."

"I'm serious. How the fuck did it get there?"

"Maybe you put it there when you were real drunk or something?"

He shakes his head. Holds up one bag, then the other, like he's comparing weight. Says, "I've never been that drunk in my life."

"Never?"

"Look, this is fuckin' *weird*. We have a chunk of crank here, and your money's gone."

I say, "I guess things just move on their own, huh?"

"No, this is serious. We gotta figure this shit out."

"Well, I think I already have, but you don't seem to agree with me, so that leaves us in a strange place. Doesn't it?"

"Dammit, Little, you gotta open your fuckin' eyes. Meanwhile, we gotta stash this shit deep and keep that wallboard nailed tight."

don't know where i'm bound

In the morning, I go outside and find another dead chicken. Opened up same as the others. I count and see only two egg-layers in the yard, plus the banty rooster. I can't find the other hen, which must've disappeared at some point in the last few days. I look all over but she's gone. So there's only two now.

I walk back toward my trailer and hear the unmistakable sound of a lawn mower on the road. There's Mrs. Trepp in her coat and sunglasses again, her gloves and her Santa hat. She pulls over onto the gravel and kills the engine.

"Hey," I say.

"Hey back." She holds out another root beer barrel.

I take it, unwrap it, and pop it into my mouth. "Thanks."

Mrs. Trepp looks off toward the Mini-Mart. A diesel truck pulls in for gas, and the driver gets out to pump. He walks around the back of his truck, and Mrs. Trepp nods like she's responding to something he said. Then she takes off her sunglasses—those big shades, folds them in her lap—and turns back toward me. She looks directly into my eyes, and underneath her sunglasses, her eyes are blue, bright blue and pale, so pale, as if the sunglasses have made them otherworldly.

I don't know what to say to her. I keep thinking about my mom when she was little.

But Mrs. Trepp doesn't talk about that again. Instead, she says, "I saw that night."

I'm still thinking about my mom, so I say, "What?"

"That night. You must not've heard my lawn mower engine because of all of the yelling. And the gunshot too. I pulled over and stopped my mower."

"That night . . . ?"

"Yeah," she says. "And I saw after too."

I nod slowly. "Okay."

"And it is what it is. I saw him that way a long time ago. Always like that. With your mom and with Derlene too."

The root beer barrel's flavor changes in my mouth. Somehow it's as if there's no sugar in it. I can feel it on my tongue, but I can't taste the sweet.

"I just wanted to say that I saw it. And that's all." Mrs. Trepp puts her sunglasses on. "And I won't be saying anything. So don't worry."

I say, "Are you sure?"

"Like I said, that's all. I won't be telling." Mrs. Trepp pops her mower's handle, and the mower spins on its rear wheel just like before. She reaches down for the pull cord handle. "I won't say anything to anyone. Not ever." She jerks the cord—one hard rip—and the engine catches. She engages the gear lever right away and drives away from me, on the gravel at first, then back on the road.

◇ ◇ ◇

I go back inside the trailer, shower, then stand wrapped in a towel in front of the tiny bathroom mirror. There are three light bruises up my left side along my ribs. In the middle of my chest, there's a big bruise, purple-dark and fist-sized. I touch it and wince. Breathe deep like I've gotta make sure I *can* still breathe deep.

I step out of the bathroom, put my jeans on and a new T-shirt. Socks and boots. JT's asleep in his bed. I check the wall, and the crank is still there. I make myself a couple of pieces of toast, throw those on the counter to cool, and stuff my backpack with schoolbooks.

I eat the toast over the sink and drink some milk from the carton. Then I go into the bathroom, brush my teeth, and come back out. Grab my coat, my backpack, and slide out the door.

As I'm about to get into my truck, Rowan walks up. "Hey, handsome," she says. One of her sweatshirt sleeves is torn to the elbow. The thick cotton hangs in strips like a wound. Rowan looks as though she's been awake all night, dark circles under her eyes.

I feel a little like she looks. I keep thinking about what Mrs. Trepp said to me. But there's nothing to do about it. I look at Rowan. "Wanna ride to school?"

She shakes her head.

"You comin' for JT then?" I try not to sound disappointed.

"Maybe. Is he home?"

"Yeah."

I don't like this feeling of hoping, of wishing she only came here for me, but I don't know what to say to make things different. I try, though. I say, "Don't go in there. Don't go be with him right now."

Rowan laughs but it's not a happy laugh. She takes my hand, and her hand is shaky. She looks down at the ground. "I never know what to do. It's not like things are simple for me."

"Just go to school with me. We can get in the truck and go to our classes and all that."

Rowan shakes her head. Looks straight at me now. She doesn't have any mascara on today, no Egyptian eyeliner, and her eyes look too real. "Little," she says, "I'm not going to school today. I'll go anywhere with you but not to school."

"Anywhere?"

"Or actually," she says, "I have an idea."

I don't know where we're going when we start walking through the graveyard, but then we hit the small trail after, stepping through the overgrown blackberries, and we come into the meadow of poison oak, the open area before the Livingston place.

We step up onto the porch. Rowan pulls on the plywood next to the front door, and it comes away from the wall. She reaches behind the board and retrieves a brass key. Then we walk around to the side of the house where the new bolt lock is. Rowan slides the key into the lock, turns it, and pops the door open. We walk in and I notice footprints. I say, "Maybe this is a bad idea. Someone else is coming here, you know."

Rowan points at her feet. "Those are my footprints."

She locks the door behind us. Then I follow her into the living room.

She makes a fire in the fireplace. At first it smokes up the whole room, billowing white, and we both start to cough. But then the flue heats and the fire draws. I pile more wood on and the room starts to warm up.

There's garbage on the floor, old garbage, ancient cans, newspapers, wadded-up toilet paper, and plastic bags. Someone first squatted in this house a long time ago, and there's an old mattress behind the couch from whenever that was, two black rings of mold in the lower right corner of the mattress.

Rowan lays down. There's a brown army blanket to the side of the mattress, not thick, but wool. Rowan says, "Come here. Keep me warm."

I lay down with her.

She slides over and rests her head on my chest, and I'm thankful she doesn't put her head right on the bruise. She's next to it. I put my arm around her. She pulls the blanket over both of us, and I think of Zaylie and get that weird feeling in my stomach again. Wonder how this moment could be so similar to the one in Zaylie's bed.

Rowan feels thinner than she's ever felt before, and I wonder if she's been eating at all. I say, "Are you okay, Rowan?"

"Maybe not," she says. "I don't know."

"What's going on? What've you been doing lately?"

"Staying where I can. Keeping warm. Eating what I can find. Staying far away from my daddy. You know, those kinds of things."

I say, "You can stay with us. You can stay in our trailer anytime."

Rowan laughs like a tree coming apart in a storm. She says, "So I should be with you and JT both, maybe add to my dysfunction?"

"No, it's just that . . ."

Rowan shakes her head a little. Because she's laying on my chest, I can't see her eyes. "You two . . . ," she says. "You're as train-wrecked as I am."

The fire is burning steady in the fireplace. The room is warm now, and I push the blanket down. I want to say "I'm worried about you, Rowan" but I don't have to. She already knows that. And maybe she's right too, maybe I should be worried about myself.

We don't talk now. Rowan breathes deeper. I can feel her chest expanding and contracting as she falls asleep on me even though it's still morning, and I lay there for a while thinking about me and JT growing up.

It was lightning that night, and the flashes came across the mountains blue and yellow, the thunderclaps like a mallet against riveted metal. I guess every kid remembers a lightning-storm night in childhood, where the world is an electrocutioner, and every few minutes, the sky issues another death sentence.

JT and I were out in the graveyard because JT told me, "Sometimes you gotta see a thing from where it really is, you know?"

I didn't understand what he was talking about, and I wanted to be back in the trailer. I pulled my wool hat low over my ears, kept the corners of the blanket tight at my collar, the wool blanket over my shoulders and JT's hand-me-down jacket zipped tight.

JT was nine and I was six, and I would've fist-fought the devil to be like him. He grew his hair long in the back, so I did too. He rolled his jeans two inches at the bottom, so I did as well. He always put his hands on his hips and spit hard while looking west at incoming weather, so I stood at the fence sometimes and practiced that. Or since he did push-ups all the time, I did too even though my first-grade shoulders shook and my knees wobbled and I never could get more than five or six push-ups at a time.

JT snuck a cigarette too sometimes from Uncle Lucky or Derlene, not often but sometimes, and I watched the way he held it in the corner of his mouth, just sitting between his lips, so I played pretend when I was alone, used anything I had, a maple twig in the corner of my mouth, a rolled-up piece of paper—or a three-inch hot-dipped galvanized nail.

JT had a cigarette now, and he was trying to light it under the cover of a tree in the middle of a grave plot, but the wind kept ripping at the lighter, putting the flame out before he could suck enough fire.

A forked bolt of lightning flashed over the hill to the north, the tines so bright I closed my eyes until the thunder followed, and I ducked back against the trunk of the tree, hoping we'd go back inside soon.

JT somehow got his cigarette to light and he puffed a little smoke. "See this storm?" he said.

I nodded.

"It's the way God starts a fire when he wants one."

"You think?"

JT laughed. "Shit. I don't know. That just sounded good in my head." JT had learned to swear that year, and I could hear the grown-up man in him whenever he did it.

Lately, I'd been practicing cusswords when JT wasn't around, and I was hoping for an opportunity to impress him by saying a cussword just right. Sometimes, on the playground at school during recess, I'd swing on the swings for a while and say "Shit" at each downswing, "Shit . . . shit . . . shit . . ."

just when I pumped my legs. I wouldn't say it loud because I didn't want to get caught by the recess duty lady, but I'd say it quiet and hard like I was mad about something important.

The lightning kept flashing and I looked at JT as he puffed his cigarette. I said, "Do you ever think it's creepy that we're in a graveyard so much? That we live next to one?"

"Creepy?" JT puffed smoke into the air in front of his face. He never sucked the smoke down the way I saw Derlene or Uncle Lucky do, like they were hungry for it. JT more puffed at it, made the smoke come up in the air around his head. "No," he said. "It isn't creepy. Creepy means you're scared, and I'm not afraid of anything. I never have been. That's a fact."

I looked at his face and I knew I couldn't tell him that I was scared sometimes, that I thought about all those bodies out there beyond our trailer under the trees and the shadows of the gravestones, that sometimes I pictured what each body looked like in its coffin, saw the bullet holes in their faces or the strangle marks around their necks, that I imagined every single one of them was murdered.

There was a lot I would never tell JT. That night was maybe the first time I realized it.

The lightning kept bursting bluish white and there wasn't much rain with it. The storm was a strange one, all that lightning close but not much wet to follow. Dry flashes breaking up the west.

"Hey," I said. "Can I try a puff of your cigarette?"

JT grinned. Took the cigarette out of his mouth. It was mostly gone now, almost burned to the filter, and he looked at it. "Here," he said, "this is how you hold it," and he showed me. Then he handed it over, and I puffed until the filter singed.

just about time

Wednesday morning, just outside of town—as I'm driving to school—I pass a pullout and see the deputy's cruiser. I let off the gas and look at the car, but I can't see the deputy's face through the windshield because of the angle of the morning light. The deputy doesn't pull out, and I keep driving.

A mile down the road, I come off a turn into a straight-away, and there he is, driving up quick from behind me. The deputy settles in off my bumper, doesn't flick his lights, so I keep driving, watching his cruiser in the mirror, checking my speed even though I know that's not why he's following me.

We drive through the turns. Past the shacks. The farm with the old John Deeres lined up alongside the road. The Mobilgas sign on the lean-to. Drive up on the creek.

Just before school, I slow the truck, flick on my blinker, and turn into the drive to the parking lot. The deputy slows too, and I look over my shoulder to see what he'll do.

He turns his cruiser in, stops it, and waits.

I drive to a parking spot, whip the truck around into the space, and look back at the cruiser. It's idling at the start of the school's drive, pulled over to the right. I can see the outline of the deputy inside the car, but not his face, not him looking at me. The weak fall sunlight reflects off his windshield, and I stare until the sun comes out from behind a cloud and the glare gets too bright off the glass.

I look at my books and consider going into school, but I know I have to wait and see what the deputy does.

A few cars pull into the drive and pass him coming up. I watch each of those cars slow, the drivers staring, wondering what the deputy's doing at school.

After a couple of minutes, I see the cruiser start to roll forward, toward me, but the deputy pulls a slow U-turn and goes out to the highway. The cruiser's left blinker comes on, and I watch as the deputy drives back the way he came, back north, up the Idaho 11, driving until he's out of sight.

I think about the deputy all day as I sit in class. Wonder when he's going to pick me up. He could take me into Orofino any-time he wants to now, any day, and I know I'm only waiting for that day to come. There's nothing I can do about it.

country boy

After school, when I drive up to the trailer, I see JT across the street in the ballfield's grass. I walk over there. See he's filming his recruiting video. He has a cell phone propped on an old milk crate, an unopened beer bottle upright behind the phone to hold it vertical.

He does a set of jump-lunges, then cone drills. He taps his phone to stop the video. Looks at me. Says, "I can edit this later. Coach says I can use the football team's computer."

"He still love you?"

"Always," JT says.

And it's true. I don't know if I've ever seen a coach love a player more. Coach would put his arm over JT's shoulders after every single game, win or lose, all through high school. Coach would laugh and talk into his ear while JT held his helmet, the eye-black sweat-smeared down his cheeks, and he'd listen and nod as if he was listening to a preacher run a sermon. The rest of the team would wander off the field with the assistant coaches, and it'd just be Coach and JT talking, walking slow down the sideline, no hurry to get to the locker room.

JT says, "If I hit Record again, can you throw me the ball just as I come out of my cut?"

"JT, you know I'm not the best QB."

"That's fine," he says. "I'll adjust to the ball wherever it is. I'm just showing that I still have coordination, hand-eye. The rest of the video will be game highlights from high school so they'll see real footage too."

"Okay," I say.

JT starts his phone again, and I get next to the four footballs he's set in front of the cone set.

"So," he says, "just throw it on a line right as I get to the last cone. I'll turn and catch it coming back."

"Okay," I say again, but my first throw is way over his head and my second throw is out of the box completely. My third goes short. "All right," I say, "sorry about those." We collect the first three balls and start over.

Then I start throwing better because I'm a little warmed up and none of the throws are really long or difficult anyway. JT is able to adjust to wherever the ball is thrown as long as I put it between the cones, and he does look like he can still play. Even though I've seen him with a football my whole life, somehow I'm surprised that he doesn't look rustier.

After 20 reps, JT says, "That's good enough. I'll edit it down to five or six and add those in." He picks the cell phone up and watches the footage, nodding a little. Then he pops the cap off the beer bottle and takes a drink.

"Workout beer again?"

"Just one today. See? I'm cutting back and getting in shape." JT smiles. Swigs the beer.

I spin a football in my hands. Grip the leather and put my fingers over the laces.

JT says, "Are you gonna play football again next year or what?"

"No, I didn't really like it."

"But you have talent. You were on varsity right away."

I shake my head. "It's not what I want."

"Then what are you gonna do?"

"What do you mean?"

"I mean, what's your plan? Maybe the basketball team? You're tall and strong enough. You could do it."

"You kidding?" I laugh. "I'm horrible on a basketball court. Tiny people doing their fancy little dribbling things and I crash around fouling everyone. Remember when I played in seventh grade?"

"Yeah, so what are you gonna do then?" JT kills his beer and tosses the bottle over the fence.

I shake my head. "I don't know."

"Well, what do you like?"

"In sports?"

"Fuck it." JT picks up two of his cones. "In anything."

"Well, I like to fish or hunt. Or I guess just be outside all day."

JT picks up the rest of his cones. Retrieves the footballs from the outfield grass. "So what, are you gonna become a guide then?"

"Yeah," I say, "I've been thinking about it. I have Big's boat and his truck too. A donkey to pack loads. All this country around me."

tall man again

Thursday afternoon, in town, I see him get out of a Century-Link truck. He's tall, with wide shoulders, light brown skin, and black hair slicked back with pomade. I pull my truck over. Watch him walk into Studio 205 with a modem and wiring in his hands. I park behind his truck. Turn my ignition key to off. Get out and wait at the railing of the Flame Bar.

He comes back outside a few minutes later. Opens the passenger door on his truck and throws a wire on the seat.

I try to think of Spanish phrases I've been practicing but I can't come up with any. I take a step toward him. Say, "Hey, can I talk to you?"

He hesitates. Looks around to see if there's anyone with me. "What?"

He's big, but not as big as me. A little shorter. Not quite as thick. I wonder how much he weighs. I say, "I don't mean to bother you, but are you Jésus Gómez?"

"Jésus Gómez?"

"Yeah."

He raises his eyebrows. Then spits on the ground.

Grinds the spit with the toe of his work boot. "Are you fucking with me?"

"No."

"No? So this is for real then?" He doesn't have an accent. None at all.

"I just thought . . ."

He looks at me. Takes a big breath and shakes his head. "So let me get this straight. You see a Hispanic-looking guy, and you think, *That's gotta be the one guy I know?*"

"I don't know him."

"No, see, that's not the point."

"I'm just looking for him."

"Right, well . . . good luck with that." He reaches into his truck and pulls out a clipboard and a pen.

I say, "I know this is, uh . . . whatever this is, but is there any chance you know him or where he is now?"

"Know him?"

"Yeah. Jésus Gómez."

He taps his pen against his clipboard. "You might wanna come up with a better plan for this. You know?" He smiles. Shakes his head. "But I gotta get back to work. Gotta bill the customer and all that. Keep my job and make some money, right?"

I watch him go into the building again. I stand there and try to decide what to do, but there isn't anything to do. I walk back to my truck. Get in and sit there for a minute.

When I turn the key and fire it up, one of my Spanish tapes comes on loud. But I turn it off.

we are the shepherds

At school on Friday, I go into Mr. Polchowski's room, find him working at his desk. "Little?" he says, and looks up from his paperwork. There are five thick piles of papers of all colors on his desk. For a moment I imagine his job, copying and grading and computer programs and meetings, keeping everything organized and helping kids to remember things, and wonder how he does it. That's not something I would ever want to do.

I say, "I'm just here to say sorry about this semester."

Mr. Polchowski slides his chair back and turns to me. Puts his hands on his knees.

I say, "I know I've been a bad student, messed up attendance and all that. Plus the suspension. And I know you were trying to help me."

"Okay." He sets his pencil down. Redoes his ponytail, then stretches his arms back behind his head. "Thank you for that."

"Yeah, I just figured that was all there was left to say." I start to leave.

"Hold on, Little. You know it might be too late in the

term for *certain* classes, but not in general. You're only a sophomore. There's lots of time to fix things up before graduation."

I nod when he says that. I know Mr. Polchowski really cares about things like graduation, and I feel bad since I don't care as much. I don't know if I should tell him that high school might not be my thing, that I'm thinking about becoming a fishing and hunting guide. Maybe building a cabin on that land if I can ever buy it.

Mr. Polchowski says, "And if we look at your grades online, you probably have a class or two you can still pass this term, if I talk to the teachers about it. And definitely art class, right?"

"True. Probably art class. I guess I should keep going to that."

Mr. Polchowski picks up his pencil and taps it on the nearest stack of papers. "But the thing is," he says, "you'd have to come to school from now on. Every single day. Attendance is everything right now. So could you do that?"

"Yeah, I could."

Mr. Polchowski stops tapping his pencil. Turns one way to crack his back, then the other. Stops and looks at me. "I know you're going through a lot right now. I know you're dealing with more than most kids."

I nod. "Thank you either way, right?"

"Either way?"

"If I graduate or not. 'Cause to tell you the truth, there are a lot of, well . . . it's just that there are so many things going on for me, you know? I might not make it. But you've always been nice to me, and I see that. So thank you."

Mr. Polchowski shakes his head. "Sounds like you're about to leave town or something."

"No," I say. "I'm not leaving town. I'm staying. I decided that."

As I walk out of the school building to my truck, I remember the joke Willa told me a few days ago. We were talking about school, and I was saying she had to go every day, even if she never liked it.

Willa made a face and smiled at me as if I was a little bit stupid, like I was a small child who didn't understand the real world. She said, "Wanna hear a school joke, Little?"

"Okay," I said.

We were eating, and Willa finished her bite and set her fork down on her plate. Then she said, "Here's the joke: The teacher says to the student, 'You *missed* school yesterday.' And you know what the student says back to her?"

"What?"

"The student says, 'No, ma'am. Not really.'" Willa looked at me and giggled, tilted her plate, and some of her venison fell off onto the floor.

guess things happen that way

When I was little, real little, the youngest I remember, I would get up from bed late at night and walk out into the living room. This was when I was still living in the big house, before me and JT moved out into the trailer by ourselves when we got older.

The TV would be on, funny shows. I don't remember the names of the shows but I remember the background laughter. Someone on the screen would say something, then hundreds of people would laugh all together, at the exact same time.

I would crawl up onto the couch, find Derlene's lap. Sit in the bright blue shine of the television screen.

The first couple of years Derlene would be drinking beer, the sound of her can tilting next to my head. The back-arching pose of finishing a can. The crack sound of a new one opening. She kept the six-pack next to her and didn't mind them getting warm.

Then, one night, as I crawled into her lap, I realized that there wasn't enough room for me, that she was carrying too much weight in her stomach. I said, "Aunt Derlene, are you getting fat?" I was too young to know what I shouldn't say.

She wasn't drinking beer that night, and I guess she hadn't been for a while. But I didn't put anything together, didn't make any connections.

"Uncle Lucky got jealous," she said, "jealous of me spendin' time with a kid that wasn't his. So he seeded me up."

money

I'm walking back from the graveyard, see Rowan at the last cemetery plot, leaning on a tall oak stump. She's chopped her torn sweatshirt sleeve, so it's elbow length on one arm. She has the hood of her sweatshirt up.

I come and lean on the stump next to her. Set my work gloves on the flat.

Rowan turns to me. She has a split on the bridge of her nose. Swelling there.

"Hey," I say.

She smiles. "I got something for you."

"But are you okay?"

"It's right here," she says.

"What is?"

She smiles and reaches into the pocket of her sweatshirt. Pulls out a fat envelope. Hands it to me.

"What's this?" I open it and see 20-dollar bills, a lot of them. A stack an inch and a half thick. "What did you do?"

Rowan laughs. "I flipped things. That's something I can do. I flipped 'em twice."

"Crank? And what else?"

"Doesn't matter," she says. "Product. Cash is cash. Untraceable. So you don't worry about it."

I hold that thick stack of bills in my hand. "But I'm worried about you."

Rowan puts her hand on my hand. "It doesn't matter, really. Nothing matters now. But there's more than $6,000 right there. And that's real. You can buy your place now."

"How'd you even know about that?"

"Shhh," she says. "Sometimes people just need a little help before it's too late. Sometimes they need someone to step in and do something for them."

I look at all that money. "I can't take this from you. You should do something with this yourself."

"I don't want to now."

"But you could do something with this money."

"I am doing something," she says. "I'm giving it to you."

"No, you could . . . I don't know. Go to Lewiston? Spokane? Somewhere new. Get a job and start over."

Rowan shakes her head. "I don't know what I would do. I don't have any idea." She squeezes my hand. "But you do. You should buy that place and build your cabin. Start your guiding business. Make your life."

"I'm only 16 years old. You really think people will take me seriously?"

"If you take yourself seriously, then other people will. Right?"

I try to hand the envelope back one more time, but Rowan won't take it. "That's yours now," she says. "It's not mine." She lets go of my hand and turns around. "Oh, and if anyone asks you where you got it, say it was from Big. That was Big's money."

"Was it really?"

"Maybe," she says. She stands up. Taps the bark on the stump with her fist. "That's sort of true. At least from his connections." She points at the envelope. "I worked for Big all last summer."

"You did? What'd you do for Big?"

Rowan taps the bark once more, then starts to walk away. Turns and takes a few steps backward as she says, "I did anything that had to be done."

six years before that night

Once—years before JT and I ever visited the site, when I was still in grade school—you told me the whole story about my mom's crash. We were outside the Flame Bar. You were smoking a cigarette, holding a bottle of Budweiser, leaning against the porch rail.

You said they found her in three parts—her body, her head, and her right arm last. You said, "That arm was a hundred feet from the frame of the car, sticking up like it was waving to everyone. Just that arm all by itself in the middle of the forest." You took a long drag on your cigarette, and the end of it shined bright red against the dark of the sky. "Kinda creepy to find it like that." You shook your head and exhaled smoke.

I tried to picture her arm the way you told me. Her hand in the air. But I never knew what either of her hands looked like.

You told me something else too.

You said that our daddy not being here all during our

growing up was something good, a gift, that JT and me would've never wanted him, that he would've never been any good to us. You told me that over and over.

And I believed you because I was young.

a new life

I go out to the property, nothing on that land, no improvements. But it's level land and there's Forest Service road access. Well depth in this area is only ten feet, and it's five acres of treed country backing to National Forest. Lodgepole pine, a few western hemlock, and larch. Good cabin wood.

The sign says: $5,000 cash, and I have that now. I brought it with me even to look. Didn't want to leave it anywhere where it could be found.

Since the mill closed and half the houses in town are abandoned or for sale, there's no competition with buying anything around here, and I heard that a couple from Boise just bought the house next to our trailer for only $17,000, but I'm still worried. I want to buy this quick before I lose it somehow.

I write the phone number from the real estate sign on the piece of paper I brought. Then I write down all the other info even though I've read it ten times before and I wouldn't forget anyway.

I fold the scratch paper and put it in my jeans pocket, stuff it to the bottom where it won't fall out.

city jail, out of jail

JT and I are out by the donkey pen. JT sucks a joint the size of his thumb. Holds his smoke and hands the joint to me. Exhales. "I think I know."

"You do?"

"And I don't blame you."

I duck a little, curl in, ready to take a punch. "You don't blame me?"

"No," JT says. "He had it coming."

He, not *she*. JT's not talking about me and Rowan. So I'm confused. I don't know what he's talking about. I say, "He, uh . . ." I try to figure it out. I'm holding the joint, not smoking, just holding it, a thin wisp of smoke is curling out the lit end.

JT points and says, "Hit it or quit it, son."

I don't hit it. I hand the joint back to him. Say, "No thanks. But wait, you know something about . . . ?"

"Yeah," he says. "I figured it." JT looks at me for a long time, and then I know what he's talking about. It clicks for me.

I say, "But I didn't talk to you about it. I never said anything."

JT puffs the joint. "That doesn't matter," he says. "Sometimes brothers are more than words, you know what I'm saying?"

"Yeah, I guess that's sometimes true."

JT has the joint between index finger and thumb. He points at the donkey with his other three fingers. "Pack mule," he says.

"The donkey?"

"Yep. He'll be part of your guiding business." JT tries to hand the joint back to me.

I wave it off. Say, "Do you wanna know how it happened?" I wasn't sure until this moment that I'd ever tell anyone, not what really happened. I watch the joint smoke and wait for JT to say yes.

But he says, "No. I don't wanna know."

"You don't?"

JT inhales but gets nothing. He taps the joint and tries again. Then he pulls his lighter out of his pocket and relights it. Shakes his head. "No," he says. "I know you did what you had to do, and that's good enough for me. So don't tell me anything."

"All right."

"And one more thing," he says. "If it comes to it, I'll take it." JT tips his head back and smokes while staring at the sky.

"You'll what?"

"Take it," he says. "I could."

"You mean . . ."

JT nods, blows smoke.

"You can't do that."

"But I will," he says. "I could take it, and I could do the time no problem. That's something I know about myself. It's the same life for me, inside or out. I don't know why." He takes a drag off the joint, holds his lips together until his face turns red. Then he bares his teeth without opening his mouth, just peels his lips back and exhales through his closed teeth like he's keeping a forest fire in his mouth. When all the smoke is gone, he looks at me and smiles. Makes a little clicking noise in the back of his throat. "It's better out," he says, "better out than in. But still the same life."

You were the North Fork of the Clearwater, the rapids and the runs. The pools of aqua water and the dark shelves at the undercuts. You were the currents and the boulders the water broke against, turned white, boiled up and changed direction, pushing at a drift boat, sucking at the flat and spinning us. You were the wet slicks and the dry tops of moss. The clean chute and the hidden strainer.

We listened to your stories and laughed until our stomachs hurt.

We ducked your fists and hid from you, waited until you stumbled to pass out, your face against the earth and your mouth open like someone screaming at God.

gone girl

I drive Willa's ATV down to Sammy's Grocery. Park and see Rowan sitting against the wall next to the ice cooler.

I say, "Good. I was hoping to see you. I needed to talk to you."

She nods and stands up. Pulls my sleeve and we walk along the side of the building, around to the back of the store. Rowan leans against the cinder block wall like she's out of breath.

I say, "Are you okay? You don't look okay."

Rowan shrugs. The circles under her eyes are darker than I've ever seen them. That bruise across the bridge of her nose is settling, small lines of yellow coming down off each side.

I step close to Rowan, take her hand and it's so cold. "Rowan . . ."

She's shaky. Her hand vibrates like a yellow jacket caught in a jar.

I say, "I'm worried about you. You gotta take care of yourself."

She doesn't have any eyeliner on. She doesn't look like the Rowan I used to know. She says, "What does that mean?"

"I mean, come stay with us. Come stay with me."

She leans her forehead against my chest. Puts her arms around my waist. "You know as well as I do that living with both of you would be too crazy."

I wrap my arms around her, hold her, her body thinning more every day. I say, "At least let me feed you sometimes. I've got a deer for this winter. Willa and I always get cheese and bread from the stamps. Plus there's eggs. I could feed you anytime. Every day really."

Rowan nods but doesn't say anything, and after a minute I realize she's crying.

I say, "You can't stay at your dad's house anymore. Look at you." I tilt her face up so I can see her. Wipe her eyes with my shirtsleeve. I lean to kiss her, but she closes her eyes and drops her head. I kiss her forehead. "You can't stay there, you hear me? You can't go there anymore."

"I know," she says. "I mostly stay away now."

"No, not mostly." I touch the bruise on the bridge of her nose. "You've got to always stay away from there."

"I know," she says. "I really do. But . . ."

"But what? He beat you up pretty bad. Other things too, right?"

She whispers, "Yeah," so quiet that I can barely hear.

"I think I have a pretty good idea, so you can tell me about it. You can talk to me."

"Not now. I can't. I have to go."

"Why?" I look at the wall, the peeling paint, two layers of gray and one of beige. "Go where?"

She backs up, and I let go of her.

"Please," I say. "Just walk back with me now. Eat some

food with me at the trailer. Just do that before you do whatever else. Let me take care of you."

"No," she says. "It really doesn't matter anymore. None of it. Plus, JT's probably home. And if he's home, well . . ." She takes a few steps along the wall. "Maybe I'll see you?"

"When?"

She looks at me. She says, "Thank you for always being so sweet to me."

I'm standing where I'm standing, my feet set like if I stay here, stay right where I am just now, she'll come back to me. "Please, Rowan."

"No, I mean it. Thank you for always being so sweet to me. You always have been." Rowan is at the corner. "But I gotta go now." She starts to walk around the corner, then stops and looks at me again. "Hey, remember when you called me a fish?" She makes the hand motion in the air.

"I didn't call you a fish. I said you smelled like water."

"Fish," she says, and wipes a tear away with her sleeve. Then she smiles and turns the corner. Disappears.

I call her name, but she doesn't come back.

goin' down the road

JT has a plate over the cast iron skillet when I get home. He picks up a spatula, and I realize he cooked something for us. I haven't had him cook for me in so long that I can't remember the last time. He says, "I made us some eggs. Had to buy them now that all the chickens are gone."

"Aren't there any left?"

"Nope. There's none. Layers, that is. There's that banty rooster. But I found the last two hens dead a few days ago. Killed by something."

"Shit." I throw my backpack down by the kitchenette table.

JT dishes us plates.

"Thanks," I say, "but why'd you cook for us?"

"To celebrate," he says, "a weird day."

I sit down. Scoot my chair in. "Yeah?"

He points at himself with the spatula. "I got an offer."

"A football offer?"

"No, a volleyball offer." He laughs. "Fuck yeah, a football offer. What else?"

"An offer from where?"

JT sits down. Trades his spatula for a fork and lifts eggs into his mouth. "Idaho," he says. "University of Idaho. They came back." He shakes his head.

"The Vandals? Really?"

"No joke."

I take a bite of eggs, too salty but still pretty good. "When?"

"I sent them my video, added in that new workout sequence with plyos, and they called me today."

"How'd they call? We don't even have a phone."

"They called the big house and Uncle Lucky came out to get me. Said I owed him one."

"Forget him. What'd they say?"

"Well, it was the DBs coach, and he said he remembered watching me play senior year. Said he knew I'd made some bad choices in the last year and a half, but if I wanted another chance, they had a safety drop out of the program this fall. The head coach said he could take a chance on somebody."

"So that's you?"

"Right. I'm the chance he's taking."

"And that's it?"

"Well, I gotta go work out for them next week. And if that goes well . . ." JT forks another big bite of eggs into his mouth, chews, and smiles.

I shake my head.

"Right, I know?"

"That's just weird. The Vandals, huh?"

JT pushes eggs onto his fork with his thumb. Puts a big bite into his mouth. Says, "I'm gonna take that spot, and I'm fuckin' happy about it. They aren't Boise State, and I'm not pretending that they are, but they're close. And maybe they'll play up against Boise State sometime. And if I got to beat the Broncos, that'd be good too."

Just then, I realize that JT isn't drinking beer. Not even a single can. He has a glass of water in front of him. I point at it. "You trying out new things there?"

"Shit." He smiles. "I always drank a ton of water. Just also drank a ton of other shit too."

"Fair enough."

JT finishes his plate of eggs. "I can't wait to tell Rowan. She won't believe it." He starts to clear his plate, but he hesitates. "The thing is, I haven't seen her much lately. You know where she's been at?"

"No," I say. I eat my eggs and don't look him in the eye. "And seems like every time I have seen her, she hasn't looked too good."

JT turns when I say that. Holds the frying pan over the table, at my eye level. Looks at me while I eat. "Yeah," he says, "I've thought about that too. When did you last see her?"

"Oh, not for a while," I say. "I'm not really sure when."

Derlene's on the porch combing nits out of Willa's hair. She has baby oil, Tide detergent, and apple cider vinegar on the step next to her, mixed in a Mountain Dew can. Willa looks cold even in her puffy jacket.

"Lice?" I say.

"Childhood," Derlene says. Pushes the sleeves of her jacket up a little farther. "She's gotta go to school, so I'm just braving the cold and a wicked headache to get 'er done."

Nothing to say to that. I walk to my truck, throw my book bag in. Hop up and turn the key, rev the engine a little, let it run for a minute, then close the door and pop it into gear.

Suddenly Derlene's next to my driver's-side window. I roll it down.

"Something to tell you," Derlene says. "You know that girl that hangs around with you and JT?"

"You mean Rowan?"

"I mean the skinny one that looks real sick lately, or somethin's not good about her."

"Right," I say, "Rowan."

"Okay then. Her. Anyway, I seen that girl go by my house

and come back every day for months. Every *single* day. You get what I mean?"

"Not really."

"Well," she says. "That girl goes up and down, every single day, and that's a normal thing. But . . ." Derlene shakes her head.

"But what?"

"But she ain't now."

"What do you mean 'she ain't'?"

"I mean, she ain't. I seen her go up there, but I ain't seen her come back."

I don't understand.

Derlene says, "If she ain't back, then maybe she's left . . . or maybe she's still up there." She points past the cemetery.

I look in that direction. "Why are you telling me?"

"Observation, that's all."

"But what does that mean?"

"Well, from where I sit," Derlene says, "you seem to care more about that girl than JT, and I'm telling you 'cause of that. So the girl went up thataway, through the cemetery toward the Livingston place yesterday, but she ain't come back. Not at all."

Derlene turns around and walks back up to her porch. Calls over her shoulder, "That's all I gotta say about that."

I put the truck back into park. Turn the key off and get out. I want to ask Derlene more questions, but she kept on going, walked up her steps, past Willa, and into the house.

Willa tilts her head sideways. Says, "What are you gonna do?"

"I guess I'm gonna head up there."

"To the Livingston place? Can I come too?"

"No, you go on to school, Willa. I'll be fine on my own."

I walk past Willa, past the house, past the donkey run and into the graveyard. The first gravestones are newer, stand straight and neatly spaced, but the old ones in the middle tip and slant, their angles changed by the oak tree roots. I walk past all those. Get to the trail and continue heading east, past poison oak nubs, blackberry snarls, to the opening in front of the Livingston place.

The morning is cold but sunny for late fall, strangely sunny, the sunlight angling through the pine trees outlining this open space. The dew is silver-white in the sunlight, a bright contrast to the house's old green paint, the boarded windows on the one side and the windows smudged dark on the other.

Through a broken window, I still can't see anything, just the living room and no one in it. I step up onto the porch. Say, "Rowan?" Lean my head through the window frame and look around. There's the mattress we slept on, the old fire poker, the shattered bottles, the shreds of magazines, the stovewood.

I pull my head back out of the broken window, walk around the side of the porch, see the back door open, and that worries me. I don't call her name again. I step inside. Quiet now. And I don't hear anything.

I see the cooking setup, the glass jars, pans, hot plates, jugs, baggies, and dips.

The bathroom door is cracked open. I lean to the gap but see nobody. I stop and listen for any noises above, movement on the upper floor, or out in front of me. But there's nothing.

I walk down the hall, past the living room, then there's a room to my right. The door's cracked open, the room mostly dark. There's almost no light sneaking past the boarded-up window, and as I come into the room, I don't recognize what I'm seeing at first. Something in the air. Something in the middle of the room. I step forward.

There's a gap at the corner of the boarded window, one small beam of light shining into the room. My eyes adjust.

Someone still. Hanging from the ceiling. I stand inside the room and try to make the person out. But I know. Just from the shape of her in that half-light. I know. Her thinness. Then I reach out, feel the edge of the torn sweatshirt sleeve.

My stomach turns over and I lurch. Gravity goes different. I step back and forth, trying to gain a straight footing as the world pulls me side to side. I bend over, breathe into my hands for a minute, then stand back up straight again. Go to the window and pry the board. Let light in.

There—in the middle of the room—she is. Hanging. Binder twine run around an exposed ceiling beam, and under her feet a block of stovewood tipped sideways, not far below the big boots she always wears, shoelaces undone, the tips of the laces touching the floor as if she just wasn't tall enough to fill the room ceiling to floor. The room is quiet, the dust particles sifting through the air like a golden ghost.

I walk up to Rowan. Look at her hanging, not spinning or turning, just still. The angle that her head is tilted at. Her loose hands. Her whole body slack. I've never seen her so relaxed, and I can't take my eyes off her. Her body is so thin that I know once again how little she's been eating the past month.

I take one of Rowan's hands. Look at her face, her lips slack and blue. I remember what we talked about the last time we were together in this house, what she said when we woke up on that mattress in the living room.

"How do you eat, Rowan?"

"Eat?" she said.

"Where do you get your food?"

She giggled. "I steal it. Always."

"From the store?"

"From anywhere." She tapped her fingers once. Twice on my chest. "I get it from everywhere."

"Like houses too?"

"Yeah," she said. "Even Derlene and Lucky's. Even your trailer."

"You steal from me?"

She said, "There isn't anyone I don't steal from."

She was tapping her fingers on my chest. I put my hand over her hand. Stopped her tapping. Said, "What did you steal from me? I never saw you take anything. Never saw a single thing missing either."

She laughed. She'd been looking at the ceiling, but now she turned toward me. She had one leg draped over my legs. She was warm against me. All alone like that, together, and no one could walk in on us. I don't know if I'd ever felt more content.

"More than food from you," Rowan said. "You and I both know exactly what I stole."

love

Standing in the cemetery, not working, not walking through, just standing. As I get older, I wonder if life becomes an accumulation of bodies, people we used to know, people around us we didn't know well.

These are the people I wonder about now. Where they are. What it's like.

I imagine the pieces of my mother put back together. Every piece found, the bones turned back to the correct lines and angles. Limbs together. The shattered pieces no longer too shattered.

Or you, driving a '69 Camaro somewhere, easing over a road at night.

Or the spirit that always was my father, no face at all.

And now Rowan. I see her hanging in the middle of that room every time I close my eyes, the dust motes spiraling around her, me sitting on the floor until I finally get up and walk back to the house to call 911.

I don't sleep through my nights, and in the morning my eyes feel like they've been raked by the shreds of a torn beer can.

I'm wearing JT's orange hunting jacket, and I slip my hands into the pockets, find a small baggie left by Rowan or JT. I take the baggie up to the Baptist church. Sit and lean against the outside wall. Pour some of the powder onto the back of my hand and snort it.

It feels like glass in my nostrils. My vision flashes yellow, and the light blinks at me. I sit there and watch the green increase. The needles of the pine trees sharpen. The daylight glittering its angles.

"Little?" It's Willa's voice. She's in the pine tree next to the fence, only 30 feet away from me on a branch, but I didn't see her hidden in the tree until now. I set the baggie on the ground, slide it under my leg.

"Yeah?"

"Are you okay?" she says. "You haven't seemed okay for a while now."

"I'm okay."

"Have you been . . ."

I breathe deep. Gulp blank air. My eyelids twitch.

Willa watches me from that branch, her one hand on the trunk of the tree, her legs dangling but still. She says, "You haven't been going to school or anything, have you?"

"No."

"But are you gonna go back?"

"Maybe," I say. "Maybe I should."

Willa climbs down from the tree. Slides through the wire fence gap. Walks the few feet up the hill to where I'm sitting.

She reaches out and touches my hair. It's the same way a person might touch an old person, a real old person right before he dies. Willa touches my hair and says, "You're the best person I got. You know that?"

"Thanks," I say.

"I love you," she says.

The blood is surging in the front of my brain. "I love you too, Willa."

silent night

I look for JT but don't find him. He's nowhere in town and he hasn't been coming back to the trailer at night. I check the Flame Bar. The Vug. The Blue Moose. The baseball diamond dugouts.

I don't find him for two days, but once I stop looking, there he is. He's in the east end of the cemetery, not far from the path to the Livingston place, and I wonder if he's been out there, wonder if he's been in that room too. He's leaning against a low oak, a plastic-bottle fifth of HRD Vodka in his hand. He looks up at me and blinks. Slow. Smiles, then hawks a loogie and spits it into the stubble.

I'm carrying my 10/22, walking to shoot at anything.

JT says, "There never would be a fuckin' funeral, huh?"

I stand above him. Release the clip into my hand. Clear the rifle's chamber and catch the cartridge as it ejects.

JT takes a swig from the bottle, and I see it's half gone. He wipes his mouth on his wrist. "Rowan's dad got her, you know? They took her there."

"There?" I shake my head.

"Her body," JT says. "To Weippe. And I guess I'll just fuckin' kill him." He holds the bottle out to me.

I take it. Gulp a swig, the liquor more like a chemical than a drink, and that seems right. I hold the vodka in my mouth, breathe once before swallowing. Hand it back.

JT puts the bottle to his lips, then tilts it. Sucks his teeth and says, "It's just . . ."

I slide down across from him and the oak tree. Sit back against a 1907 gravestone that says TURNER. Lay my rifle across my lap. "Yeah," I say. "It's fucked up."

JT raises his eyebrows. He leans forward to hand me the bottle again. I take it and swig another gulp. Swig a third.

JT pulls a clump of grass and looks at it. Says, "I just don't know what I'll do." His tongue is thickening. Mouth loosening.

I look to see if he's crying, but he's staring at the ground and I can't see his eyes. "Nothing to do," I say. "Nothing to change now."

"No." JT wags his finger back and forth. "No, no. There's something. We could kill him."

"Yeah, we could, but what would that do?"

JT leans and holds his hand out for the bottle. I pass it back. He sits against the tree, rocks the bottle in a circular motion, and watches the clear liquid swirl. "Go in today," he says. "Break in and wait for him to come home tonight. Then take him away."

"Away?"

"Just speed the travel to the good Lord. Or in his case, speed it to hell." He swigs the HRD.

"You know we can't do that."

He points at me, the bottle shaking in his hand. "Why the fuck not? Give me one good reason."

"Because you're gonna get out of here. You're gonna go play football next semester and start over. You're gonna leave this place and do something else."

"I don't give a fuck about that now."

"But you do. You've always loved football. So you gotta get out of here and go do that Idaho Vandal thing."

"No," JT says. "We gotta go kill him first. Hide it after, make it seem like something else and all that, but that's our job now. He's a piece of shit, and that's the whole honest-to-God truth. That's why she did it. So we gotta kill him and make up for it."

We walk back to the trailer together, me holding my rifle and JT stumbling along with the bottle in his hand. I walk us down the cemetery lane, through the middle not to trip on any gravestones, across the gravel, and up to the trailer.

JT hands me the bottle and I swig from it, the liquor coming in smoother now that I've started a buzz.

JT says, "Let me switch my clothes, then we can drive."

"No, JT. We really can't go there."

At the door of the trailer, JT turns and grabs my throat, and now he doesn't seem drunk at all. He doesn't blink. His face is so close. "We're going," he says, "and that's fuckin' final." He lets go of my throat. "Get your truck keys."

JT switches into new jeans and a hooded sweatshirt. He grabs two pairs of gloves. Hands me one of them.

I say, "I'm good. I'm not cold."

He says, "It's not for cold. So put those on."

We both put gloves on.

We leave the trailer and get in the truck. JT's holding the HRD bottle between his legs, taking a sip every once in a while. As I drive south onto Highway 11, the rumble of the engine purrs JT to sleep. His head rolls forward. I think about driving past Weippe, continuing on down the Grade, letting JT sleep for a while, cool off, sober up, but part of me feels like he does. Part of me wants what he wants.

Before I can decide what I'm gonna do, JT's head snaps up. "Are we to Weippe yet?"

"No," I say. "A few more miles."

"All right." He nods, and his eyes start to close again.

The road winds through the late fall stubble, the fallow fields and the long grass along the highway, wind-beaten, pale yellow under a late gray sky. We pass a cow-creek slough. A Mobilgas shed from the 1960s. An old John Deere with the green paint peeling. A farmhouse with a wraparound porch that's dropped to rot at the west end where the weather comes heaviest.

I drive us into Weippe. Almost to the split. Think JT's asleep but he says, "We're close now." He points left, and I turn. Drive slow along a row of manufactured double-wides.

He points again, and I go right. "You tell me which one."

JT takes a swig from the bottle. "Don't worry," he says. "I will."

We keep going as the road winds. JT reaches down into the well and pulls out a framing hammer. Sets it across his thigh. "Here," he says, and points out his window at a house

347

that's faded blue. "That's it." He tilts the HRD bottle again, swallows, and stares through the truck windshield.

There's no car in the driveway. Rowan's daddy isn't home. I say, "Should I park down the street?"

JT turns to me and blinks slow, his eyelids heavy. Opens and closes his fingers around that hammer's handle. "Right. Not a bad idea."

I drive to a gravel lot behind a feed store, two blocks down. We get out of the truck. JT's still holding the bottle in one hand, the hammer in the other. He hands me the bottle and I take a big drink. Swallow and cough. Look at JT. He lifts the hammer like he's gonna hit something. "Let's go," he says.

We walk back to the house, step up onto the porch. JT knocks at the front door, but no one answers. We walk around back, and JT tries the sliding door on the porch. It's locked too. JT says, "Check the windows."

I try each one, moving along the house. At the bathroom window halfway down, the window with the cloudy glass, I push up and it doesn't catch. It slides, eases open all the way. "They don't have a dog, right?"

JT shakes his head. "Can you fit through that?"

"No," I say, "but you might. You're smaller than me."

JT steps up next to the window. Hands me the hammer and puts his arms through the opening, one shoulder, then the next. He reaches the counter inside, kicks his feet up, and starts wriggling his middle while he pulls himself in. His feet scissor in the air as he walks his hands down onto the floor. Then he pulls his legs inside and pops up to his feet. "Got it," he says. "I'll unlock the back door, and you meet me there."

I walk back along the house to the sliding glass, and JT appears on the other side, undoing the click lock. He opens the slide. Holds his hand out and I give him the hammer. "Okay," he says, "let's check things out." He flicks on one light, a living room lamp.

I step into the house and look around. There are dirty dishes in the sink. Dirty dishes on the counter. Dirty dishes on the table. Piles of junk mail. Newspaper inserts. Amazon boxes and Styrofoam peanuts. Plastic bags. Clothes crumpled on chairs. Clothes on the ground. Pepsi bottles. PBR cans. DVD cases. CDs. Natty Ice cans. Stained napkins. Stains on the carpet. Video games. Doritos bags. Utility and house bills. Empty pill bottles.

It's the kind of house where you wouldn't know where to sit down if someone said, "Have a seat."

JT is looking at knickknacks on a shelf.

"Anything interesting?"

"No," he says, and knocks a little figurine to the floor on purpose. It doesn't break, so he steps on it and the glass crunches under his boot.

There are two sides of the house. JT points east. Says, "Don't go into that room."

"Why?"

He swigs from his vodka bottle. The vodka's mostly gone now, and I wonder how he's still walking, still talking.

"Just don't," he says. "We'll go in here, though." He points to the other bedroom.

It's Rowan's dad's room. Filthier than the kitchen. Stained bedding, the blinds drawn, a bad smell everywhere. JT flips on a bedside light.

There are nudie magazines on the bed but not the kind of nudie magazines I'd ever want to look at. "Hey, those are . . ."

"Yeah, that's some fucked-up shit."

The girl on the cover looks younger than Willa, halfway wrapped in a blanket. I flip the magazine over—so I won't have to look at that girl anymore—but the back picture is much, much worse. I look away.

"See," JT says, "that's why we're here."

I shake my head.

JT hands me the vodka bottle, only a few ounces left. I tilt the bottle and guzzle it all. Breathe and keep it down. Set the empty down on the bed. There's a TV in front of us, on milk crates, stacks of movies, and a lamp without a lightbulb.

JT says, "We should wait in here. Keep the lights off, huh?" He goes back to the living room. Turns the light off out there, then comes back in and kills the bedside lamp.

I stand where I am and try to adjust to the lack of light. The vodka swims through my bloodstream. I look around but the far side of the room has turned to shapes only, lines and shading, nothing distinct.

JT sits down on the floor and leans back against the foot of the bed. I can't see the hammer, but I picture him holding it across his knees. He says, "I hope that fucker comes home soon."

"Yeah, me too." I sit down next to JT. Lean back against a bedpost. I stare at the dark room, feel the vodka flattening pieces of my brain.

I don't know how long we're sitting there before we fall asleep, but it probably isn't long.

◇ ◇ ◇

I hear a car door slam shut and I open my eyes. It's even darker in the room now. No light at all. I push up to a seated position. Hear JT snoring on the floor next to me. "JT, wake up."

"No," he mumbles. "I'm good."

I shake him harder. "Get up."

He groans. "What are we—"

"We're at Rowan's dad's house. We fell asleep."

"Oh, shit." JT sits up. Sniffs. "Is he home?"

"I don't know. I thought I heard a car door. But maybe not." The clock by the bed reads 3:13. I feel for the bedpost, grab it, and stand up. Realize that I'm still buzzed from the vodka. "Come on. Let's go look."

"Okay," JT groans. "Wait for me."

I find the bedroom door and open it. JT follows me, holding the hammer. The window shades are up, and a distant streetlight shines yellow along the block, yellow seeping into the room. We walk to the living room window, lean against it, stare out at the front yard, and see nothing but an empty driveway. Empty road. No car and no Rowan's daddy coming.

I say, "He never came home at all."

JT rubs his eyes with the knuckles of his gloved hand. Says, "He's a real piece of work. A great guy."

I press my forehead against the window. Feel the cold coming through the glass. "So what should we do?"

JT shakes his head. "Probably time to go home. I've got a hangover ridin' this train."

I look out on the street, the row of manufactured homes. Old cars. Gravel yards. "This is a fucked-up town, huh?"

JT laughs. "Little," he says, "this is a fucked-up life."

I put my hands on the glass. Feel the cold through my gloves. Say, "Not always, though, right?"

"I don't know about that."

"It's not always gonna be like this."

"I hope not." JT takes the hammer and taps it against the glass. I feel the vibrations in my hands, and against my forehead since I'm still leaning against the window. JT taps harder and I can feel how close the glass is to shattering.

I say, "Sometimes I feel like . . ." but I don't know how to explain what I feel.

"I know it," JT says. "I know it."

JT hits the hammer against the glass one more time, harder than before, and the sound it makes is both deep and high-pitched at the same time.

JT says, "I thought a lot about you when I was in jail. I thought a lot about us when we were kids. And I was wishing you had it better."

"But what about you?"

"I'm good," he says. "I'm doing fine."

"You're fine?"

"Well, I've accepted that life is the way it is, and that's all."

"But we gotta hope for more than that, right? I mean, don't we?"

JT cocks that hammer back like he's going to swing it through the glass.

I flinch.

"Do we?" JT says. He looks at me, then back at the

window. He's holding the hammer six inches from the glass. Even in the small light, I can see how strong his forearm is, the rounded lines of his muscles as he holds that hammer in the air.

I say, "Let's go home. You need to start training to play football next year."

"And you?" he says.

I grab the empty vodka bottle, and we walk out the front door. Leave it unlocked. There's no reason not to. There's no one around at that time of night, and we walk down the quiet road without talking. When we get to the truck, I think of something, an idea comes to me. "Wait," I say. "Hold up." I open the passenger-side door and look under the seat. There's one of Big's old flannel shirts under there. One of his red ones. A few of his tools. I find a flashlight and look around. Find two pieces of old mail with his name on it, a water bill and a piece of junk mail.

I grab an armload of stuff and jog back to the house. Go in the front door, walk to the bedroom, flip the light on, find the closet, and open it. There's a lot of junk in there. It's a mess. Clothes piled up, old shoe boxes, more terrible nudie magazines, and full cigarette cartons.

I hide Big's stuff in the back of the closet, underneath a pile of random stuff, then move everything back in place to look like it was before.

I turn the bedroom light off, go back to the front door, lock it from the inside, then head out and pull the door shut behind me. At the road, I jog back down to the truck.

JT's up in the passenger seat, dozing. When I shut the driver's-side door, he lifts his head. "What were you doing back there?"

"Nothing," I say. "Just had to run back in real quick. Finish something."

JT's one foot is hanging out of the car. He pulls that foot in and closes his door. I turn the key, start the truck up, and give it some gas.

On the way home, JT sleeps, his head leaning against the door. I crack my driver's-side window to let in the cold middle-of-the-night air, clean and sharp, breathe deep to stay awake. Fight sleep and fight harder to stay between the lines.

the timber man

I call the deputy's office from the Mini-Mart pay phone. Say, "Ma'am, this is Little."

"Excuse me?" the woman says.

"This is Little McCardell, ma'am, I mean, Gavin McCardell of Pierce, Idaho."

"Gavin McCardell," she repeats, and I can hear her pen scratching on paper. "Of Pierce, you said?"

"Yes, ma'am. And I need to leave a message for Deputy White."

"Oh," she says, "okay." She writes some more. "I can get him a message through dispatch."

"Can you tell him to come up?"

"To Pierce?"

"Yes, ma'am."

"Is it important?"

"Yes, ma'am, for sure. It's real important. He asked me to contact him if I had something."

"Okay then," she says. "And to what address?"

"Oh, he'll know, ma'am. You just tell him I need to say something important, and he'll come right up to my place."

"All righty then . . ." She pauses and I can hear her scratching a little more. "I'll let him know then."

"Thanks," I say, and hang up.

I walk back to my yard and wait. Spend the time hunting eggs, trying to find whatever the last chickens left around. I discover one egg behind a fence post. That's all.

I go inside my trailer and cook that egg, but the deputy knocks on my door before I've had a chance to eat it. I let him in, point to the kitchenette table, and say, "You want an egg?"

"No thanks," he says, and takes off his hat. Sits down.

I slide my egg onto a plate. Salt and pepper over the top. Get a fork from the drying rack and sit down.

The deputy says, "So what's going on?"

I cut my egg with the side of my fork. Let the yolk run out. "The thing is, I heard something."

The deputy uses a finger to spin his hat on the table. "And that was?"

I take a bite of egg. It's runny enough that I can slurp it. I swallow. Say, "I heard that Rowan's daddy—not sure what his name is, but he lives in Weippe—he had something to do with Big. I heard they were into something together." I keep it vague the way JT and I practiced it this morning before he left. I let the deputy jump to his own conclusions.

Deputy White spins his hat in a circle. "You mean the father of the girl who . . . ?" He looks up at me.

I look back down at my egg. "Right," I say, "her daddy."

"And what was it that you heard?"

"I don't know. That's the thing. It wasn't specific, but something. They had a deal go bad maybe? I heard about it up at the Flame Bar. But as soon as I asked questions, nobody wanted to talk anymore."

"And who was it that you heard say this?"

"A guy from Weippe. Middle-aged guy. Pretty tall. Looked like he'd lived hard for a lotta years."

The deputy nods. "And the story was that these two had been partners on something? Something like meth?"

"I don't know what," I say, "but Big and her daddy were in on something, something not good."

The deputy spins his hat on the table again. Breathes in deep, puckers his lips, and breathes out slow. "So maybe a deal went bad, and something happened?"

"Could be."

"And now Big is . . . ?"

I finish my egg. Say, "I don't know. This is just what I heard."

"Right," he says, "but it doesn't seem too good, does it?"

"No." I scrape my plate and lick my fork. Then I stand up and put my plate in the sink. Run water over it. Scritch at the yolk under the running water, then lean down and take a drink from the tap. "Do you know where he lives?" I say. I have my back to the deputy.

"Unfortunately, yes. I had to notify him after his girl . . ."

"Right," I say, "so you know it."

"The thing is, it's tough to get a warrant without some kind of probable cause. And without a body, I don't know . . ."

"You mean Big's body?" I look at the deputy.

He taps his hat with his index finger. "That'd be the body I'm looking for."

"And no warrant without his body?"

"Well," the deputy says, "there ain't a lot of wiggle room. So did you have anything else on him? Anything at all that we could make probable?"

"No." I shake my head. "Nothing else." I put a little dish soap on the sponge. Scrub my plate and fork. Rinse them.

The deputy says, "Think hard now. Nothin' else at all?"

"Well," I say, "actually, I got a question: Is it legal to have pictures of little girls?"

I look at the deputy, and he stops spinning his hat. "What do you mean?"

"I mean, is it *illegal* to have bad pictures of little girls? Maybe buy and sell them?"

"Like naked pictures?"

"Right," I say. I see the magazine covers in my mind again. Shake my head.

"That *is* illegal." The deputy flips his hat and puts it on his head. "Is he into that sort of thing?"

"That's what I heard. I heard he had nasty pictures of little girls in his house. Magazines and stuff. That's what they said."

"And would you be willing to sign a note for the judge that you heard that?"

"Yep."

"Okay then. That'd be enough. Let's get you to write down what you heard, and I'll see if I can get a warrant to go into his house and look around. Maybe add that to any connection I find to Big."

I get out a piece of school paper and write the note. When I finish, I sign my name at the bottom.

"Date the top there." The deputy points.

I date it and hand the paper to the deputy. "Here you go. I hope that's enough."

At the door, the deputy stops, his fingers on the handle. "You know, this wasn't what I thought I'd hear from you today."

"What'd you think you'd hear?"

"Not this," he says. "I was expecting to hear something else entirely."

I'm not sure what he's really saying, and I don't ask. Instead, I say, "So does this mean we can let the poaching charge go?"

"If I find something pretty good, then we'll move on. If not, you're still on the hook."

"How good does pretty good have to be?"

"Pretty damn good," he says, and adjusts his hat. Tilts the brim down low. "So we'll see." He opens the door. "And we'll talk again soon."

december

over the next hill

JT and I work five days on the new property. We fell trees and run a debarker off a generator. Use cant hooks to roll and stack lodgepoles.

JT flips the generator off. Says, "I'm leaving in a few days. Gotta get on campus and enroll a term before spring ball."

I can see his breath in the air. The first snow hasn't hit but the sky is a promise.

I say, "You staying for Christmas?" and smile.

JT laughs, and I do too. We've never had more than a sniped Christmas tree. Tinfoil tinsel. The one year he got me a box of .22 cartridges, the one year either of us ever gave.

I say, "Thanks for helping me on the property here."

"Shit, Little. You know I would." JT steps over to his cant hook. Snags a log and rolls it into place. Then he picks up the chain saw and winks at me. "And you know what?" he says. "This is a *fuckin'* good workout." He pulls the cord, steps over with the saw running, and chops the crown.

sunrise

Zaylie pulls up as I'm stepping out of the trailer on Saturday morning. She gets out of her Corolla. Says, "Merry early Christmas?" Goes to the trunk and opens it. Pulls out a four-foot spool of coop wire and a lamp. She sets those on the ground. Then reaches into the back of the car and pulls out a two-foot box.

"What are you doing?" I say.

"Getting you back on your feet. Do you have a 120-watt bulb?"

"Probably."

"Good. Because I just remembered that I needed a stronger bulb than this." She hands me the box.

I unfold the cardboard flaps and look inside. There are 15 yellow chicks in there. They're scuttling and stepping over each other. Cutting back and forth with the tilt of the box.

Zaylie says, "The feedstore guy tried to sex them but he said it's not a perfect science. So you'll have to eat any roosters in a few months."

"That's fine."

"But other than that," she says, "you'll be good to go."

"Thank you, Zaylie." I'm holding the box.

Zaylie reaches out and flicks me on the back of my hand. "No problem," she says. "Should we build this sucker now or what?"

"All right." I fold the flaps back closed, take the box inside the trailer, and leave it on the kitchenette table. When I go back outside, Zaylie's already carried the coop wire over to the fence line.

"Will this work?" she says. "Right here? Do you have wire cutters and pliers?"

I step to the shed. "Got 'em right in here."

"Then we're building a coop, sir. Get ready for more eggs in your life."

"Oh, I'm ready." I find a pair of needle-nose pliers and two pairs of cutters.

"If you're with me," Zaylie says, "you better be ready."

so do i

Three hundred yards from the road, I'm not even sure how the raven got there. I see it struggling in the underbrush and I walk up. Black hidden under the green. Tangled in a fern growth. I pull the bird out and see that both wings are broken. What should be four feet across and straight, the wings are snapped where they connect to the body. The left leg too. I set the bird down and look. Only the right leg is still working, and that one good leg pushing the bird in a circle.

I try to figure out what happened, what accident, how a bird that big could be crippled up like that. The day is hot, and the raven opens and closes its mouth for water.

I look up at the trees, the triangle tops above me, try to imagine a mistake, a series of choices this large bird had made.

The raven turns, its neck showing a sheen of gasoline blue. The bird looks at me, its body unable to turn and follow its own head.

I know I have to put it down. I know there's no other way. There's no leaving it here. There's no walking away and forgetting. So I kneel down over the bird. Hold it loose.

Don't want to hold it tight and feel it struggle before the end. I hold it loose and count to myself.

Then I close my eyes and grip quick. Turn the neck as I flex my hand, and the spine makes a sharp crack. The raven's mouth opens and closes once more, but its eyes are wide, and there isn't anything living in it.

Willa said, "I can't do this. I really can't." She shook her head. Her one eye was swelling shut from where he'd hit her.

"No," I said, "you *can*." I took her face in my hands, looked her in her good eye. "We don't have any other choice."

She stood there, her face tilted up to me. "I don't know, Little."

"No," I said. "Listen. We're gonna hide this. We're gonna hide it now, starting *right* now. And we're gonna keep hiding it as long as we can. But if anyone ever finds out, I'm gonna say it was me. And that's how it is." I shook her a little. "You can't tell me anything else 'cause you don't understand."

"But I do understand." Willa pointed at the bushes. "It's not right."

"The right thing is this," I said. "You helped me. You did the best you could. It would've been wrong if you didn't . . . okay? But you did."

Willa put her head down and started to cry. "It was in his coat. I just found it in there while you two were fighting. When I pointed it, I wasn't even sure if it was loaded . . ."

"I know, Willa." I hugged her. "I know. And I'm sorry."

"But what can we do? I really need to know."

I was hugging her and I could feel her shaking in my arms. I said, "You let me have this, okay? This was me. I did it."

My mind was storming blue-black clouds, a wind picking up, branches swinging through the front of my brain, hard pine dropping heavy in the forest.

I pulled back so I could see Willa's face, that ugly eye, swollen top and bottom, meeting in the middle like a cat's eye turned sideways. I said, "You promise me right now, Willa. This second. You never did it . . . or it didn't happen, okay?"

She closed her good eye. Tears running from the corners. She nodded her head, and I held her again. I said, "That's our story from now on. You promise me now, okay?"

She nodded again.

"And that story never changes. No matter what. So I gotta hear you say it."

"Okay," Willa said.

"Okay what?"

"Okay," she said. "It was you."

I held her coyote face in my hands. "That's right," I said, and hugged her again. "If anyone ever finds anything out, if anybody ever . . ."

We stayed there, huddled like we were braving the cold, but this was Indian summer and it was hot and still, past dark but warm, no wind at all except in my mind, like there were two worlds and the only way to cut one world out was to keep my eyes open and keep looking around. Make sure nothing dark and cold was coming from behind.

Neither of us said anything as I patted Willa's back. She looked up at me again. I smoothed her hair. Said, "I should probably dig now 'cause it's gonna take a long time. You walk over there and stand lookout. And stay awake. Sit down or stand up, do whatever you have to do, just stay awake and let me know if someone's coming."

Willa nodded. Then she walked over to the small rise. From there I knew she could see the road way below us.

I took up the shovel and broke ground, the loam thin in that spot and the earth rocky, thick with clay. Each shovel strike made a clink. Steel on stone. And I wondered which might break first.

author's note

While none of the characters in this novel are based on real people (other than Mr. Polchowski), the location is real. Pierce, Idaho—just west of the Bitterroot Mountains—is an incredible location for a book. Stunning natural beauty. Nationally renowned trout and steelhead runs. A landscape that includes moose, bear, elk, wolves, bobcats, and cougars. There are very few places left in the United States as wild and rugged as the foothills and mountains of North Central Idaho.

The people of Pierce are engaging as well. Independent yet mutually supportive. Proud and capable. These are not people wasting their lives staring at cell phone screens or worrying about the latest celebrity gossip. It's strange being in a town where people are generally capable of wiring their own homes, acquiring their own meat, storing up wood for a long winter, and fixing their own cars or trucks, but that's Pierce.

In many ways this town is a place set back in time. The main event each year is the Pierce 1860 Days, a celebration of the town's gold-rush roots, a celebration that seems never to end, as trapping and taxidermy are still common vocations in modern-day Pierce.

Unfortunately, the poverty, both financial and cultural, is stunning as well. The racism and the lack of higher education. There's little legal oversight, almost zero police or sheriff presence in the town. Many times in Pierce I've seen a twelve- or thirteen-year-old ride an ATV on the Idaho 11 through the middle of town with a shotgun or rifle on his front rack.

Some residents are fiercely loyal to this former gold-mining and logging town of 508 people, while others—some teenagers—can't wait to leave. I wanted to write about young people in Pierce because that conflict (between the lure of home and the desire to go out into the wider world) is both powerful and universal. Teenagers everywhere consider leaving their hometowns, yet most don't.

The first time I stayed in Pierce, I was talking to a teenage checker at Sammy's Grocery, and I said to her, "We're on vacation here."

She stopped and looked at me like I must've been recently released from a state mental hospital. She said, "Why would anyone *ever* come here for vacation?"

I just smiled and shook my head, because how could I respond to such a perfect quote?

But there was another big element that I wanted to develop in this novel, and it had nothing to do with Pierce, Idaho.

My mother didn't find out about her Mexican heritage

until she was an adult. When she was a child, her mother would dress her in long sleeves, gloves, and a large hat and tell her to keep out of the sun. She would say to my mother, "Do you want to look like a dark little Mexican?"

My mother knew nothing about her grandmother, didn't know about a name change from Isa Alvarado Chavez, didn't know anything about the lies on the US Census in 1920 and 1930, about burying Spanish as a first language. My mother said, "Why would I look like a dark little Mexican?"

But her mother never told her.

I remember how terrified my grandmother was of the sun. She never allowed it to hit her skin, always afraid of tanning. She hid in her house during the summer, wore an enormous hat when she went outside, got in her car while it was still in the garage, and would never roll down her window.

I saw a picture of her as a teenager and I said, "Wow, you're so beautiful, Grandma, so tan and dark-haired."

She got incredibly awkward and didn't know how to respond to me.

I didn't understand what she was hiding, but I felt the tension and never forgot that strange moment.

I was an adult when we all found out. My mom said, "So many things in my childhood make sense to me now. There were so many clues, but I never put it all together. There was a lot of racism in my home growing up, and maybe some of that racism was just hiding the truth."

My daughters are enrolled in a Spanish-language immersion school, and I've learned to speak and read Spanish as well. I want my Mexican heritage to be as much a part of our lives as my Swedish heritage or my Swiss last name. It matters to me that my daughters recognize the complexities of the US melting pot, the tragedy of anti-immigrant rhetoric, and the cost of assimilation.

Also, as someone trying to understand his own complicated background, I wanted to write a character who was trying to come to terms with a mixed identity. I wanted to write as someone attempting to acquire his own background, to acquire and understand something bigger than himself. And this brought me closer to Little.

acknowledgments

Although *Too Shattered for Mending* is my fifth book (and third novel), I didn't know if it was going to be a book when I wrote the first few drafts. I wasn't sure anything was working. So I asked a few trusted readers to give me some feedback. Thank you to that four-person group for pushing this novel forward:

1. To my wife, Jennie. Thank you for your advice to go darker, to submerge the draft and not allow it to rest on the surface.

2. To my good friend Jackson Darland. Thank you for your feedback on the school scenes, on Zaylie, and on tone and shading.

3. To my sister Maddie Hoffmeister. Thank you for your help with Jésus Gómez and the Spanish thread. For your advice to ease back on the fishing terminology.

4. To my superagent, Adriann Ranta. Thank you for letting me know that this was in fact a book worth pursuing and revising, that I should continue to work and develop this story.

I'm so grateful for my team at Knopf as well, especially

my incredible editor, Katherine Harrison, for her insightful, funny notes, her reactions and ideas written in the margins, and for her metaphor about the layers of a filbert.

Also, thank you to Catfish Sam Terris, the best young publicist I've ever worked with. And to Josh Salmon Redlich for adopting the book halfway through. To Laura Antonacci (The Swimmer) in library marketing; Rebecca McGuire, hustling in school marketing; the elegant Jenny Brown—who, truth be told, *does* like suspenders—VP and publisher; and Adrienne Waintraub, director of school and library marketing. Also to Kristin Schulz, who seems to get so many things done for everyone.

Thank you to the copyediting team, especially Barbara Perris for her poetic ear, and the sales team, Felicia Frazier in sunglasses (ready to rock-climb). To the design group and Angela Carlino for the cover. Random House Children's Books is a wonderful company to work with.

Thank you to my parents, Pamela Hoffmeister and Charlie Hoffmeister, for always supporting art and writing, and for modeling the working life for me.

To the town of Pierce, for good days of Idaho fishing, snowshoeing, chopping wood, eating wild meat, and hiking with the dogs.

Love to my siblings, Hill, Coop, Haley, El, and Maddie. And to my in-laws and outlaws, Carrie, Sarah, Nate, Aimee, Horace, Bitz, Caleb, Courtney, Kari, Jay, Dan, Kathie, and Patrick.

To the real Mr. Polchowski, my fellow teacher Brian Naghski. Your students are incredibly lucky to have you in their lives. I am as well. Bri Bri forever.

Thank you to my friends and colleagues who are always willing to talk about writing: Jeff Hess, Katie Meehan, Dusty Smith, Ben Temple, Luke Mazziotti, Anna Grace, Sarah Prater-Eichner, Ingrid Bodtker, Lee Baker, Zeb Rear, Bobbie Willis, and Zach Stewart.

And to Ben Leroy, the King. Always.

To Laura White, Jeff Zentner, Kathleen Glasgow, Evelyn Hess, David Arnold, Sabaa Tahir, Estelle Laure, River Donaghey, Brendan Leonard, Michael Copperman, Seth Kantner, Willy Vlautin, Pete Fromm, Lidia Yuknavitch, and Brian Juenemann, wonderful people in the book world. And to the Sweet Sixteens, an excellent collection of authors.

Since I worked on the first draft of this book while in Joshua Tree, thank you to the Joshua Tree National Park Association for allowing me to write in the Lost Horse Cabin, and for my writer-in-residence position in the spring of 2015. Thank you to Caryn Davidson for running such an incredible program.

Finally, thank you to Rain for your sarcastic, fun sense of humor, and to Roo for your glorious love of the natural world. Pieces of both of you are in so many characters that I write.